THE
FLAX FLOWER

To Grace
Best wishes
Amanda [illegible]

Published 2015 by Amanda MacLean on Lulu.com

ISBN 978-1-326-08842-2

Amanda MacLean was born in Glasgow and lives in London. In her free time she sings traditional Scottish songs. *The Flax Flower* is her first novel.

For Annie and Andrew,
and the singers
of the song

Prologue

At twenty-six, there were lines around his mouth that were not from laughter, and the curls of his hair had grey in them where they nestled against his neck round behind the back of the ear. Women liked to think of those curls coiling around their fingers like the tips of tiny serpents' tails. They saw something too, in behind the broad-spaced eyes with their long lashes and the high cheekbones that made people call him handsome, something beyond that and deeper, a sadness maybe that made a woman want to take him close and to comfort his face in the soft space between her neck and shoulder. So he had plenty of opportunities, if he had wished to take them, but mostly he left them to think those thoughts to themselves. He wasn't too interested in women for their own sake, and it was only now and then that he would notice a lass, hear her laughing, sonsie-like, and watch her for a while and the sparkling life of her would draw him in. After a while they would be going to bed together, and soon after that, a week or a month or so at most, they would be lying in the dawn light after the heat of passion, and she would look at him that way and reach a hand round to the back of his neck to pull a curl straight, and he would look down at her and see that it was the wrong face. Young enough, but the eyes and the chin were wrong, and the hair splayed across the pillow was brown or yellow or black, or the wrong shade of red. It was then that he would begin to plan his escape, a few days later he would cough into his hand and say, 'I'm awa back up north next week,' or some other excuse, it sounded like a lie to him even if it fooled her, and a week or two later their eyes might meet in the Grassmarket or the High Street or the Canongate while she was carrying a brace of chickens back from the market. His eyes would wander over her face and he would blink and give a wee half-smile, and he would nod, vacant, and look away. That would be it, for half a year or maybe longer. Because he never could stay with a girl once she started doing his own lass's things.

He was easy to spot in a crowd, being taller than most and wearing the blue and silver livery of the Earls of Balcarres. That was in the mid-seventies, long before Balcarres went to France to support the Old Pretender in his exile. He liked to go into the coffee houses in Edinburgh where he would meet with friends and smoke tobacco and drink short shots of the strong coffee, and the light would come palely in through the wee windows high up on the walls. Inside, the rich smells of tobacco leaves and coffee with its bitter tang would mix together, and he would think that was why he liked to drink the coffee, the bitterness was there and you nodded to it but you didn't let it overpower you, and it would not stop you from savouring the warm richness too. When he started to speak like that, whoever he was with – another man from the servants' hall or just one or two of the regulars – they would give him a sideways glance and say 'Aye, man, it's well you dinny tak a dram, you talk enough nonsense sober.' He would look up a bit sheepish and grin, and then he would join in the nothing-talk, the city gossip, why the market was short of hens and the price of fish, and he would feel fine, he could walk away from the sadness when he wanted to. Only there were times when they were friends to him, sadness and memory, he did not take them for a curse the way other people might, and you could go and visit them for a while, for a long time if you liked, as long as you did not settle with them.

There were rare occasions when a mood would come on him and he would talk for hours, flights of fancy that were calculated to make his companions laugh.

And that would make a man new to the servants' hall ask, jovial, half-joking, making conversation in the break before he went back on duty, 'Have you never had a mind to marry? A man like you should draw the lassies in no bother, but I'd lay a good bet even an ugly bastard like me has had mair luck than you these last six months.'

He would look up from the side of his bed where he sat polishing the silver bell of his trumpet. He would run his fingernail *click click click* over the engraved filigree letters that circled the rim and that read *Thomas McCuir Glasgowe 1669*, while he looked past the man as if he did not see him, and there would be a strain in his voice when he replied, 'No, it's no so easy...' and his words would trail off.

'Aye, but still – do you never think of it?'

And he would close the conversation, 'No, I never,' the three words like the click of a padlock closing shut on a box, and go back to his polishing. Most men would know well enough not to take it further, but anyone who tried to pry the box open would get his fingers trapped sharpish. If he were of a mind to ask around the place he would hear the story, bits and pieces of it anyway.

In the spring of 1676, he found himself in a company of men in a coffee house just off the Royal Mile. The wind was whipping down the lanes and vennels of the city like a dominie in a rage. They were not well known to him, the men in the coffee house, one or two regulars and a whole crowd of students from the University, and then him and a couple of other men in the Earl's service, to whom he had said, 'Come out for a bit we'll see the town thegither.' They had dressed their best in the tight silk coats that were then coming into fashion, and together they had jostled through the streets to the coffee house. Younger men, his companions joined in easily with the student crowd, and he found himself drawn in too. The students were in high spirits and after a while the songs began, raucous and bawdy, songs they could all join in with, *Saw ye my love Maggy* and *The Braw Lads o' Gallawater*, it was as well there were no women in the house.

Every song ended with a round of cheers and clapping and shouts for more, and he was drawn out of himself into the spirit of the occasion. He threw his head back and laughed with the rest, joined in when he knew the words, and sometimes when he didn't, he could walk away from sorrow when he felt like it.

'And now, here's one for you, you'll ken it maybe from the play a wee while back, Unfortunate Celia it was called.'

He had not heard of the play, but the nods and murmurs around the room told him that many of the others had. The student singing it stood up in the middle of the room, in the centre of the ring of wooden tables and chairs. He had a mediocre voice, high and thin, but it suited the role and he played up to it, twisting his fingers in his wig and eyeing his companions coquettishly. It was a daft song about a girl, Celia, forced to marry an old man she didn't love. But she swore to get the better of the situation,

'It's a thousand to one that before I have done
I'll deceive him and leave him to himself all alone.'

When the last line – 'I'll be happy and poor, with the man I adore' – was over and done, he gave a shout – 'Good on her!' – and he drummed his fist on the table and called for pipes and tobacco for himself and the singer.

There was a break in the singing after that, and men shifted in their seats, turning animatedly to talk to each other, and ordered more drinks. He took the opportunity to go for a piss in the privy. When he got back to the public room, he saw that his friends were gone and his seat had been taken, so he installed himself next to a pair of students on a bench near the back of the room. There was still a lively murmur going on in the place, and at last there was a call for another song, 'Come on now, lads, who's next? That's no the lot, surely?' Heads turned around the room, searching for the next singer to put himself forward, but he held back, it had been a long time since he sang a song in a company. The atmosphere in the room had settled, the time for bawdy had passed, and so the next man to clear his throat uttered his words quietly, and reflectively. He was too old to be one of the students, though he knew one or two by name, and had joined in energetically with the singing earlier on. A wee man, wrapped in a plaid, not a city man, but a Northerner.

'Now I winna pretend to be the singer John Aird is –'

Scattered cheers, and attention turned towards Celia, who pouted prettily for his audience.

'– but yon last song put me in mind, and I canna say why it did, but it brought to mind another song about a lass that fell in love wi the wrang man. They say it's true, mind, up there in Buchan, and you can see the lassie's grave in the St Peter's kirkyard up in Fyvie if you care to mak the journey. It's a long song, mind, so be sure that you want to hear it.'

Cries of 'Aye, let's have it, now.'

He heard little of this introduction because the students next to him were blethering to each other, but as the man started the song, the sorrowful tune quieted the air and the room fell still, as if the chairs, the tables, the walls and even the embers of the fire were listening. Noises came in, dull and distant, from the street outside: the quick clop-clop of a child running in wooden pattens, the impatient whinny of a horse, the clank of a pail. But inside the coffee house the air held its breath. Before the first verse was over, his right hand had closed tight around his china cup, and his fingers did not loosen throughout the whole span of that long long song, while his knuckles turned white and bloodless. His eyes appeared to be fixed on a blank space on the whitewashed wall opposite, just above the fire, but his gaze was unfocused, and the skin around his eyes and the corners of his mouth twitched minutely, making his face seem to flicker. In the last verses, he squeezed his eyes shut, as if there was something he was trying not to see, or perhaps trying to see better inside his own mind.

When the ballad reached its conclusion, the room was silent and still for a moment or two, while the listeners made the journey back from the mill-lands of Buchan to the smoky basement room in

Edinburgh. Into the quietness, he released a half-stifled sob before letting his head sink into his hands. The deep breath he took stretched his tight red waistcoat across his chest with such force that the buttons on it strained against their stitching and then swung, dangling loosely on their threads.

He sat with his face in his hands, oblivious to the heads that turned towards him, and the suppressed snigger of a student. He stared downwards at the time-smoothed grain of the table between his elbows. A few men started some scattered applause, and the rest of the company joined in, awkwardly. There were some half-hearted attempts at banter – 'No more of they tragic ballads for him! Sing us something cheery instead!' – but the atmosphere was gone and the crowd soon thinned out.

After a while he and the ballad singer were the only customers left in the shop. The singer had been watching him with curious eyes and now came over to sit facing him across the table, clearing his throat before he spoke.

'Eh, man,' he began, 'It's nae often one of my songs taks a man like that. Either you're a wee bit saft in the heid, or you've a story to tell.'

I

In the summer gloaming the Miller of Tifty pulled the door of the mill shut behind him and followed his son and servant up the steps towards their supper, leaving the mill to squat on its own by the side of the burn. The air was fresh, with a slight chill about it, and William Smith sucked it in vigorously, clearing away the dust of oats and peas that had grabbed at his throat since the dawn, when the first grain of the day had arrived. The great stone of the miln had turned with barely a break since then, while the water wheel juddered and shook with its own slow slapping rhythm. Through the day, more men had arrived from the neighbouring touns to share the farmtoun gossip while they waited their turn. To the miller they had said little, nodded a stiff greeting – 'Aye, Tifty' – and turned to each other, while he stood apart overseeing the progress of the work.

He took the steps slowly, and at the top, when he emerged into the warmth and light of the evening sun, he stood for a while to catch his breath. A tabby cat, with its tail erect, trotted briskly across the yard and pressed herself against him, and he brooded as it weaved in and out between his legs. It did not matter to Smith whether his neighbours liked him or no. But respect, that was something else again, and not every man had given him respect that day. Still, he remembered a time when all the folk of Fyvie had had far worse things to say about him. Even now, the memory of it made his jaw clench, and his brows furrowed above his rheumy eyes with their irises pale and blue as a winter's morning. The long white hairs of his eyebrows quivered as he fought against those bad old thoughts by taking account of the assets that kept him in good standing in the community. His fairness in the gathering in of the rent and the multures: he would take his due from the tenants, every bit of it, but he would not cheat them, not by using false measures, nor by slipping extra handfuls of meal into a sack hung in a handy place out of sight. No man could speak ill of him on that score. And to any man who said a miller did no work, only gathered in the product of others' labour for no labour of his own, he would reach out his hand and silently display the proof of his labours. It was there before him now, as he reached down to stroke the cat. He looked ruefully at the missing finger, his badge, that showed that he had earned his place in life as well as being born to it, the Gentleman Miller of Tifty.

With that, he straightened up and the cat mewed in protest. The sound of his daughters' singing at the milking drifted across the yard from the byre. He had aye liked to hear the singing of women. Women, aye, so they were – it was strange to think how fast the years crept on. And to think how long it had been since he had come up into the yard, just like this, and found them playing there with their brother, and begun a chase, swinging a wee girl off her feet and throwing her into the air above his head, catching her with steady sure hands, the pair of them laughing, delighted, into each other's faces. Now the days for games were a long time gone, and soon there must be serious business afoot, with three fine husbands to find for them.

But find them he would, soon enough. And then, with the lassies married off, he would learn to sit back and kick his feet up on a cushioned chair all day if he liked. And it would not be long before his children would bring their own bairns, his grandchildren, in to see him, and he would indulge them as a grandfather should, and play the old games again, though he might be creaking in his joints. Agnes's would have red hair like her own, and like his had been, and there would be a joke about it, they would have the same temper as the pair of them, even when they were still unsteady on their feet.

As he creaked open the house door, a chicken dodged his feet and ran across the slate floor of the kitchen, then fluttered up to its roost in the inglenook. He sniffed in appreciation at the good smells of cooking, muttering a brief greeting – 'Aye, Helen' – to his wife. She glanced quickly over her skinny shoulder and grunted a reply before returning her attention to the blackened pot that was suspended from a chain over the fire. Smith removed his apron, and hung it on a hook on the back of the door next to Gibb's and Young Will's. Then he turned to his left and filled a basin from the water barrel, to scrub away the day's filth from his hands and face, and went to take his rightful place at the head of the broad table where Gibb and Will stood waiting. Smith sat down heavily, and contemplated his wife's back – still stick thin after bearing four bairns, he had never been able to credit it – while the rest of the household gathered. The womenfolk came in one by one, washed their hands as he had done, and stood patiently at the table until they were all ready. Grizel carried each of their wooden bowls to the hearth in turn and filled them with broth. Then Smith pushed his chair back and rose to his feet to lead his household in a short grace. Together they uttered a quiet 'Amen'. The women swished their skirts neatly out of the way before sitting and they all sat and took up their spoons.

In the silence as they ate their supper, Smith looked around at his family and servants. Sourly, he contemplated Young Will, who was clapping his skinny dog as it rested its head on his knee, hoping for a scrap of food. What a useless, shiftless loon, a son who had taken from him little more than his name – thank God for Gibb, who made up for Will's blunders in the mill. And Grizel, too, handy in the work of the house and the land, alongside his own womenfolk. Helen. And his three bonnie lasses. Jane, yellow-haired, slim and proud like her mother when first he courted her. Bessie, good lass. Agnes, smiling away to herself, aye his bonny rose. Then, thinking of the talk he had overheard earlier in the day, he cleared his throat.

'Did you see what a bad match auld Camalouns made for his daughter?'

As he spoke, he saw Agnes shift on her stool, and her eyes flicked up at him and away. There was a brief silence, but he knew it was coming before she opened her mouth, the way she half-smiled as she flicked her hair back over her shoulder with one hand.

'How is it a bad match, father? She looked gey pleased wi her man when she wed him in the Kirk.'

'He's naethin but a poor cottar's son. Camalouns is wealthy enough. He should be wanting better for his grandchildren. Nae that his daughters can expect as much as you three Tifty lasses.' He looked around the table, nodding contentedly. Then he continued, 'Na, there winna be any worries about that, the young men will be beating a path to our door soon enough, with aa three of you coming into bloom thegither. And hear this,' – they had heard it before, but they might as well hear it again – 'there'll be nae man can say I stinted on my daughters' tochers.'

No, he would offer a good dowry with each, for he had wealth, plenty of it, from the multures that he collected each year, and good money that he made at the market and hoarded next to his silverware in the carved wooden kist that stood at the foot of his bed.

'But mind you,' he carried on, holding up a finger in warning, 'it winna just be any kind of man for Tifty's lassies. Nae even a miller like myself, if I get my way!' Smith watched with narrowed eyes as Young Will rose from the table, crossed to the door and left the house without a word. Then he carried on, 'Na, mark my words, your mother and I will be taking good care in choosing – because I winna be handing over three hundred merks per lass to just any man!'

Aye, he would have the folk know that he had married his daughters to fine grand men, so that they would come up to him on a market day and say, 'I heard the minister reading out the banns for

Jane' – or Bessie – or Agnes – whichever one it was, 'you're a gey fortunate man.' Aye, it would be fine, he would nod in agreement, and next time he did his accounting he would add that grand wealthy son-in-law and his daughter's good fortune to his goods and the silver piled in the wooden kist.

He sat back in his chair and took some small pleasure at the thought, and his belly shook gently up and down as he chuckled to himself.

Then she started up again.

'Ocht father, you aye think we're so grand. Half the tenants in Fyvie are the sons of some laird or other. Their fathers aa had wee bits of land here and there.'

'They're nae the sons of lairds like Inveramsay!'

'Aye, but they're nae fourth sons, either.'

'Dinna start, lass. That's mair than enough.'

It took both him and Helen to quiet her.

She had aye been thrawn like that, she could drive a man mad with it, 'I winna,' and 'I canna,' and 'How should I,' even when she was wee, 'Eat your kale, Nan, while it's hot,' and she would say, 'Na, I winna,' and no manner of coaxing or cajoling would change her mind. It had made them laugh, then, but now she was of an age to wed, it was a different matter. She wouldna gie the eye to any of the laddies, which had been fine by him up till now, but it would do her no favours when the time came to marry, and he would have to hope for a brief courtship since her tongue had its own will. Not many husbands would stomach that kind of talk, and no gentleman worth his salt would want to hear it all his life. So a quick courtship it would have to be unless they could find a man with a broad latitude where it came to women, and there werenae many of them about.

II

'Andrew Lamb will sing you a pretty song.'

'Lamb?'

'My trumpeter. I keep him for a trumpeter, but he's good for a song and aa. Are you no, Lamb?'

The Laird's raised voice sounded clearly from the high end of the table, where meats were being served. At the low end, where the servants waited in hope of a half-eaten carcass, Andrew Lammie looked up.

'My Lord?'

'You're good for a song, Lamb, are you no?'

Before Andrew could answer, the Laird of Fyvie continued with a wink, and a nod that made his curled wig bob above his brows, 'You'll sing for us after dinner. The story of Sir Patrick Spens we'll have. Aye,' and he turned to his guests, 'we'll hear a tale of shipwreck later. Now, my Lords, would you care for a pinch of snuff?' and he waved his hand, inviting his guests to help themselves from the gold-trimmed horn of an ox.

Andrew nodded assent, ignored by his Laird, as well as by his companions below the salt.

The banquet in the Great Hall progressed. Servants clattered up the wide staircase with silver ashets piled high. Most days the Laird of Fyvie's table was nearly as spartan as his peasants' – kale broth with a few wee lumps of mutton; porridge or sowans; ale to drink. But on those occasions when he had guests, he liked to put on a show. Finely etched glasses from Holland, filled with good ruby wine from France, sparkled in the light of many candles. On the table, the best his estate could muster in meats and wheaten bread; and fruits and spices from far foreign lands, laid out on white linen. Above the salt, the Seton coat of arms added its weight to the silver cutlery that was already heavy in the hands of the guests. Where Andrew sat, bare-headed, with the rest of the household, the pewter tankards were filled with ale as they were on any day, but the picked-over dishes being passed down were richer. At least the music of the viol players was free for all to hear.

A chicken, glazed and stuffed with prunes, came his way, well picked but with the wings still in place. As he pulled one off, it brought to mind the miller's servant who had brought the birds from Tifty that morning, Gibb with his squint in the right eye that meant you never could tell if he was looking at you or not. A dour, disagreeable old loon, but because he lived with the Smith family at the Tifty mill he had immediately reminded Andrew of the lass who lived there. It was the same with him whenever any of the produce of the mill came to his attention. When he saw the sacks of meal piled at the storeroom doors, he would be filled with a spreading warmth that lifted him from his daily tasks, while it also pained him because of her absence. Pork, when it was served, most likely came from one of the mill's pigs that was nurtured on the abundant supply of grain, and so it lifted his heart.

Now, he suppressed a smile as he imagined her that morning, choosing the chooks from the squabble in the mill yard, expertly catching them and holding them firmly by the feet while they flapped in confusion and their baffled heads screwed around to turn the world the right way up again. He imagined her striding across the mill yard, a wee bit flushed from the chase, and handing them over to Gibb, and all the while thinking maybe of him and whether he would be eating them tonight, or maybe thinking of someone else, not him but a richer man, and that made him shrink away inside, until in his mind's eye he made her look up at him, and he reached out to push behind her ear the wayward strands of hair that had fallen across her face when she bent to catch the birds. He imagined her blushing with surprise, and he could almost feel her warmth in his palm as he slipped his hand around the back of her neck and he drew her towards him, and then –

'Lamb!'

He fumbled and almost dropped the chicken's wing-bones, long stripped of the little flesh they had carried.

'My Lord? '

'So you're nae deaf, then, Lamb?'

'No, my Lord, I'm no deaf.'

'You'll gie us a song now. And mak a good job of it – Ha! Ha! – I dinna want these good lords thinking I've been boasting for naethin.'

The Laird of Fyvie was usually soft-spoken, diffident almost, even with his servants. But today, like the food on the table, he was transformed. The Urbane, Sophisticated Laird. Andrew Lammie preferred the everyday version to this over-seasoned one.

'Mak it a song of bravery, something martial, to inspire my guests. Ha! Ha!'

'You dinny want me to sing about Sir Patrick Spens, my Lord?'

'Na, na, nae that one, good God, na.'

Andrew thought for a few moments.

'Then it should be Otterburn, my Lord.' He knew the story well, and he had a good tune for it. The words would come, in their good time, when he called on them.

He stood up. As he did so, the man next to him turned half-around but did not catch his eye, saying for his neighbours, rather than for Andrew himself, 'Sing it well, and you'll maybe get thrown a big bone to chew on, eh?'

'Come and stand here, Lamb, so my Lord Balcarres can hear you. Let the viol players rest. Quiet, aa, I winna have any of your racket.'

Andrew passed behind the long line of the men's backs to the top of the table. He walked slowly, directing his attention away from the cold regard of his fellow servants that he could feel like a chill in the back of his neck. He, an Edinburgh lad miles from home, was a foreigner to them. *Forget them. Remember the story, the battle just like the one in the tapestry there on the wall.* One of Fyvie's greyhounds slunk under the Laird's chair as Andrew approached and lay with its thin snout, carefully aligned between its forepaws, poking out between the tassels that hung from the edge of the chair. It watched him steadily with its shy, bulging eyes.

When the pieces of the story were set right in his mind, settled in order like the beads on a necklace, he said, 'My Lords, pray listen while I sing to you of the victory of Scotland at the Battle of Otterburn and the death of Earl Douglas.'

Their Lords watched him, and waited. He spread his feet within his boots, and settled his shoulders wide and loose, and took a good look at that poor sad warrior in the tapestry, him that was sombrely looking out straight at him from the middle of the raging battle, holding his hand to his wounded head. He let one breath in and out again, and as he did so, he fell deep into the silent place at his centre. Then he took the first breath that would give life to the song, and from that silent place there came a voice that he recognised as his own, singing the first words that would draw out all the others after themselves. The still, stitched eyes of the old warrior were fixed on him, and as Andrew sang, 'And Percy wi his good broad sword that could so sharply wound, has wounded Douglas on the brow,' he saw not him but the face of Earl Douglas himself. And he spoke the words of the Earl of Douglas and Lord Percy for them, the same words or something like them that they had said themselves nearly three hundred years ago, and they were living and real there before him, as real almost as the audience that sat there listening. The story was coming through him, through his words, and so he was careful with it, giving it the right shape and the right pace, and leaving the right spaces between the words to allow them time to see what it was that had happened so that they would understand it.

The tune he was using was the one he always used, the one that his father and grandmother used for other songs, but that he thought was best for Otterburn, because it had the right pace and rhythm to it and somehow it helped him find the words to fit it. Each time he came to sing it the words would come as sure as the tune just when he thought of the next thing to happen in the story.

You had to be careful with it, though, and not step into those old knights' places too far or you would be like a mummer on the stage, turning your head this way and that and making the audience snigger at you, who did you think you were, they didn't want to see you act out the story but to see it just themselves in their own minds, carried by the song straight from your imagining to theirs. You had to stand aside, but your will had still to be there strong enough to hold them to the song, because if you went in weak and all kind of shamefaced and embarrassed it would be just as bad, all they would see would be you still, and they would laugh the harder. So it was a skill you learned, and when you had it right you were away in your own place during the singing, you felt the story and the song filling you and it was as if you were reaching into that past time, and with your voice clear as the peal of a bell letting those old ghosts tell the tale themselves.

Then he came to the end, and for a few moments he was suspended, until he was called back to the great hall of Fyvie Castle by the sound of the Laird clapping, loud in the stillness that followed the song, and his guests and men following suit.

'Well done, Lamb, you've done me proud,' the Laird was saying as he turned to his guests, 'What did I tell you, my Lord Balcarres? You see why I had to bring him up frae Edinburgh? Now let's have a tune frae the harpists, I have a fine pair of harpists from Ireland, you'll never have heard the like.'

Andrew stood in his place, awaiting his orders.

'Is that aa, my Lord?'

The Laird cast a warm eye over him, 'Aye, Lamb, thank you,' and dismissed him with a blithe wave of the hand as he turned back to his fellows.

Andrew turned and walked back to take his seat.

The man on his right, who had spoken before, caught his eye as he sat down. 'Nae bad, Lammie, you've a skill there right enough. Near as good as one of our own Buchan singers.'

He nodded in acknowledgement of the compliment.

III

Andrew Lammie took his time shaving, slow and careful as the sharp edge of the razor pulled against the skin of his cheeks and chin and upper lip. He liked to make a good job of it, and on a day like today in particular, when the Laird had chosen to do the ridings of his lands, which Andrew well knew included the Mill of Tifty. He did not want to be visiting Tifty's lands with nicks and cuts all over his face like a lad after his first shave. When he was done he turned his head from side to side to admire his reflection in the rippling surface of the tin mirror. Then he gave himself a wink to steady his nerves and stepped out of the servants' hall and went across the castle courtyard to the dilapidated stables where the strong smell of horses and their manure made him wrinkle his nostrils. The stable man handed him the lead reins of two horses, the Laird's black gelding and his own chestnut mare, the both of them decked out in gleaming polished harness. The shining dark leather softened the sun's rays as they fell on it, and the brass glinted and winked at him when he turned to look back at the pair as he led them across the courtyard. Their hooves made a sharp din as they clipped the cobbles, and the sound echoed around the courtyard, clattering against the four walls of the castle. He waited at the yett, the great iron gate that penetrated the south wall and that was left open in these times of peace. On either side of him, the grand south wall lifted its turrets and gables five storeys into the air, dressed all in white like a proud bride.

The mare flicked her ears and stamped her hoof, impatient to be off, and he tried to quiet her by stroking her long nose with a slow and steady rhythm, enjoying the soft velvet sensation beneath his fingertips, but he felt much the same himself, for beneath his surface calm there was an excitement stirring like a colt that wanted to leap and buck and not wait for the Laird but to gallop away and not stop until he got to the farmtoun at Tifty, making the chooks scatter and trampling the kail until she came out from the big house to tickle him behind the ears and run her hand along his flank. And at the thought of it he had to press his face into the side of the mare's neck, in among the long coarse hairs of her mane, to keep his calm.

But he was no horse, and in any case he was on a tight rein, so he had to wait until his Laird was good and ready, and when he did come stepping down the stair in his riding gear – 'Ah Lamb, I'm glad to see you ready, have you your trumpet? And your sword? Oh aye, aye, good,' – there was more delay, for he had his Factor with him and Andrew had to dash back to the stables to saddle up a third horse, a good strong one for the Factor was fond of his dinner. So by the time they were finally ready for the off, and he had assisted the Laird of Fyvie and the Factor to mount, the latter red and puffing and only succeeding on his third attempt, he sprang into his saddle as if he had been fired from a gun and had to circle the mare around in front of the castle walls at a quick trot while the Genial, Indulgent Laird smiled over at him from the yett and instructed him, 'Now Lamb, just hold steady and gie us a good blast on your trumpet to send us off, will you, and gie us a fanfare every mile or so, and that will do us fine the day, thank you.' Well then Andrew reined his horse and himself back in, and took a deep breath before raising the trumpet to his lips and sending the notes dancing across the landscape, and then they all set off at a trot, with the Laird's three greyhounds bounding ahead. With the greyhounds at the front of the small party there rode Andrew Lammie, in red and gold and with his sword at one side and his trumpet at the other, and his cloak flapping in the wind and his hair blowing and his horse stepping high, and behind them the Laird and his Factor, side by side, deep in a lugubrious conversation that acted like a dead weight on their progress.

'Do you see the state of the east wing, Factor? My grandfather never got around to it wi the restoration, and it's suffering for it now. We must see if we can scrape something together for it. Now I have one or two ideas if you'll lend me your ear…'

Andrew could not fathom how someone as rich as the Laird still had to scrape money together, but he had no intention of finding out today, so he gave the mare's sides a squeeze with his legs and slapped the reins against her neck, and she picked up speed. Following the River Ythan northwards against its course, they quickly left the others behind. When they rounded a bend and passed out of the Laird's sight, Andrew gave the mare her head and they fairly flew along under the tall beeches and the shifting dappled light of the Wood of Fyvie, with the greyhounds streaking ahead.

At the confluence of the Tifty burn and the Ythan, he clicked his tongue and pulled back on the reins, and the mare slowed to a walk, clumping with a hollow sound across the wooden bridge that lifted the path over the Tifty burn. He let her drop her head to graze on the long grasses by the burn, while his gaze wandered across the Howes of Fyvie. The crops had been shorn here, leaving only a short stubble to cover the bare earth. The greyhounds weaved among the cut stalks, following trails of scent. A startled hare leapt from its scrape, and the hounds silently sprinted after it, but at Andrew's shrill whistle they slowed their steps and returned to him with their tails between their legs.

Andrew waited, and waited, and began to fidget. Halfway there, only a mile to go, and now he had waited for as long as he had taken to get here. His heart was still beating with the joy of riding, and the joy of where they were going, and he wondered whether it was age, or the weight of responsibility, or both, that made the Laird and his Factor so slow, when they could have flown along the track like him and got to Tifty already.

The greyhounds trotted back over the bridge to the burn's south bank, ranging among the wide spaced trees that climbed the steps of the long hillside, following the course of a faint path that curved away from the water's edge and led to a broad, shallow glen. Andrew jumped from the mare's back and followed them a short way to stretch his legs, thinking he might come across some of the lassies that came there to gather rushes for the cruisie lamps, but there was no one about.

When, at last, the Laird and the Factor reached the bridge – 'Gie us a blast, will you, Lamb? So the folk can hear that their Laird's about, eh?' – Andrew was glad to oblige, and although he was no calmer, he let the mare go at a slower pace. He looked back and raised a hand in greeting as they overtook a cottar from Cardonwell, plodding slow and steady with a great sack on his back, as he followed the gentlest of slopes eastwards along the side of the Tifty burn. Then they arrived at flat meadow-lands, where the miller of Tifty's kye looked up and shook their horns at him, and then lowered their heads again to seek the sweet grasses amongst the meadowsweet and the willow herbs.

They paused to rest their horses in the shade of the willows where the Tifty burn ran out from the ravine where the mill stood. Andrew drew the back of his wrist across his brow to clear away the sweat, for despite the light breeze the day was hot, even for August. He leaned forward to give the mare an appreciative pat on the neck, and when he looked up the Laird caught his eye with a great big broad smile across his long thin face, and so Andrew was happy to oblige him with another good blast on the trumpet, hoping she was listening. Then he dug in his heels and the mare picked up his excitement and cantered up the steep path, and around the tight bend to the right and into the yard at Mill of Tifty, busy with men carrying their sacks of meal, and half-grown piglets rooting about among the sheds. The greyhounds, sprinting ahead of him, sent a flock of chickens scattering and the birds' squawks of alarm were echoed by a small skinny woman who was working a cheese-press by the door of her house. She turned her head to shout over her shoulder, still keeping her eyes on him, and was joined by another woman, taller than her mother and with none of her skinniness, and with red hair falling down her back and a high colour in her cheeks, and at the sight of whom his insides turned over, twice.

He was vaguely and uncomfortably aware that it was the older woman who was looking at him with something like the intensity of his own gaze. But the eyes of the woman who had stopped him from breathing passed over him, briefly, without a flicker of interest, and she passed some brief comment to her mother, and then looked beyond him to the Laird and his companion as they arrived, at a slower pace, in the yard behind him.

He took a deep breath in and held it before letting it out very, very slowly, looking away over the top of the house. He dismounted and helped the Factor to dismount, then took the reins of the three horses and waited, while the Laird and his man strode up to the house and engaged the two women in conversation. The cottar he had passed on the way arrived in the yard, dumped his sack down to take a breather, and started a discussion about oats, in which Andrew struggled to keep up his part, and not only because he was a city man.

The cottar soon found someone better informed to talk to, and Andrew was left to himself, which suited him fine. He looked around the yard, to stop himself from staring too long at her. Such places were still new to him, only a few months come from the city, and they held an interest that the Fyvie folk would laugh at if he let on about it. He was standing near the byre, a long low building at the entrance to the yard, turf piled on stone like a cottar's houf. The yard itself was no shape at all, just an open area of trodden earth that was dry now, but must turn to a slew of puddled and pockmarked mud in the wet weather. Across the yard, near the edge of the ravine, the glazed windows, two storeys, and lime-pointed stone of the house gave out the status of the family that lived there, a far cry from the rubble and turf of the cottars' houses scattered over the neighbouring hill to the south of the Tifty burn. Over the door the engraving on the lintel read *W. S. & H. B. 1649.*

There came the sound of a woman's laughter and his eyes flickered briefly over to where the Laird was smiling down at the red haired woman. She seemed to be laughing at some joke he had made, which Andrew thought highly unlikely, he had seldom heard the Laird say a word that was more than extremely dull.

As he wondered whether the patched wicker fence around the kailyard would really keep the pigs out, one of them slipped through it and he had his answer as it bit off a dark green curly top of kale and chewed it, while wandering aimlessly among the twisting stalks of pea plants, some of them still brightly flowering. Then the pig got through a gap in a dyke of cut turfs, into a small orchard, that must give the buildings some shelter when the wind turned and blew from the west. The pig had no luck in the orchard, it being too early for the small hard pears and apples, and sour green plums, to ripen and drop to the ground.

Snatches of the conversation crossed the yard to him. Now it was mainly the Factor who was speaking – 'finish the shearing on the Mains this coming week... needing five hooks sent frae Tifty... a week if the weather holds, God willing...' Soon the two men took a well-trodden path between the house and the kailyard and descended to the mill. From the speed with which their heads passed out of sight, he could guess at the steepness of the steps.

While the visitors were down at the mill, the red haired woman and her mother set to work turning the screw on the granite cheese press. Still he waited, waited, and looked over from time to time, trying to catch the younger woman's eye whenever she looked up from her work, but she ignored him as successfully as if he were not there at all, as if the horses' reins were tied to a dead stump instead of being held in his living hand. As he stood waiting in the glare of the sun, a trickle of sweat made its slow progress down his spine.

Eventually the Laird and the Factor reappeared, peching a bit with the effort of the climb up the steps, and followed by a big solid man wearing a long apron, and grey with dust from head to foot. The only colour in his face was the strong pink of exertion that showed through where the trickles of sweat had eroded channels in the dust on his temples. Andrew recognised the Miller of Tifty, not only from the Kirk, but from the coarse imitations that he had seen. There were some – Jamie Buchan and the like – who, after a few glasses in the alehouse at Woodhead, would imitate the Miller's stance, feet planted square and folded arms resting on their bellies, and his staccato speech, pretending to snap out orders to Young Will and Gibb as they went about their tasks. And they would laugh at how his belly was bigger than the year before, it was no wonder when he took so much from them in multures, he had to be putting them somewhere. Sometimes the laughter would stop, and their voices would drop as they hinted at other things, things that were never spoken of directly, not to an outsider like him, anyway. Watching the man's bearing from close quarters, he guessed that those same folk, who were happy to poke fun at the Miller in his absence, would not dare say a word against him to his face.

As the Miller reached out to clasp the Laird's hand before he mounted, Andrew noticed the smooth stump, all that remained of the right index finger. Andrew had heard the story sure enough. How the Miller had been lucky to keep his hand, one time when he had lost his patience with the stuttering mill-gear and reached in, without thinking, to make an adjustment while it was still turning. If Gibb had not seen and leapt in to help him, well, there were stories of millers whose hands or arms had been crushed in the mill-gear, and worse than that even, there was the tale of the mill that had been abandoned after the miller's body was found contorted and crushed, stretched around the great cogwheel as it still strained to turn. That was somewhere way far away, down in England, in Cornwall he thought they had said, but the story had legs and had travelled the length of two countries to disturb Tifty's sleep.

The Miller turned stiffly on his heel. Andrew's greeting died in his throat as the Miller's eyes raked across his face and past him without a flicker of recognition, ignoring him even more thoroughly than his daughter had. Before mounting, Andrew watched his wide back as he crossed the yard and started down the steps to the mill.

The rest of the day they rode the lands around Tifty, taking the ale and cheese that the tenants' wives offered at each farmtoun, and the sound of Andrew Lammie's trumpet could be heard from far off as it marked their progress between the touns. At Meikle Gourdas, on the north side of Tifty's hill, they made a long stop to admire the grand new building work that was in progress, for Ironsyde was having built a long, broad byre that would hold many kye when it was done, although that was more likely to be next year than this. And Ironsyde said that if it was done by Christmas, then the Factor himself could come at Hogmanay and christen his new fiddle and the byre both, and the Factor was gey pleased at that. It was a challenge, he said, for the pair of them, for it took a load of work to do either to perfection, and the folk of Fyvie would judge on the night of Hogmanay who had done the better job when his fiddling spurred them on to dance until the byre was shaken to the ground. Old Ironsyde laughed at that and clapped the Factor on the shoulder, and said it was more like that the Factor would have his fiddle smashed over his head by some drunken dancer, for all that it might have taken him a year and a half of winter nights to fashion it. And so they shook hands on it, and called on Andrew Lammie and the Laird of Fyvie himself as witnesses, and with the Laird as a witness there could be no backing down.

As the day lengthened, they turned their horses' heads back towards the castle. Tired now, the greyhounds trotted along close behind the mare's hooves. As they crossed the long low hill between Camalouns and Cardonwell, Andrew turned his gaze east, to where the thin trails of peat smoke from Tifty's cooking fires rose into the still air. He breathed deep, then turned his head in the other direction, to look down on the smooth flow of the Ythan in its wide valley. The low, round topped hill fell in rippling ridges towards the river, and then the land mounted in the same easy way from the western bank. And in the distance, blue against the pale sky and the still-glaring sun, rose the high peaks of the far Highland hills, the rough lands where lawless Hielan men gathered to plan their raids on the douce Lowlanders' cattle.

When at last they arrived back at the Castle, the sun was low in the sky and the harling plaster on the walls glowed rose-pink. The Laird and his Factor dismounted, and throwing the reins into Andrew's hands, strolled towards the gardens to take in the last of the sun, with the greyhounds slinking like cats around the Laird's long legs. The horses' heads drooped as Andrew led them through the yett. The courtyard was shady and cool. He allowed the horses a long drink at the trough before leading them over to the stables, where he hung his trumpet and his sword in its scabbard carefully on a nail on the wall. Then he helped the ostler with the tack, hefting the saddle from each horse's back. He liked to see the quick shiver of pleasure that passed over their hides as they welcomed the release. The chestnut mare chewed contentedly on a mouthful of straw, flicking her ears back one at a time to hear his humming as he drew the curry comb in long strokes across her flanks, and bent to tease out the knots that the day's sweat and dust had tied in her fetlocks.

And as he hummed, he smiled to himself, and thought of the day just passed, and the morning at Tifty, the woman with the red hair and how, when the Miller had passed out of sight, and just as he was turning to place his foot in the stirrup, she came across the yard carrying a muck rake on her way to the byre, and as she brushed past him she muttered something, barely moving her lips, and still without a glance in his direction. And how he had to twist his lips down to stop himself from smiling as he leapt into the saddle, and he was laughing through the trumpet as he gave the blast that sent them on their way, because despite all the time she had spent talking to the Laird of Fyvie and his Factor, all polite as if she gave a damn about whatever it was they had to say, there was only a single word in all that time that mattered one bit to her, and that was the one word she had muttered to him as she went past him on her way to the byre, and that word was, 'Tomorrow.'

IV

Annie lay staring into the dark above her bed, and listening to the rush of the burn in the glen below. In all that land, it was the only place where the burn hurried in its course, cutting between two hills that pressed themselves together, running faster down among the boulders in a steep sided glen. Her sisters snored gently beside her. The house creaked as it cooled and settled. Her parents were still awake, talking quietly in their room across the narrow landing. She could hear their voices rising and falling, but not their words. She thought of the day just gone, and saw Andrew riding into the yard again with the wind ruffling his hair, and thought of how well he looked in the red and gold, and of how it would be with them tomorrow, when she slipped away from the toun and the chores and took the path to the south of the Brig of Skeugh. She would go on until she came to a clearing where a great beech had fallen, and you could sit or lie easily in the dry hollow space under the old dead trunk, and no one could see you or know you were there, and in the spring the wood anemones lay sprinkled like stars on the ground, and the celandines shone like little suns. She would crawl in under the old tree, and Andrew would be waiting for her. That would be twice in the same week that she had seen him, two feast days with which to fatten her memory. Her mother, too, had maybe had a taste of something forbidden when she saw him riding into the yard today, because there had been a suppressed excitement in her voice that Annie had never heard when her father was about the place, 'Agnes, come see, it's the Laird's trumpeter! Is that nae a pretty man!' And she had laid down the broken pith of the reed that she had been stripping of its green sheath, and had had to slow her steps on the way to the door, and she had not allowed her eyes to rest on him, but had merely given him a quick glance once over, and shrugged as she said, 'Oh aye, I've seen him about the place afore now,' giving no hint of how often, and how recently, she had seen his pretty face.

It made her laugh, the way her mother thought the Laird's coming to Tifty was such a great, grand thing. When she heard the sound of the trumpet blowing close to Tifty she had given her one of her funny wee smiles, 'Och, Agnes, that'll be the Laird of Fyvie come by. We're aye glad to welcome him to Tifty,' but it had been the sight of Andrew, sitting up proud in the saddle, that had animated her mother's voice, not the Laird when he came slumping along behind with his fat Factor. An image formed in her mind: the Laird, gawky and awkward in servants' livery, holding the horses' reins, while Andrew strode across the yard in a powdered wig and entertained her mother with his conversation. Well might she nod and laugh and curtsey then, like some daft puppet, as she had done that afternoon, while the Laird droned on and on, colourlessly, about his harvest and his hunting and his hounds, and enquired after the health of the entire household in minute detail. That was one thing you could say in the man's favour, at least – that he took an interest in his folk, not just the lands that they farmed and that he had never expected to inherit. And then she felt some pity for him, and a little guilt for laughing at him and his grey, solemn ways, it was no wonder he was slow and sad when he had lost both his father and his brother earlier the same year. And she was glad that she had made him smile a bit at least, when he had turned to her and said, 'And Agnes, you're looking bonnier than ever. Tell me, there's surely one or two loons in the parish breaking their hearts over you, is there na?' and she had looked him straight in the eye in answering, 'Na, my Lord, naebody that I ken, and I'm nae breaking my own heart over any of them, either.' That had made him give a wee faint smile, 'Na? Are you sure?' Then he had glanced up at her mother as he continued, 'Well, well, I'm sure your mother and father will find someone for you if they try hard enough, eh, Helen?' And her mother had stretched her lips wide at that, and nodded, nodded, nodded, 'Och I've nae doubt, my Lord. Look at her so bonnie now, you would never think she was sic a wee skinny shargar when she was born, would you? Do you ken I had to tak her down to the Shargar Stane, to stop us from losing her?' Annie had blushed and laughed and put up with their nonsense, and held her peace, and given no hint that she had not given a quite truthful answer to the Laird's question. For you could not well admit to such things when the Kirk Session was aye on the lookout for such scandalous conduct as a kiss on the cheek. And neither she nor Andrew had a mind to suffer Mr Jaffray's rebuke for it in the Kirk. Nor was she yet minded to give her parents the news that her sweetheart had to work for his fee because he had neither birth nor lands nor silver, even if it was an Earl who paid him. The thought of her father's red clenched face, and the click of her mother's tongue, loud in the silence that would follow that news, kept her quiet on the matter.

But it was hard, holding it all inside her as she had to, and not being able to say a word about it. Within her, his name circled with its own rhythm, *Andrew Lammie, Andrew Lammie*, like a catkin in a pool in the burn. When she was alone – which was not often – she might say it aloud. But in the house, or around the mill, or at any time when others might be about, she only allowed his name to ebb and flow within her. Now, as she turned onto her side with her back resting against Jane's, she did not even dare to whisper it into the darkness of the room, though she could feel it pressing against her lips, as if she had only to open her mouth and it would pop out, like a bubble, of its own accord. And in the day, too, she had to take tight control of her tongue, in case she were to ask her mother a question, 'Did you see my brother Will?' and instead of saying 'Will' she were to say 'Andrew', and then her mother would look at her in a funny way and she would blush and stutter and correct herself but it would be too late.

So there was his name, filling her up like water in a well. And maybe he was filling up with her name too. Only that was the odd thing, he had given her a new name, and how it had happened was that he had a new name himself now he had come to Fyvie, Andrew Lamb he had been in Edinburgh but the Fyvie folk had taken his name and made it their own, Lammie, the same way they took the name of a place like Backhill and made it into Backie, it sounded more friendly-like. So anyway he had said, since he had a new name now, then she should too, and she had said, 'Aye aa right then, what's it to be?' And as they sat side by side, on the dry leaf litter under the fallen trunk of the beech, he had played with her fingers as he had played with her name, 'Agnes – Nannie' (because that was the play-name she had had as a child) '– my Nannie – mine Annie – my Annie, my bonnie Annie, Annie and Andrew Lammie, what do you think of that? Mill of Tifty's Annie and Bonnie Andrew Lammie, it sounds right, do you no think?' And she had cuffed his shoulder and said, 'You're nae as bonnie as all that,' and he had said, as they laughed into each other's faces and he pulled her to him, 'Oh aye, but I am, you ken I am, that's how you like me.'

And since then she had been Annie to him and never Agnes, though she was Agnes still to her family and everyone else, and never Nan any more at all.

She snuggled her head into the bolster, as if it was Andrew's shoulder, and her breathing grew deep and regular, and she dreamed.

William Smith blew out the flame of the cruisie lamp and the room was plunged into blackness. He closed the drapes around his side of the bed. Helen was already lying under the covers, her feet cold against his bare calf. Her breath was quiet and even, and listening to it, he hoped he would be joining her in sleep soon. It had been another hard day at the mill. A long line of tenants with grain to grind, he had had to turn some of them away, telling them to return tomorrow, and they had argued, and left with sullen resentful looks. There were never folk for arguing like the Fyvie folk, it was the same when he called the tenants in for their mill service, when the heather-thatch was leaking or it was time to fetch home the new millstones. But however they might grumble over the mill service, he would hold them to it, every day of it, they were thirled to his mill and he made damned sure they knew it, *What, man, would you rather your oats rotted in the damp of a roofless houf?*

So there had been that. And then the Laird of Fyvie riding by, with the Factor, and asking for five hooks from Tifty to finish off the shearing on the Mains. Who would he send? Jess, as usual, and her son's wife, Mary. Jean, and Barbara. Who else? Not one of his own womenfolk. No, he would keep their strength for his own shearing, start it Tuesday, if the weather held. Oh aye – Margaret Urquhart he could send down. She had been a good enough hand with the muck-spreading. It was five hands lost from his own shearing, but you couldna naysay the Factor, not right in front of his Laird's face.

His thoughts were beginning to blur together when he was jerked back into consciousness by a racket in the kitchen downstairs. The door opening and slamming shut, feet stamping on the flags, mutterings. Young Will back from his drinking. Tonight he would sleep downstairs. Until a few years ago, Young Will had slept in the hurley bed that pulled out from under their own French bed, but these days Will more often than not fell onto the pallet in the kitchen next to Gibb, instead of staggering up the creaking stair. Tifty preferred it that way anyway. He had had words about it with his son, 'You winna lie snoring like a pig wi that reek of drink on your breath while your mother sleeps in the same room.' It also meant that Young Will was forced to rise early, ready for work in the mill, when Grizel started her clatter in the kitchen, and Gibb stirred next to him. It was a better arrangement than the days when Tifty had had to go back up the stair to kick his snoring stupefied son out of the hurley and into consciousness.

Helen stirred beside him, and then spoke from the darkness.

'William. I canna sleep.'

'Is it any wonder, wi the racket that lad's making?'

'Na. It's nae that.'

He had an idea she was going to ask for a third servant. Again. He had made it plain already: there was room and work for more than the two servants if he chose, but too many servants gnawed away at a man's wealth the way rats gnawed at grain. He had no mind to take on another with four women of his own blood in the house. There were plenty hands to feed the chickens and pigs, make soap and butter and ale, spread the dung on the rigs, and shear the crops.

'Let it lie until the morn, wife. I'm needing my sleep.'

They lay next to each other, listening to each other's breathing. After a while, Tifty sighed.

'What is it then, wife?'

'The Laird came by the day.'

'There's nae need to keep me awake to tell me that. You ken I saw him myself. '

'Aye, William, I ken, so you did. But you never saw what I saw.'

'What, then?'

'Him talking to Agnes.'

'To Agnes? What of it? He aye asks after our daughters, and Will.'

'He does, William, but there's been something in it this last wee while... I canna say for sure, but it's the way he speaks, and the way he smiles at her. I've had an idea in my head these last months, and it's time we spoke about it. And there's a way she has, too. She started up like a snipe the day, when she heard the trumpet at the foot of the hill. William, have you thought why it is she's been gey hard to find about the place when her work's done?'

'She's aye been a one for wandering, Helen.'

'I just think there's a way they are with each other. Just the way they are in their speaking and their looking. And her awa walking in the woods by herself whenever she gets the chance. Well... how are you minded about it?'

'I'm minded about naethin, woman, except that your mind is wandering. Let me sleep now.'

But he did not sleep. While his wife snored quietly beside him, he stared into the blank darkness. Thinking of the times when the Laird had passed by the mill on his hunting trips, and Sabbath mornings in the kirkyard after the service, and now it seemed to Tifty that on those occasions the Laird had liked to speak to Agnes more than to others, and that sometimes she would say something to the Laird – Smith himself had never managed to hear what it was – that made a smile come to his lips and linger there as he rode off. And Seton had not wed yet, though there must be plenty rich and landed ladies in his world to choose from. So he had maybe been waiting to have his head turned, and a lass like Agnes could surely do that to any man, whatever his rank, if she had a will to. And if she did not have the sense to keep her mouth shut for long enough? Well even then, they said that the Laird's mother, the Lady Seton, had had a hell of a tongue on her, and it was maybe true that a man might suffer it better in a wife if he had been raised on it. And if his main concerns in a wife were for beauty and bairns, well, Agnes had the first, and could give him the second, no doubt of that. He was away high above them of course, a great Earl as well as a grand Laird, but in a funny way that might count for Smith's suit, rather than against it, for Alexander Seton might be happy to take a modest tocher, with all his wealth he hardly needed to drive a good bargain.

When he called these things to mind it seemed to Tifty that his wife was maybe not so fanciful after all, and a wee bit encouragement might be all that was needed. Only he would have to be sure, good and sure, if he was ever to take action on the matter. So he must make sure of Helen, unless – until? – unless they were sure of their catch. She had got them into difficulties before with her claiking tongue. That business with Sinckler. They had been careful, once they had known the danger, and lucky too, and they had escaped the worst of it. But it had still taken years before the hard stares in the Kirk had softened, and the handshakes had taken on a warmer feel.

If Helen was right, then once again they would give their neighbours' tongues no rest for a long while. Only this time – more than twenty years on – he would be glad of it. His pulse began to quicken.

He argued with himself in place of sleep, and the next day, Saturday, he spoke to Helen as soon as she woke, 'Dinna breathe a word to any soul about what you said last night. This is a matter to be sure of, before anything. Nae a single word, mind?'

V

As Grizel rose from the table to take the dishes for cleaning, Tifty gave her an order.

'Go down to your mother's and tell her she's to go to the Laird's shearing the day after tomorrow, her and Mary. And find Jean and Barbara, and tell them the same, and Margaret Urquhart too. And when you see Margaret Urquhart, dinna forget to tell her man he's to finish that dyke the day, or he'll owe me another day's work.'

'Margaret Urquhart, sir?'

'Aye. You heard right.'

'But Margaret's wi bairn, sir.'

'And what's that to you?'

'Naethin, sir. I'll go.'

So she went, and Tifty went down to the mill with Young Will and Gibb, and thought no more of it until there came a soft knock on the door at dinner-time when the household was gathered around the table in the kitchen once more.

Jane got up to open the door when his call of, 'Enter!' went unheeded. He heard a quick exchange – 'Peace be here, Mistress Jane, might I speak to your father a minute?' and Jane came and laid a hand on his shoulder, 'It's Margaret Urquhart, she's wanting a word wi you. Na, she winna come in.'

He scraped his chair back and went to the door. Stood beneath the lintel. Arms crossed. Looked Margaret Urquhart up and down. The frown lines between her brows spoiled the look of her pale, pretty face. Her plaid was gathered around her but did not hide the swell of her belly.

'I'm sorry to bother you at your meat, sir.'

'What is it you want?'

'Grizel came this morning to send me to the shearing.'

'Aye, so she did. What about it?'

'Well, sir...' she opened up her plaid to show him her bulging middle. 'I'm wi bairn. I thought maybe you had forgot about it...'

Margaret looked up at him, waiting for his answer.

'And so?'

Her eyes fidgeted away from him. 'I canna bend, sir. How can I go to the shearing if I canna bend?'

He cleared his throat. Looked over his shoulder back into the room. 'Helen. Tell this lassie how you spent the whole summer digging peat when you were carrying Jane.'

He did not wait for Helen to start up, and she did not try to.

'You're in service at Tifty, Margaret Urquhart, and Tifty is to send five hooks to the Laird's shearing.'

'I thought maybe another of your cottars' wives...'

There was a pain coming in his jaw, and he resisted the urge to press the stub of his finger at it to relieve the tension.

'All of my cottars' wives are to go.'

She made no reply, and he waited for her to turn and leave, but still she stood before him, one hand picking at the hem of her plaid at the elbow, looking to the wall at the side of him. Finally she lifted her eyes to his face again and went to open her mouth, and he could feel a vein starting to throb in his temple. But before either he or Margaret could speak, he heard Agnes's voice from the room behind him, 'Let me go, father.'

He looked round over his shoulder to see Agnes standing just behind him, smiling at him that way she had. Beyond her, at the table, Jane made a sour face and rolled her eyes at Bessie.

'I've told this Margaret she's to go.'

'Aye, I ken, father. But the Laird winna mind who you send down to him. And you ken I've aye liked to go down to the Mains.'

He narrowed his eyes and thought for a bit. Truth was, he had forgotten how far gone the Urquhart woman was. Here was a way out. And another thing – here was his daughter more or less begging to go down to the Laird of Fyvie's own rigs, not far from the Castle where he lived. There was maybe a reason for that. The pain in his jaw began to slacken off. He gave an abrupt nod. 'Aye. Fine. You go in her place, lass.'

He turned back to the Urquhart woman as she stood outside the door, still waiting. 'Right then. You'll be getting back to your work.' He closed the door over before she turned to go.

Annie had her own reasons for wanting to be near to the castle. And she had been glad to help Margaret when she had heard the iron starting to come into her father's voice. Three months only Margaret had to go before the bairn came, how could she be stooping and swinging a hook all the day? And she knew that Margaret had been sick, awful sick, for much of the time. She thought back to the May-time, when she had first guessed that Margaret was carrying a bairn. Margaret and her husband, John Duncan, standing in the yard outside the mill-house with all the other Tifty folk. Two dozen souls gathered together in the pearl-grey light of the first morning of May to sain the whole farmtoun with fire and prayer. Two piles of wood had stood ready to be lit while they bowed their heads and her father intoned a brief prayer, calling on the Father, Son and Holy Ghost to grant them protection in the year ahead. Then, with a flick of his fingers, her father had indicated that the fires should be lit, and Peter, the broad-backed ploughman, had bent to his task. The members of the five households of Tifty had stood solemnly around, while the dawn light grew stronger in the east. When a fine white ash was falling from the embers, and the sun appeared on the horizon behind a thin strip of gold and purple cloud, the women took up rakes and deftly spread the embers, making two long smoking rectangles with a narrow path between them. Then all the bairns of Tifty were sent along the path, to purify them and keep them from ill-health. It was only four-five years or so since she herself had walked between the fires, and well she remembered how the heat had hit her cheeks and made her step quickly and carefully, looking straight ahead at her mother's stern face, waiting for her at the end of the aisle. Now, the bairns walking between the embers had the same look, wide-eyed and solemn. Peter and Jess's three grandchildren held hands in a line, and ran to James and Mary when they had done, 'Father, Minnie, did you see us?' Then came the two Reid boys, and their sister awkwardly balancing the youngest Reid bairn on her hip. Skinny wee things, clothed in little more than rags, all four of them, for their father had no trade. John Duncan, and his wife, Margaret Urquhart, new come to Tifty at Martinmas, stood by and Annie had watched as a secret smile passed between them, and it was then that she had guessed that next year Margaret would be carrying a bairn in her arms as she walked between the embers, and no doubt that was what Margaret was thinking of as she ran her hand down the apron that covered her belly, still flat but not for long.

Then finally John Scott, the herd, too big for this almost at fourteen, sauntered through with his hands in his pockets, while George Scott and Jean Cheyne, his parents, looked on with pride. When the bairns were through, it was the turn of the cattle, to protect them from elf-shot and sickness. Skinny and weak as they were after a winter foraging on stubble and little else, John still had a job with them, for the first of their number kept shying away to one side, until he took her by the ear and pushed her nose right in between the embers and gave her a hard slap on the rump, and away she went. Then all the others followed on wobbly legs, and John, nonchalantly swinging a stick, followed the last one and drove them all away to the pastures.

When the kye had all passed between the needfires, then the men took up brands from the fire and all the folk of Tifty followed in a line behind her father around the bounds of the rigs, to make certain that all of Tifty's lands would give a good yield of oats and bere barley and flax. Already the new growth was sprouting a fresh and brilliant green, and the larks were rising, and peewits quartered their territories. When it was done, each man led his family home to the hill across the Tifty burn to relight the fire in his own hearth with a new and potent flame for thc safekeeping of his family.

So that had been Margaret's secret on the dawn of the first of May, and by the time the sun had set that same day, Agnes – she had still been Agnes then – had a secret of her own. Her mother had sent her the half-mile west to Cardonwell to pick up the new shoes for Young Will from the cottar there who made a wee bit extra living as a cobbler. She had let her bare feet choose the best way among the twining network of paths that led to Cardonwell, taking her time, for being the first of May it was a holiday. She had taken up the shoes from the cobbler's wife and admired the workmanship – he had done a fine job – and then she had wandered further off down the Tifty burn, and it was then that she had first spoken to the old Laird's new trumpeter, who like her was taking his holiday in the Wood of Fyvie. He had come from Edinburgh some months before with Alexander Seton, when Seton had received news of his brother's death and his father's illness.

On the tenth day of May, the old Earl had died, and Alexander Seton had succeeded him and become the Third Earl of Dunfermline, and the Laird of Fyvie. And by that time, she was already thinking up her excuses to go back to the Wood of Fyvie, and soon the house was filled with more reeds than they could use for lamp wicks or scouring brushes in a year, for they grew very well in the woods near the Brig of Skeugh.

VI

To the south of the Castle the Mains of Fyvie were ripe with the Laird of Fyvie's own crop. The heads of oats bowed low with the summer's gathered sunshine and the larks and pipits sang as they climbed into the air. A great brown hare lying in her scrape sat up from her late summer dozing and listened, ears upright and twitching, eyes swivelling in their sockets, and then sprang suddenly away, leaving the tall stalks shivering as they closed like a curtain behind her. Then to the place where the hare had lain, there came the rhythmic sound of the shearers' singing, and soon a line of women passed by, bending and rising all together, and their hooks flashed in the sun as the stalks shivered a last time and fell in bundles. Then soon behind the shearers came other hands, quick hands gathering the fallen stalks, gathering and tying and setting the stooks on their ends, and then men's strong arms to carry them to the Laird's cornyard.

At one end of the line of shearers, Annie stopped to lay her hand to the small of her back and rub away the pain. In the heat of noon, sparks swam in front of her eyes. They were nearing the end of the rig, and in the distance she could see the serving men bringing the luncheon down from the castle at last, carrying the ale, cheese and fish, butter and bread that they would eat in the welcome shade of the Mains's small orchard. Quickly, she bent to her work again, and was not far behind the line of shearers when it reached the end of the rig and split into groups of two and three. The women's light voices drifted back to her as they walked up the slope ahead into the orchard. There were a dozen or so women doing the shearing, including the five of them down from Tifty.

At the end of the rig she tucked her hook into her belt. As she walked slowly up the slope, she held her wrist in her left hand, rotating and flexing it slowly, to test for sprains. The men who had been following behind the line of shearers, gathering the stooks, began to overtake her, and so she was the last to arrive in the shade of the orchard, and had to wait while the labourers clustered around the four serving men. Her heart began to beat when she saw that Andrew was one of them. He was pouring out ale for the labourers, filling to the brim the wooden cups that they held out. He was taking his time about it too, talking to two of the girls down from Meikle Gourdas, asking after them, and how the work was doing, and when they would be shearing the corn at Gourdas, and whether Ironsyde was likely to win his bet with the Factor. Jealousy slithered suddenly awake in her belly, and then vanished just as quickly when they moved off, and he turned his full attention to her. While the other serving men packed up, and the labourers dispersed into the orchard in search of shade, they played the game of conversation, 'Ah, Mistress Agnes of Tifty, and how are you the day? And how is your father? And your mother?' with as many smiles and glances as they dared. Then reluctantly she made to move away. His curly head bobbed near to her own before they parted – 'Dinna wait for the others when the work's done,' and she whispered back, 'How's that? You'll maybe be off to Meikle Gourdas the night,' thinking she was better teasing him than testing him over the Gourdas lasses. But her fingers fluttered as his hand brushed hers lightly when he at last handed her a full cup of ale, and she caught his eye and nodded yes, yes, before turning away.

She looked around for a place to sit and eat in the shade. All through the orchard, the labourers had spread themselves on the ground, and were arching their backs to clear away the pain of the morning's work, spreading their limbs in the dappled shade. Jess's voice close by startled her.

'Come and sit by me, Mistress Agnes. That tree right next to mine looks like a good one.'

She looked down to see Jess sitting propped up against one of the old apple trees, wriggling her back and shoulders with pleasure against the knobbles on its trunk. The fine network of lines on Jess's round face deepened as she smiled at Annie, patting the ground beside her. As Annie lowered herself to sit, Jess asked, 'How are you finding the work the day, Mistress Agnes?'

'Ocht nae so bad, Jess. Only it's hot!'

'It is that. And it doesna look like it will break for a day or two.'

'That's good for the shearing.'

'Aye, but nae for my back. The Lord alone kens how many more years of this work I have in me.'

'Ocht, Jess, you're nae old.'

'Aye, I am, Mistress Agnes, I'm fifty-six year old and I feel it, and dinna say I dinna look it, because I do, and I can remember three Lairds in the castle at Fyvie. And –'

Here Andrew, who had been gathering together his ale kegs and corks, straightened up and walked on past on his way to the Castle. Jess paused, and Annie, out of the corner of her eye, saw Jess peeking round the edge of her mutch towards her.

Then Jess continued, '– and nane of them had a trumpeter as bonnie as him that's in the Laird's service now.'

Annie blinked, then stared back blankly at Jess, refusing the invitation in her dancing eyes. She shrugged, and tried to sound offhand as she answered, 'Do you think so?' Then she changed the subject by making a show of coughing, pretending she had sucked a flake of fish down her windpipe. Jess patted her on the back gently until it cleared, and let her hand rest between Annie's shoulder blades for a moment before withdrawing it.

'Are you aa right, there, lass?'

'Aye, Jess, I'm fine. It just went down the wrong way, that's aa.'

She pulled her knees up and rested her back against the tree. Sure enough the knobbled bark felt good where it pressed into her tired muscles. She looked up through the low branches with their ripening apples at the brilliant white clouds that floated lazily above. They ate their meal in silence. When she had done, Annie slid the hook from her belt and took a sharpening stone from her pocket. Spitting on the curved blade of the hook, she began to grind its edge. The stone made the sound of the sea as it ground the curved edge sharp. After some time, she cleared her throat and broke the silence.

'I've aye wanted to sing the story about Jeannie of Saltoun. Would you learn it me, Jess?'

There was a pause before Jess answered, 'Aye, you've aye liked that one. And you're maybe ready for it now. But mind, if I learn you that song, I want you to sing it right, sing it proper, and sing it real.'

Annie stopped her grinding for a moment and looked Jess steadily in the eye. 'Aye, Jess, I can do that.'

'Then you come down to my hame any night and I'll learn you it, just like I learned you your other songs. But wait until this shearing's over. It's aa I can do to get back up the road to Tifty after this work. And speaking of the work, it's time we got back to it, though I'm loath to leave the comfort of this tree. Here, Mistress Agnes, tak my hand and help an old woman to her feet.'

Annie jumped up quickly, stretching out her hand to Jess. Around them, the other workers began to stretch and rise, grumbling, to their feet, and set their faces down the slope where too many rigs still waited to be sheared.

The sun was past its zenith, but still the heat shimmered over the rigs. Annie took up her place once more at the end of the line of shearers. Before the work began, each woman bent and with two deft swipes caused the stalks to fall in a cross on the ground, a charm against hurting the wrist. From the other end of the line, Jess gave a long call, a high, nasal, wavering cry, and then they bent to their work as one, bending and swinging, bending and swinging throughout the long hot afternoon with the sun beating on their backs and their shadows lengthening, until the red sun came close to the horizon and the air began to cool. At the end of a rig they halted at last, welcoming the chill of the breeze in the blue evening air, and stood blethering while the men gathered together the last stooks of the day.

When it was nearly dark, Jess looked around her for the other women of Tifty, and found only three to walk home with, for Mistress Agnes had not stopped to blether with the other women, but had taken the road home as soon as the last calls of the evening trumpet, sounding from the castle nearby, had died away.

VII

He was waiting for her on the bridge. When he saw her, he held his arms wide open in welcome and she ran to him. He caught her and swung her around, his kisses warm on the skin of her neck, and then they joined hands and ran away up into the wood, so that the shearers would not see them together when they passed by on their way home.

When they were sure they were out of sight and sound, he leaned his back against a big tree, and pulled her close in towards him, and for a while the only thing there was for them was the sweetness of kissing and the softness of each other's lips and skin.

Then Annie linked her fingers behind his neck and swung back so that she could look him full in the face, 'Andrew, it's a whole week the shearing will take, a week! Will you aye bring the ale like you did the day?'

'I'll mak sure of it.'

'And we'll meet at the brig the nights, when the shearing's done.'

'Aye, each night we can do the same, just like this.'

'For a week.'

'A whole week.'

They were laughing, swinging gently from side to side. And then he dropped his hands to her hips and pushed her back to take a good look at her.

'Look at you, Annie, my Annie, I never saw sic-like a lass in aa my life before, I never kenned you were here waiting for me.'

'And I never kenned I was waiting for you at aa, until you came, and then I thought I must have called you to me, aa the times I was thinking on the world awa frae Fyvie.'

'Did you think on Edinburgh?'

'Aye, I thought on Edinburgh and how it must be there.'

'And what if I had never came? What if the auld Laird had never brought me here?'

'You'd have came some way or other.'

'Aye, so I would, if you were calling me.'

'Tell me what like it is in Edinburgh.'

He told her, and she listened, and questioned, and did not believe half the things he said, and told him so. And all the time as they talked, she twisted and twined the curls of his hair in and out through the tips of her fingers, and his arms were wrapped around her to hold her close to him.

They were quiet again for a while, looking up through the branches of the tree and watching the clouds change from pink to purple, and feeling the dew-damp begin to cool the air. Then she heard a noise from the direction of the path, the other shearers returning to Tifty, and they were both suddenly alert. 'Andrew, it's time we were awa,' which was true – it was nearly dark, and there was a chill coming in the air. Reluctantly, they walked down through the woods to the Brig of Skeugh, and here they could hardly part for kissing, each time one went to move away the other reached out for another last kiss, they could never have their fill. Finally, she resisted him, refusing a kiss but lifting her fingers to caress a patch of stubble that grew on his upper lip, in the crease between his mouth and nose. It made her feel proud of him and tender for him at the same time, proud because it showed he was a man, and tender because of the way he had missed it when he shaved that morning, like a wee boy trying to look after himself. Then she stood up on her tiptoes to kiss him there, the wee ends of the hairs tickling her lips, whispered, 'God gie you a good night, my Andrew,' in his ear, and then she was off and running. She had to run fast and long to catch the other shearers as they stopped to bid each other good night by the willows on the Tifty burn. She deflected their curiosity as best she could, and Grizel, better than a sister, asked nothing as they walked together up the path to the mill-house.

VIII

The weather broke at the end of the week of shearing, just when the maidens had taken the clyack sheaf, that was the last sheaf to be cut, into the byre at the Mains, and dressed it in women's clothes. Water sheeted out of the sky for three days with barely a break. At Tifty, the mill turned from dawn to dusk, and the Miller cursed under his breath at the bad weather that gave him power to grind the Laird's harvest while it left his own grain to stand rotting on the rigs. Annie, her mother and sisters and Grizel, were busied about the house with the combing of flax and the spinning of linen. In the evenings, the menfolk came back up from the mill through the rain, jogging to stay dry, and threw themselves down in the wooden chairs by the fire to get warm.

On the Tuesday, the weather began to clear and Annie bridled the pony and hung over his back a pair of wicker panniers, which she loaded with cheeses wrapped in muslin. She took the path to Woodhead with her father and brother, the pony splashing resolutely through the puddles while she kept as much as she could to the tufts and ridges of turf along the sides of the path. The sky was lowering, dark clouds full of rain, and as they reached Woodhead large, heavy drops began to fall. She threw her plaid over her head as she led the pony in between the ramshackle stalls that sprawled around the mercat cross. Trade was slower than it had been in the summer, and the Fyvie folk went about their business hurriedly, heads down, wasting little time in gossip as they rushed to finish their business and get out of the rain.

The weather brightened around midday, and young Jamie Buchan came up to her with a great broad grin, saying 'Is that the tempting cheese of Fyvie you have there, Agnes? Gie us a round of it and I'll maybe have more luck wi the lassies,' for the Fyvie cheese had a reputation thereabouts as a love potion, strange though it seemed to Annie who had sweated in the making of it at the cheese-press. Her father stared coldly at Jamie, but was still happy to take his money off him and drop it in his deep pocket along with the other coins. She picked out one of her best cheeses for Jamie and was just handing it to him when suddenly the dull market crowd parted, and heads turned as Andrew Lammie and the Laird of Fyvie passed through, the Laird on his black gelding and Andrew on his chestnut mare with the harness sparkling in a shaft of sun that came in the break between the showers.

She did not think he saw her as he rode straight-backed above the crowd, looking neither right nor left, but her eyes were drawn to him of their own accord. Following behind, the Laird gave a brief, wan smile in her direction, half-heartedly raising a hand to her and to the rest of the crowd around him. Then she felt a nudge in her ribs and she started guiltily, and was surprised to see her father looking down at her with some satisfaction, or so it seemed from the smug look on his face. Before the horses passed out of sight, he nodded his head in their direction, saying with appreciation, 'Now there's a man, Agnes, eh?'

She could never have thought he would say such a thing, and her heart lifted with unexpected gladness. She opened her mouth to speak, but could not think of a single thing to say, because the right thing would be if Andrew came up to speak to him after Kirk, or came by the mill, to ask if he might walk out with her. She had never thought she might have to tell him herself, like this, with no time to prepare what she wanted to say. So she shrugged and gathered her plaid around her and avoided his eye in confusion, reddening a bit as he nudged her again. And then he continued, 'Aye, he's a fine man, the Laird of Fyvie, a very fine man indeed.'

An empty sad disappointed feeling washed through her. 'Oh aye,' she said, and added slowly, 'nane better.' But strangely enough there was a feeling of relief that came with it as well, quite unexpected, and she did not understand why or where it came from.

When they returned in the evening her father was in a good humour, although they had not got such a good price as he had wanted for their cheeses. He went up the stairs, rattling the few silver coins in his pocket, and Annie, in the kitchen, heard the creak as he opened the lid of the wooden kist in the bedroom above. When he came back down the stairs, he was carrying a very thick, very well-thumbed book, and he took a pair of glasses from his chest pocket and sat down to read by the fire. She recognised Markham's *A Way to Get Wealth* from the dirty red tassel that hung between its pages, and the dark brown of the cover. It was always either Markham or the Bible. But on market days it was rarely the Bible.

He read for a while. Jane and Bessie murmured together over their spindles. Her mother dozed. Gibb snored, already in his bed. Young Will had not yet returned from Woodhead. Drinking, most likely, after the market. Annie spun flax into linen, and hummed to herself, thinking through all the song-stories she knew and how to tell them, and in her imagining putting Andrew into some of them because he suited them. She would see him riding into a story, just as he had today when he passed through the market crowd. Now, by the fire, she played with the thought that instead of coming from Edinburgh, she had called him to herself out of one of the old songs. Instead of riding all the way from Edinburgh to claim her, maybe he had come over the sea from Norway in a ship with a golden mast and silken silver sails, and stepped ashore and gone to the great castle of Fyvie, a great lord or a king's son in disguise. And she started singing through the story of Hind Horn, but Andrew kept interfering with it and she lost the thread of the song and had to go back right to the start again because she could not remember where she had got to, but she had not got as far as him going to sea when her father closed his book over and laid it very deliberately on his lap, and she could feel his eyes watching her as she worked.

'So, Agnes.'

'Aye, father?'

He seemed to hesitate. Then he continued.

'The good Laird of Fyvie hasna married yet. I'm thinkimg we could maybe help him find a bonnie wife, of good blood.'

She lost the rhythm for her spinning and, confused, laid her spindle in her lap. At last she found a voice.

'Well, I dinna ken what way we could do that, father.'

'He wouldna settle for a lowborn wife. A gentleman's daughter with a good tocher, that's what he'll be wanting, eh?'

She could feel the colour rising in her cheeks. Always the same things.

'I dinna ken, father, what wife he might want, or what way *we* might find him one. But what would be wrang wi a lowborn wife, if they loved each other? Why is it aye birth, and land, and silver wi you?'

Then he surprised her, because instead of putting her in her place for answering him back, he chuckled away to himself, 'Well, highborn or lowborn, he'll maybe find one soon enough is what I'm thinking. Aye. Soon enough.'

There was a silence between them while she searched for the meaning of his words, and her father continued to watch her while she shifted uncomfortably on the creepie stool. Then he looked away, seeming somehow satisfied, and addressed her mother, talking over the day's news from the market. Annie listened with less than half an ear, while she examined the puzzle of his words from every angle, and thought of what he had said at the market, too, as they had watched Andrew riding past. And as she turned these things over in her mind, an uneasiness came to her and stayed with her for the rest of the evening.

The news from the market was that Cat Campbell from Ardlogie was carrying a bairn. At first she had refused to say whose it was, but the Kirk Session had leaned hard on her, and in tears she had at last given them the name of her lad, and so they were both to do penance for the grievous sin of fornication. And also, that Highland men had raided cattle from a toun beyond the Ythan, fifty head of fine black kye fattened on the pastures of Strathbogie. They had come in the middle of the afternoon, in broad daylight, as the kye strayed and the herd lay back in the long grass, dreaming of his sweetheart maybe and playing a lazy tune on a reed pipe. So quiet and skilled had they been that the lazy lad had neither heard nor suspected a thing until a sudden shower had smattered him in the face, and jumping to his feet to run for the shelter of a dyke he had seen not the wide eyes of the kye staring at him from beneath their polls, but empty pastures stretching to the moors, and just cresting the hill of the high moor, his herd at a frightened gallop and men in long dark plaids running alongside of them. That was his story, though some said that he had had some help from his master's daughter in forgetting about the kye, which would explain why he was so deaf and blind that he could not hear the pounding of two hundred hooves. But that was just dirty talk, and the poor lad had been thrown out by his master, so if any herd came by looking for work you should be sure to ask him if he could hear you well enough. Poor lad, he would have a trouble to find a place without a letter of good conduct from the minister, and might end up wandering the country and take up in the company of all wrong kinds of folk.

Anyway, that was the word that had come round, and so at Tifty the menfolk were put on their guard. From the storeroom at the end of the kitchen, William Smith took out his steel bonnet and a thick leather jerkin and an old sword, and put them ready by the door in case the alarm were to be raised and they must ride out after raiders.

'You must tak tent and watch, my lasses, if you are out on the road alone, for it's nae just kye that the Hielan men are after,' he said, and Annie thought of Eppie Morrie being carried away by the four and twenty Highlandmen. But they were far enough from the high hills for the news to raise more excitement and talk than fear, for it would be on the far side of the Ythan that they would be setting up watchmen at the head of the deep glens that ran up into the hills, and only when the cattle there had been harried and stolen would the raiders cross the river to take the beasts from Fyvie's lands.

On the Saturday night, when her work was done, Annie crossed over the Tifty burn by herself and went up the brae to Jess's cott. It was a poor, shabby structure where the smoke from a single grubby hearth stained the heather thatch black, and the roof frame creaked in the wind, and rain came in through the leaks in the roof to puddle on the bare earth floor. But Jess and Peter gave a warm welcome to all comers, nevertheless. As she approached she was met only by Bella, Jess's old, bony cow, who gazed at her over the open half-door, blinking at her lazily as she chewed the cud. Annie gave her an affectionate scratch on the nose before going in search of Jess, all the time thinking she was glad not to be a cottar, to live like that, and to be quartered together with the beasts.

She found Jess on a bench round the side of the building, shelling peas in the last of the sunshine.

'There you are, Mistress Agnes, will you sit yourself down and sing for me Eppie Morrie? For I'm thinking of her often wi this news of the Hielan men, and it will be a lesson for you to remember and abide by.' Jess smiled as she patted the bench beside her, and Annie found the song and let it out bit by bit into the summer air. When she was done, Jess quietly nodded her head in approval.

'That was the first of the big songs I learned you, was it nae, when you first came to me asking to be learnt them?'

'Aye, Jess, it was.'

'You sing it good, but you could sing it better. Do you ken why?'

'Na, tell me.'

'You still put too much of yourself into it. You see when you sing the bit where she says "There's nae a man in aa Strathdon shall wedded be wi me", it's like it's you that's speaking, no Eppie Morrie herself, because you're thinking it yourself, nae just seeing and telling it. Do you see?'

Annie began to shuffle her feet the way she had done when she was ten, when she had first come to Jess asking for her songs. Then, Jess had looked down at her and asked, 'But dinna you ken a wheen o songs already?'

And Annie had said, 'There's some I just ken, like, the ones aa folk sing. You dinna have to learn them, you just ken them. But there's others you have to learn, like your big story songs. Will you learn me them?'

And Jess had seemed gey pleased with that answer, and said, 'Aye, then, I will. What song do you want to learn first?' And when Annie had answered 'Jeannie of Saltoun,' Jess had shook her head, 'Na. I'll nae gie you that one yet. That's a song for big lassies. You can start with Eppie Morrie.'

'Is it true? Eppie Morrie. Are the things it says true?'

'Now there's a question! Tell me now: does it matter if they are or no?'

'Well, if you're telling a story, you mustna tell a lie, must you?'

'Na. Na, you mustna tell a lie. But you see, wi these auld songs, it's a different kind of a truth they're telling.'

Annie had bitten her tongue and learned the song, listening first to make sure she had got the air and the gist of the story, and then getting the ins and outs of it straight in her mind. At first it all jumped around so she would start and stop and start up again, not knowing what was coming next, and it was all mixed up in her thinking. But then, as Jess sang it over for her, all the time stopping to ask her questions, 'Now how is it he says this and nae that? And who is it that's speaking the now?' it began to lay itself down in a pattern, until it was all settled down in her and she would always be able to remember it straight, however long it might be before she sang it again, because each bit called forth the next and the story and the tune were all wedded to each other. It was like learning a path. The first time she went a new way, she wouldn't know where she was at all. And then as she went along it more often, she started to recognise landmarks – a rock or a tree or the line of a hill – but she did not know what was coming next. And then at last it got so that when she saw one bit she knew what was before and after it so that wherever she was there was only one thing that could come next and she could never be lost again.

So she was still learning, learning songs and learning the right and proper way to sing them. To draw them up out of your belly the way you might draw water out from a well, and to forget everything around you and in you except the song itself. She wanted to sing the way Jess sang, and the way Andrew sang too. He had sung that way the first time she had ever seen him. On Fastern's Eve, it had been, way back in February. He had been right here in Jess and Peter's cott, and he had sung the story of Hind Horn, who had gone away to sea for seven years and come back in disguise just in time to claim his love for himself before she married another man. Afterwards, she had thought little of it, except that if someone had asked her who had been there on Fastern's Eve, she would have been able to say with confidence, 'Andrew Lammie', though she could not have told you whether or not most of the other folk had been there at all.

Then that time on the first of May, he had been walking in the woods close to the Brig of Skeugh. He had nodded to her as he passed, 'Aye, Mistress Nan, it's a fine morning,' and carried on without a second glance, and she felt like a cat that had been stroked the wrong way, from its tail up to its head, because she was not called Nan any more, and no one had any business to be telling him that she was. So she stopped in her tracks, and turned round to call after him, 'It's nae Nan, *Mister* Trumpeter, it's Agnes,' and he turned around on the path and replied, 'So you ken me after all? I thought you hadny seen me,' and she liked his Edinburgh voice, the way he said the words different. And she said, 'I ken you alright, you're the Laird's new trumpeter, up frae Edinburgh. You sang about Hind Horn at Jess's place, I like that song.'

'Aye, that's right. So you liked my singing then?'

'I did, you sang gey well.'

Then a moment's silence had come between them, awkward, and she felt that she was babbling when she carried on, 'You wouldna mind me frae that night. I was sitting on a kist awa at the other side.'

That made him look up, straight at her, with a searching look as if he was asking a question and waiting for an answer, but when he spoke she had no answer to give, 'I do mind you, Agnes, you were sitting on a kist and when I finished my song I looked up, and you saw me. And I saw you. But I haveny seen you since.'

She looked back at him, and blinked, once, twice, and then she gave him an answer, 'I've seen you in Kirk.' And he looked away, up into the tops of the trees, and thought about it before looking back at her and giving his reply, with a grin that grew slowly, 'Aye, but that doesny count, does it?'

It was Annie's job to feed the chickens, morning and evening. When she was very young, she would watch as her mother fed the chickens and she would stand in a trance, hardly taller than the cockerel, surrounded by pecks and clucks and beady flickering eyes. Soon it had become her task, and hers alone, to feed the chooks, although they all could easily have done it in turns and it would have saved her the walk down to the mill whenever the meal kist was empty. That evening of the first of May, as she fed the chooks in the yard, she had listened for the sound of the trumpet blowing from the castle, and imagined Andrew, standing high on the walls with the wind ruffling his hair, and his lips pursed to blow the notes. Then a laugh had risen in her, because she could see his cheeks all puffed out and red and his eyes popping, the way he had looked that afternoon when he told her about learning to play and he had demonstrated the wrong way to blow a trumpet. They had laughed and laughed, if someone had found them they would have taken them for two dafties, it wasn't that funny, but it was, the way he had said it. But all the while the trumpet was sounding, she had kept on sending the grains flying as the chooks scrambled, in that undignified way they had, to get there first, and she had not turned into the wind to let the notes of the trumpet kiss her cheek. And this evening, one of the last of August, as she walked home from Jess's cott carrying the song and the story of Jeannie of Saltoun within her, she listened for the trumpet blowing from the castle, and the sound came across the rigs, carried on the wind with the first leaves of autumn, red and gold and glistening with rain.

IX

'These reeds are too dry to be stripped, I'll go and get mair.'

'They stripped fine last night,' said Jane, 'there's nae need.'

'Na, they're dry, better for brushes, I'll get some fresh afore it gets dark.' Annie tucked her hook in the belt of her apron, threw on her plaid, and was out the door before her sister could argue further. Then she was down by the Brig of Skeugh and into the woods and Andrew was there before her, 'You're here! I was thinking maybe the Hielan men had taken you.'

'Na! But I couldna think how to get awa. I'll need to tak some reeds back wi me.'

'Again?'

'Aye. It was aa I could think of.'

'Tifty must be lit up like a Halloween bonfire these nights!'

They carried on the joke as they gathered a few desultory handfuls of reeds and stowed them in the dry shelter of their hollow tree trunk. Then he took her by the hand and they walked for a bit without saying much, until suddenly he asked, 'Do you like the sound of Edinburgh?'

'Aye,' she said, 'I do.'

'Would you like to go there wi me, some day?'

She thought that would be fine, her and him travelling down the long road together, seeing all that there was to see in the land of Scotland. She would sit close behind him on the chestnut mare, holding tight onto him, and they would come to Edinburgh at the end of a week, and already she would have seen more things in that one week than she had seen in her whole life in Fyvie. But something about it made her uneasy, and she hesitated, and answered only, 'Ocht, but what like could I do there?'

'You could keep kye and sell milk and butter and cheese to the city folk, for they would never have tasted the like of your Tifty cheese.'

She laughed at that, for how you could keep a cow in the city she didn't know, and when she said so, he said, 'Well, it's true, and you'll see one day, if you come wi me.'

They walked on, listening to their feet shushing amongst the leaves, and after a while she turned her head to look at him and judge whether he was in the mood for a game. 'Maybe we could go to sea instead. I've aye thought it would be a grand thing to go to sea.'

'Dinna be daft. A lassie canny go to sea.'

'I thought of that. I could dress up as a boy and we could join a ship thegither, how about that?'

'There's plenty songs and stories about that kind of thing, you've no need to start your own.'

'Aye, but I might anyway. Then I would see the sea. Think on it – the waves and the foam and the gulls crying, and nae sight of land for months, and I would see whalefish and flying fish and mermaids, and the mermaids would be the only ones who kenned I was like them, naebody else would guess, they would just think I was a laddie.'

Andrew gave her a look of horror, rolling his eyes and shaking his head in mock dismay. 'That would be an awful waste.'

She thought to herself, aye, maybe, but then you could walk down the road, and whistle, even, if you wanted to, and no one would give you a second glance or stand in your way, 'Gie us a smile, Agnes, dinna be so dour.' Why you should smile for them you could never guess, they did not know what you were, they thought they did but they didn't know a tithe of it. But she did not say it, because it would spoil the game.

Then he turned to her, looking at her with the same searching look he had given her the first time they ever spoke together.

'So. You want to go to sea. Would you no rather get married and have bairns?'

An uneasy thought flickered briefly through her mind, a man and a woman huddled around a pitiful fire with barely enough peats to catch light. Then she looked up into the full warmth of Andrew's smile, and the thought vanished, but still today she would rather play a game, and so she tossed her head playfully in answering, 'Och well, I'd have to find a nice husband first. That might be a hard job!'

He laughed out loud. 'Ocht, there must be some lad, Annie, that would tak you.'

'Do you think so? Who do you think would mak me a nice husband, then?'

'Now let's see...' He scratched his chin, pondering. 'That lad frae Gourdas, Ironsyde's son. He's a fine figure of a man and no mistake.'

'He's skinny. I'd be aa grated to bits wi his ribs.'

'Mm-hmm. Now I ken, it must be Gibb! I hear he's been widowed for years. He'll be looking for a nice young wife to warm his bed again, and you would only have to move your bed down the stair.'

'What, that old bodach? Him wi his skeely eye? I wouldna thank you for him.'

They giggled together as they crossed their eyes to impersonate the old man.

'Well then. If you canna find a husband for me, I'll have to find you one myself. It would have to be Jamie Jaffray.'

'Eh? The minister's boy? Yon streak of nothin wouldny ken what to do wi you when he got you to his bed.' His arm tightened around her waist and she leaned into him.

'Would he na?'

'No from what I hear.'

'And would you ken any better?'

'What do you think?' His hand slipped around the back of her neck as he kissed her on the mouth, long and warm and deep and dark.

Later, spinning by the hearth after supper, she thought how it could be, if she had the courage to marry him. They would cross the Forth, and come to Leith and see the boats rocking at the pier, loading cargo for Holland, and fishwives from Fife with their loads of split herring on their backs, and then the rock and the castle of the great city of Edinburgh. The markets where all the people of the world came, the French and the Dutch and the English too, and where you might even catch sight of a black man, as Andrew said he had, although she only half believed him. Earls and barons being carried in their chairs holding their handkerchiefs to their noses, the lanes and vennels and high narrow buildings all clustering together, and above it all the great Castle on its dark rock, and the King's Trumpeters riding down to the Mercat Cross. Andrew had seen them often when he was a bairn, riding by with their glitter and glamour, and that was why he had wanted to be a trumpeter, so he said, that and the chance to get out and see the land of Scotland in a Laird's service. Which was what he had done, while all the time she stayed at Tifty and milked the kye and made cheese and butter, and imagined the sun glancing off the sea and the white sails of ships heading to the Indies. Or sat by the fire at night, as she did now, with her mother and sisters and Grizel, sewing or spinning or carding the wool, Gibb tip-tap-tapping at a piece of leather work, the chickens clucking quietly in their roosts by the hearth, while she pricked her ears for news of the wider world amongst the gossip her father and brother brought back from the market on a Tuesday. But unless she went to the market herself, which was seldom, she heard little of it, for her father and brother brought back little but silver and the prices of things. It was the travelling chapmen who brought the real news of the broad world to Tifty, unpacking it with pins and lace and spoons and pewter cups, rolls of cloth and rabbit skins and hair for wigs and knitted stockings. Sometimes her mother would offer a bed to a chapman, if he was weary and had had no other offer, and then he would tell them all the news of the land of Scotland, and Annie would eat it up with her ears, and question him for the details of everything that he had seen as he led his pony through hail and sleet and sunshine along the trails that crisscrossed their way out from Tifty's door. Often, he had been west to the highlands, or north and east to the fishing villages where the women could not sleep on winters' nights for fear of their men's lives among the tossing waves, or even south as far as Edinburgh where Andrew came from. These chapmen's stories would make her mind stir and wander away from Tifty, in search of new things and unknown places, while all the time her feet wandered only as far as the market at Woodhead or the Fyvie Kirk.

Such travelling chapmen might quarter with them a night, or a week, or longer, and always before he left she would press a coin into his palm in exchange for one of his wee folded chapbooks. And when the day's work was over and again they sat by the fire, she would hand it to her father. He might wave it aside with an impatient gesture, but if she was lucky and he was in a better mood he would put down whatever else he might be reading and read it out in measured tones. His glasses would glint in the light of the candle as he read out a murderer's last words on the scaffold, or news of foreign battles, or of ships lost at sea, or of the burning of witches. And afterwards, although the conversation might turn quickly again to the weather, or the price of crops, Annie would be able to mull the words over in her mind, and picture the like of scenes she had never witnessed herself.

Gavin Sinckler had been one such quarterer. He had stayed a while, and her parents had had reason to regret it, before she was born and not long after they had come to Tifty, when still the English were in Scotland and there was no king.

X

The air in the Kirk was dim. It carried a shiver with it, and the musty, musky smell of mice and bats and cobwebs. Pale light struggled down from the pair of narrow slits high up in the eastern gable wall. In the pulpit, Mr Jaffray was preaching with great fervour, his eyes flashing, raising his hand again and again and bringing it down with a swift cutting motion to emphasise the points of his sermon. His black robes billowed with his movements, as if the righteous winds of heaven blew on him already. Annie, seated in her pew, heard the long slow creak of the door opening and closing at the back of the Kirk, and instantly the storm of the minister's preaching was stilled, right in the middle of a word. She looked up to see Mr Jaffray, frozen in his pulpit, one hand still raised towards the roof, glaring the wrath of God down on whichever poor latecomer it was who was even now making his way down the single long aisle that ran the length of the Kirk, directly in the line of the minister's sight. Along with the rest of the congregation, she dared not turn her head to see who it was, but out of the corner of her eye she caught a movement and knew that it was her brother who slid, red-faced, onto the end of her pew, bowing his head in contrition. He would hear plenty about that from their father later on, no doubt.

'—horrent before the Lord our God.' Mr Jaffray continued from exactly where he had left off, and the whole congregation breathed a little easier, although it seemed that the latecomer had incited Mr Jaffray to even greater zeal, and the godly words that formed in his mouth rang out over their heads and up into the spaces among the thatch.

Despite Mr Jaffray's enthusiasm – for a husband's right to keep godly discipline in his household – Annie's attention began to wane, and she cast her eyes around the Kirk, looking for distractions. At the front of the Kirk, at right angles to the other pews, was the high carved back of the Earl of Dunfermline's pew. The new Earl, the Laird of Fyvie, was there, as he had been every week since the spring when he had first inherited. No doubt the mortality of his race was still playing on his mind. There were some who said that, like his father and his grandfather before him, the new Laird of Fyvie would soon occupy his pew only twice a year, when he came to share the communion bread and wine, and be reminded that there was no high table in the house of God. There was talk even that the old chapel at the castle, where Mass had been said in the century long past, was still in use, but that was surely a lie, and you should not listen to such gossip, nor be the one to spread it.

An unusually strong blast from Mr Jaffray returned her attention to the sermon for a few more minutes, but soon her eyes dropped from the minister's face to the unadorned pulpit and then swiftly to the bench of repentance that stood on a raised platform just below it. This Sabbath, three sinners sat in plain view of the People of God in Fyvie. Annie could not read the word that was printed in neat black letters on the placard hanging from Cat Campbell's neck, but she knew what it must say: *Fornicator*. The twine that suspended the placard looked rough, and every few minutes Cat reached a hand up to scratch her neck where the fibres irritated the skin, which was red and sore-looking. Then her hand would take its grip on the placard once more. She would hold it out in front of her, clear of her body, for a while. Then when her arms tired she propped it on top of her belly, but that looked uncomfortable too because of the way its thin edge dug into her. Her body looked bulky in the rough sackcloth. Cat's loon should have been sitting beside her, but he was noticeably absent. No doubt the Kirk Session would pursue it vigorously, and he would be making his appearance there in the following weeks, whether he willed it or no. Annie wondered whether Cat minded him not being there and having to sit there without him. Cat hardly needed the written sign because it was plain for all to see, and while her loon would be able to cast away his placard at the end of his three appearances, she would be left carrying the sign of her shame in front of her for months yet.

There were only two other sinners on the bench next to Cat. Two men, a *Sabbath-breaker* and a *Drunkard*. There was space for three more at least – a quiet week in the parish. When Mr Jaffray turned and leaned down towards them from the pulpit, Cat's fidgeting with the placard ceased and she froze, with eyelids dropped and her mouth set, seeming not to breathe. Mr Jaffray began his rebuke, and his words reverberated between the narrow walls of the Kirk.

'You sinners that appear afore the people of God, you must repent and turn from your path of sin and seek the forgiveness of him who will otherwise banish you to the Fires of Hell.'

Annie thought that he loved to say the word Hell, stringing it out – 'Heeeellll.'

'You, Catrina Campbell, outside of the sanctity of marriage you have committed filthiness with a man, indulging your carnal appetites wi nae thought for the salvation of your own soul. But your sins have found you out, and now you must repent sincerely, afore God and afore his people. You must ask God to forgive you for the sinful weakness of mind that led you to submit to your carnal desires...'

And Annie watched as Cat sat, frozen like ice but scarlet from the dip between her collar-bones right up to the roots of her hair and her ears, as if the fires of Hell were licking at her skin already in a foretaste of the punishment to come. And if that was the case, then it was Mr Jaffray, and not the devil himself as you might have thought, who was stoking the fire.

Annie shifted minutely in her seat. The Minister's admonishments had rarely touched her before, except to instil a feeling of cool superiority over the daft wee bodies who ended up on the bench of repentance because they had acted like animals and not like the elect of God, and had allowed a man to do that thing to them without the sanctity and blessing of marriage. But these last few months, she saw how it could happen. Not that it had to her, not yet. But each time she met with Andrew their kisses were deeper and longer, and sometimes when they went to sit in the shelter of the old tree trunk, his embraces would set a fire licking in her belly, and there would be long times when no words passed between them, until they broke apart with difficulty. As Mr Jaffray carried on, her stomach clenched and turned over as she imagined walking in the marketplace all swollen up like that with the eyes of every passer-by drilling into the big bulge you carried ahead of you, as if they could puncture it with a look. She felt a flutter of panic as she imagined herself in Cat's place, looking for Andrew's face in the crowd and not seeing him, and looking into the sea of faces, and knowing the thoughts they would be having, the same thoughts the whole congregation were having now, as they sat stern and unforgiving and righteous and upright in their pews, imagining just exactly what it was you had done and where and who with and how often, and seeing you throwing your head back and hearing the grunts of your lover and imagining how his hands had crept over you, and you would squeeze your knees tight together and sit quietly with downcast eyes just as Cat was doing now, and they would be thinking how you had not always kept those knees together, you dirty, filthy, carnal wee bitch.

Somehow, although it was not said out loud, it seemed to her that the Kirk made out that women like Cat were in some way filthier than the men who had got them that way. There was supposed to be something low and filthy about women, anyway, something to do with blood, and she remembered how it had been, not long before her sixteenth birthday when she woke one morning with wet between her legs and stared in horror when her investigating fingers emerged stained with blood. Her agitated movements had wakened Jane, who stirred beside her, and saw.

'Have you started, Agnes?'

She nodded, mute with the shock of it, it was happening and already she hated it.

'I'll tell mother.' And Jane dropped her feet to the floor, dressed quickly and left the room to come back minutes later with their mother.

'Here's cloths, you fold it this way and that, like that, you must be careful to keep clean at these times or you'll get a rash,' her mother speaking in a low voice, lips pursed, telling her the few things she needed to know to cope with it for the rest of her life and make sure it never showed, the shameful dirty thing that made her a woman. It should be kept a secret, not to be mentioned by her or anyone else, and Annie stiffened at the thought of the men in her family finding out, 'You winna tell father or Will?'

'Na. There's nae need for them to ken about it.'

She had hoped it would not happen to her, alone among women, and as she cleaned herself up she felt disgust at the betrayal her body had played on her. She had preferred her clean hairless girl's body to this dark bleeding mess that was not her or anything to do with her. That was how it was for her that first time, and every month for the following year, as her body continued to betray her by changing its shape. She felt increasingly uncomfortable about the mill when the tenants and cottars brought their sacks of corn to be ground. She could tell they saw the change in her and she hated them for it.

But as time went on it came to her mind to wonder why it was such a dirty thing this. It was blood only, no one made such a fuss if they cut themselves on a knife, you simply bound up the wound and no one minded it, but this was a different thing, you couldn't understand it. It was something to do with Adam and Eve and original sin which was Eve's fault though Adam had been keen enough himself it seemed, but no one blamed him, just the wife, if it hadn't been for her Adam would still be in Eden living forever but he would be awful lonely and he would have to play with himself an awful lot. She knew about that because she knew Will did it, Grizel had told her she heard him sometimes now that he slept in the kitchen, and she had to lie very still in her bed across from his, praying he would think she was asleep. And that thing that he did was a terrible sin too. So maybe it was better that Eve had done what she had done or they would none of them be here, it made her laugh, that, maybe what they said about the dirt and the shame of it and Eve's shame was only part of the story. She wondered if her mother and sisters had the same thoughts, but she kept them quiet within her own mind, they thought she had enough to say as it was, although really she had less to say to her parents and sisters as time went on. Around the big wooden dining table where they ate their kale broth and barley meal, the conversation was seldom anything now but marriage marriage marriage, 'Did you hear the banns being read?'; 'Nae a good match'; 'God knows why his parents didna object to it'; 'The bairn was born just six month after the wedding, a scandal, they'll appear before the Kirk session next week', on and on, until Will would come in late, kicking his dog and smelling of drink, and put the miller into a spell of ill humour. She would sit and feign interest, while in her mind she wandered along the Tifty burn with Andrew.

XI

The Miller of Tifty pinched a few grains of oats between his left thumb and index finger, dropped them into the hollow of his right hand, and selected one grain to nip between his front teeth. It fitted neatly into the half-moon of his lower incisors, which had been worn to fit its shape over the decades. The grain cracked with some effort, and gave a slight burnt taste. He looked sideways at his neighbour, who stood next to his sack of oats.

'Ach, man, you've left them in the kiln over-long. I'll grind this load for you, but you winna be wanting to send it up to the Laird's table. You'll want to be mair canny wi the rest of your harvest. But dinna come next week, mind. I'll be resting the miln now until Young Will here fetches home the new stane.' He gave a nod over towards his son, who was cleaning the oat dust out from around the miln, and did not bother to look up.

'Aye, Tifty, I was thinking that auld stane's seen better days right enough, there's nae enough weight in it to crack a nut.'

'Na, you're right, so Young Will here will be off with a pile of men on their mill-service to fetch hame a new one. It's only right, Will, is it nae, that you do the work, since it's been your ill care that's worn down the auld one so fast, eh?' Tifty gave a low laugh, and stuck his jaw out, waiting for his son to answer him. Young Will looked up, giving him a dirty look, but gave only a grunt in reply. The lad had little enough to say for himself these days. But it was time he started to take on his responsibilities, now that he had learned his way about the mill. Long enough that had taken. Tifty was not a man to go easy on a labourer just because he was his son. And he had been slow to learn. God knew, if he had wanted another trade Tifty would not have stopped him. But when he had asked, ten years ago – 'You'll be coming to start your work at the mill, Will, now you're fourteen' – the lad had assented quickly enough. It was a long time ago, now he thought of it. Time to let the lad have his rein, see what he could do.

'And tak tent you balance it well this time, so it doesna grind the stane, or I'll be sending you back to the quarry to fetch hame another one by yourself. Hear me?' He was determined to get some response out of the lad.

'I ken how to balance a stane, father, you'll see.'

'And you'll set up the auld one by the wall outside there, next to the other two auld millstanes.'

They were the old millstones that the bairns used to clamber over when they were wee, now covered in a thin sheen of moss and lichen. He thought back to the last time they set one up there, how they had fetched home a new runner stone from the quarry on the north coast, two days' journey away, and the men had rolled it on an axle made out of a fir tree. How they had gone in dry weather because that was the only time they could roll the stone without it foundering in the mud and leaving a rut that would make travellers curse him for months after, and how the rain had come and how the men came down to the mill soaked to the skin and without the stone, saying they had left it on the road up by Seggat, and he had cursed them and the stone and the mill and the weather. And it always seemed to be that way, fetching home a new millstone never brought him luck. But he would have to trust to luck that the weather would hold this time. It had come clear again in the last week or so, and the earth with a long summer's thirst had drunk in the rain and was dry again. If the job was not done now, it would have to wait until the spring, for by the second week in September you could count on the weather for nothing.

There would be expense, too, in the matter. The men who fetched home the millstone must be fed well, for it was hungry work and deserved a welcome at the mill house with ale and good bannocks and cheese, and even meat, in return for their efforts.

So three days later Young Will went around the neighbouring farmtouns to gather a party of tenants and cottars for the labour, and four days after that, the women of Tifty worked all morning and into the afternoon in the kitchen of the mill house, and when the work was all but done, Helen Black said to her daughters, 'You three lasses go and pick the men some good ripe geans. Grizel, you bide and help me here.' And so Jane and Bessie took baskets and went out arm in arm. Annie followed them out into the breezy warm end-of-summer air, to the steep path that led up past the cottars' houses, where the branches of the wild cherry trees hung low and dangled their clusters of fruit within the reach of passers-by. Annie went a wee bit higher up the hill than her sisters, and set to work, sending a sharp, tight glance, but no words, in answer to Jane's pointed exclamation, 'Would you look at Agnes eating all the geans herself?' But their lips and tongues and hands were dyed just as deep a purple-red as her own with the juice of the geans, because they ate one for every three that they put in their rush baskets. When they had had enough, they worked faster, trying to finish the job before the men returned, and before the chattering starlings in the upper branches stole them all.

Then above the racket of the starlings, Annie heard the men approaching with the millstone on the path above her, giving orders and encouragement to each other, her brother's voice amongst them.

'Hold on there, John.'

'Straighten her up now!'

'Over your way a wee bit.'

'Nae far now!'

And then, without warning, the yells of alarm.

'Below! Tak tent below!'

Beneath the men's cries, she heard a low, heavy rumbling. She looked up. At the top of the steep slope, the men were waving and shouting frantically. The millstone was rolling free down the steep incline. She stared in frozen horror as it gathered speed and began to bounce, leaping high and hurtling down the slope towards her. She threw herself backwards onto the ground, scattering geans from her basket, and she felt the wind on her face as the stone whistled past. As it reached thc flat, it hit a rock in the middle of the path and smashed it to pieces with an ear-splitting report that echoed from the surrounding hills and sent starlings exploding from the branches and the crows flapping and cawing from the trees in the mill glen. The kye that had been grazing by the path bellowed and kicked their clumsy heels above their backs in fright as they ran off, and John Scott the herd threw curses after them. The millstone took off again, wobbling crazily through the air, and bounced twice more. But it was losing speed as it rolled along the flat, and finally, it turned in a slow half circle before tipping over onto its side, fluttering like a coin before it came to rest with a low *boum* and a puff of dust.

The six men who had rolled the stone from the north coast ran in a clatter down to where Annie and her sisters sprawled in the stone's wake.

One of them reached out a big hand and pulled her to her feet, 'Are you hurt, lass?'

'Na, I'm fine.' But she was shaking from head to foot. Jane and Bessie had got to their feet too, white-faced and trembling like herself, and for once they took refuge in each other, huddling together in a tight knot, while the men descended to where the millstone lay. They trampled the spilled geans into the earth as they went.

The three sisters cried a little into each other's shoulders, until they stopped shaking. And then, suddenly, it was the funniest thing that had ever happened to them, and they doubled up, helpless, in the shade of the gean trees, spluttering and barely able to stand.

When they were able to walk, they followed the men down to where they clustered around the millstone, which lay, now harmless, with a big chip out of one edge. Others were coming to join them, the cottars from their houfs and young John Scott, who had not followed his startled kye to the far side of the meadows. An undercurrent of shocked laughter was still rippling through the three sisters, so that as the men muttered serious things between themselves, one or other of the girls' shoulders would start to shake, silently, and she would have to turn her lips inwards so far that she felt she was swallowing them. Their father, half-running, came down from the house and elbowed his way through the group of men.

Peter, Jess's husband, was the first to address the miller. 'It's cracked, Tifty. And there's a big chip out of it. You'll be needing to fetch hame another one yet.'

'How was it the stane got free?'

The answer came in bits and pieces.

'We've had ill luck with it the whole trip.'

'Did I nae tell the laddie the axle was too thin, when we cut it?'

'Acht, the axle was fine, that rock it hit would have snapped another one just the same.'

She watched her father's profile, the twitching muscle in his jaw, as he took her brother aside from the group of men. Then the laughter that had been quivering inside her drained away as her father lifted his arm and gave Young Will a single back-handed slap across the face with such force that he stumbled backwards and dropped to the ground, there in front of all the folk of Tifty and their neighbours.

Young Will sat on his backside, shaking his head as if to clear it, and looking up at the miller with dark and burning eyes and a red mark blossoming on his cheek. Annie saw his shame and his cowardice as if he was naked in front of her. And she thought to herself, *He's feart. If he was a man, he would answer him back. He's feart, like a bairn.*

While she was staring at him, thinking such things, he looked up and right into her, and she was sure that he must know what she was thinking. He covered his darkened eyes with his lids, and then he got to his feet and walked away up the road to his mammy at the mill house, without a word to his father or to her or to anyone else. His eyes spat his shame and disgrace at her as he passed.

Before the men dispersed, she heard Peter talking to her father, aside from the others, 'It wasnae the laddie's fault, Tifty, he did a good job on the way hame,' and her father answering, 'He's aye been a careless fool.'

The men wanted to leave the cracked stone by the side of the path. There was little point, they said, taking it back up the hill, but the miller was having none of it. He would find a use for it, he said. It would be good for a door-stone, when the passage of feet in and out of his kitchen wore the old one down. And so he made them roll it up the path to the mill house, where after much labour and sweat and grumbling they propped it against the wall by the door, across from the cheese press, and Helen Black welcomed them in for a drink and a meal.

The fetching home of a millstone should have been a cause for great celebration, but there was a heavy feeling in the air that not even Peter's banter could lift, and the infrequent laughter sounded forced and unnatural, what with the miller of Tifty sitting silent and proud at his end of the table, and his son slumped at the other, sullen and brooding. The guests soon made their excuses and dispersed to their homes, and Annie could hear their voices lifting and the flow of their conversation starting again as they passed out of the yard. Some of them looked back with a rueful shake of the head at the stone that had caused them so much trouble. But from then on Young Will always averted his eyes from it, although he went in and out of that doorway many times every day.

XII

For nearly a week more, the late summer refused to give way to early autumn, and on a Sabbath in mid-September Annie met Andrew after Kirk in their secret place in the shelter of the old fallen beech, just as the grey rain-clouds began to form overhead. He had heard the story of the runaway millstone many times already, of course, there had been no other talk in Fyvie since. But she had to tell him herself, her own way, and at the thought of how it might have been, her lying hurt and broken beneath the stone, he hugged her to him, and kissed her, and she kissed him back and held him close as he rolled her on to her back in the dry leaf litter, and their lips and hands grew urgent. Then the thought of Cat Campbell on the repentance bench came to her and extinguished her desire in a moment, leaving her lying rigid beneath him while he continued to press himself against her, until at last she had to take him by the shoulders and push him away, 'Na, Andrew, we mustna,' wriggling out from underneath him, and leaving him lying on his front, breathing hard.

She drew her knees up to her chest and sat with her back against the dry curve of the old tree's inside. A thin rain had begun to fall outside, and she could hear it pattering lightly on the ground and on the leaves of the trees. From close by, a robin sang. She bit her lip as Andrew propped himself up on his elbows, and gave a wee desperate groan. Then he slapped his open hand to the ground, making the leaf litter jump. She was about to speak, when without warning he flipped himself backwards, so that he lay with outstretched arms half in and half out of the tree, with the light rain falling into his face. 'Aaaaaahhh...' he went, half a cry of frustration, and half a laugh. When he had cooled down, he adjusted himself and crawled back into the shelter on all fours, shaking his head and smiling wryly, 'Oh, Annie, you've got me caught on a hook alright. Look at me, coming to heel like a young dog that's been caught stealing the meat frae the table.'

She let herself relax a bit. 'You're nae angry wi me, then?'

'No. No really.'

'It's just – you've seen Cat Campbell in the Kirk these last weeks –'

'You're right. We canny risk it. And I'm in no hurry to father a bairn anyway.'

'It seemed like it, just then.'

'Ocht, Annie, you can always gie me a good kick if you need to.' He paused. 'But it seemed like you wouldny have minded, yourself, until you went aa stiff.'

They were sitting side by side, leaning their backs against the knobbled inside of the old tree trunk, with only their little fingers hooked together.

'Aye. But I was feart aa of a sudden, what would I do if there was a bairn?'

She did not look at him, but out of the corner of her eye she saw his head turn towards her.

'What would *we* do, you mean. *We* would get married. And if the Kirk wanted to hold us to account when the bairn was born a wee bit early, well – we could gie them even more scandal to gossip about, holding hands on the repentance bench.'

'My father wouldna like that, nor my mother either.'

'Aye well, neither would mine be best pleased, but still – once it's done it's done.'

'I dinna think my father would like you for a son-in-law, Andrew.'

'Aye, well, I'm thinking maybe I wouldna like him for a father-in-law either. But how does that matter so much?'

'I dinna think he would gie us his blessing, if you asked him.'

'As long as we both went freely to the Kirk, we could be married whether he blessed us or no, do you ken that?'

'Aye. But –'

'But if it bothered you, Annie, I'd change his mind for him. He might deny me the first time, and maybe the second, but he would have to gie us his blessing one day.'

'Na, Andrew. You dinna ken what kind of a man he is when he doesna get his own way. He's nae a yielding man.'

He took both of her hands in his own. 'Aye, well, maybe you dinna ken what kind of a man *I* am if you think I'd let you go that easy. I'd marry you, and we would be thegither, and naebody would be able to point the finger at us. Understand, my Annie? And after that, we'd have our own bed, and lie thegither the whole night, wi no fear of whether we had a bairn or no.'

'But it would be a gey hard, narrow bed we shared thegither.'

'And how would that be?'

She turned her head away, and he had to ask her to repeat herself because she mumbled the words. 'I dinna think he would gie you my tocher.'

His hands holding hers went slack.

'Your tocher? How does that matter?'

'We'd need it, to live well.'

'Aye, right enough, it would be a help. I canny deny aa the silver I've got is a silver trumpet, and even that belongs to the Laird. But I earn a good fee. I'm no one of your poor Tifty cottars.'

'We'd need it, Andrew. But I dinna think he would consent to it. He would gie it to a gentleman. Or some small Laird. But nae a Laird's trumpeter.' She felt ashamed. Miserable. They had never spoken of it directly before, and she had barely thought of it until then, except that now she saw clearly that it had been part of the uneasiness she felt sometimes when they had talked of going to Edinburgh.

He dropped her hands as if they had burnt him. When he spoke, his voice was hard.

'Oh. Oh I see it now. Am I no good enough for you, Annie? No man enough? Just a wee servant-boy, fine for a summer, for a bit of play when you're in heat, is that it? You like to heat me up and leave me burning, and aa the time you're just waiting for some rich gentleman to make the right offer. I dinny ken what your father will say until he's asked, but seems like your answer's plain already. Well, Mistress Agnes, you can find another man to play your games and beg for your tocher. I'm no wanting it.'

He had never made her cry before. But as he spoke, something inside her crumpled and she could feel her chin wobbling while the tears streamed into the corners of her mouth, down her chin, and into her hair as she rocked back and forth, rolled tight in a wee ball, trying to comfort herself. Andrew watched with hard eyes. Then he pushed himself from the ground, dusted the leaf litter off his knees and his palms with disgust, scrambled out into the rain, and was gone.

In Kirk the next Sabbath, she could only mouth the words of the psalms as he stared stonily past her.

XIII

Agnes was mooching and moping about the place. The Miller of Tifty could see no reason for it, until the news came around that the Laird of Fyvie had gone for a visit to another great Earl in Beauly. He and half his household, it seemed, had gone up the road toward Turriff early one morning, waking all the folk of Camalouns and Cardonwell with the noise of that damned trumpet as they passed. The Laird was not expected back until November, although why he wanted to travel at that time of year was anyone's guess.

And so Agnes was moping about the place, and the Laird was away. It was enough for William Smith. He watched his youngest daughter's lowering mood with growing satisfaction as the weeks passed, assured that they both had their sights set on the same mark.

It was a high target right enough. How high, he was not prepared to discuss with any of his peers out in the world, because they would have told him straight that Fyvie was out of reach, and that was not an opinion that he wished to hear. But he was not a man to lower his sights once he had set a mark. And so at night, he and his wife watered their ambition and gave it room to grow in the warm, dark, secret space between their bed curtains. Late into the night, long after the cruisies were extinguished, they would talk, and their daughters in the room next door would wake in the dark and hear the rise and fall of their voices, muffled and made senseless by the bed-curtains and the walls between them. Around the table he began to make a joke of it with his wife, making a wee dig every now and then, 'Are you thinking the Laird will come by Tifty on his road hame, Helen?' and Helen would answer 'Ocht I dinna ken, William, ask one of our lasses, they'll ken better than me.' Agnes never said anything much in reply, at most she would give a half-hearted shrug, but that was the way the lassies liked to play along, aye pretending they couldn't guess your meaning when they knew it fine.

Now that he was convinced there was an interest on both sides, the question was one of etiquette, but that was not a simple matter. Truth was, it seemed the Laird might need a wee bit encouragement, him being slow to act so far. But by God, there must be a way to persuade the Laird if the Laird was half-persuaded already. Agnes was aye one to play down the family's standing, so the Laird was hesitating maybe because of that. Tifty would have to find a way to set his mind at ease on that score. But to ask outright was to risk a rebuff, and he would not stomach that from any man, whatever his title.

He argued the matter back and forth with Helen, and at last he decided. He would write a letter. A letter would be good. He could set out his assets, and remind the Laird of his standing, a son of Inveramsay, brother of the Bailie Dean of Guild and Treasurer of Aberdeen, the baron John Smith who himself had met with General Monk when the King was being restored to the throne. Brother, too, of a Burgess of Aberdeen, Nathaniel Smith. But he would only allude to the matter in hand. He would not state it plainly, not in a letter, no. In his letter he would only invite the Laird to visit him at Tifty *on a matter of importance to both our families* – he took some pleasure in turning that phrase over in his mind – and if the Laird agreed to come, well then Tifty would state the matter plainly. And if not – if he turned the invitation down – well, it might sting for a while, but there would be little harm done in the long run.

Then when the Laird came – and surely he would – they would entertain him in this very room, the grandest in the house, filled with all the treasured possessions of a Laird's fourth son. The four-poster bed with the rose and gold needlework on the green silk hangings. They were worn a bit now, but still they gave out his status. The carved oak kist that sat at the bed's foot, and the delicate varnished writing desk where he would write the letter itself.

Helen took great delight in listing every item they had at their disposal. 'Now, there's the two silver cups and the silver spoons, half a dozen of them, and we'll get out the candlesticks, the good brass ones, mind, no the cruisies. And your lovely linen napkins, the ones with your father's initials,' – aye, the ones that his eldest brother had condescended to let him have when he succeeded as Laird, little enough that had been – 'and we'll put away the wooden bowls and the pewter mugs, and I'll have Grizel polish the silver, make sure she gives it a good high finish, and we'll wash and press the linen, William, until it's soft and supple and runs between your fingers like water, you'll see.'

He let her run on, taking as much pleasure in it as she did, imagining how, when it was all laid out and gleaming, he would be careful to make sure his guest knew the value of what was in his hands. If he did not remark on it, Smith would clear his throat and point out the initials on the linen, 'That's my father's initials, ken, you see the JS there? He had them done for him in Holland,' and the Laird would stow that fact in the kist of memory alongside the others that the miller would carefully let escape him and that would add to Fyvie's estimation of him. And then at last Tifty would tactfully raise the question of his youngest daughter's future.

It was a good plan. A sure one. He would have a stab at writing the letter soon. Read it to Helen before he sent it down to the Castle. And then wait, and see what Seton made of it.

Ach. It was too much to hope. But mind – no harm in trying. Maybe it would not be the Laird of Fyvie in the end. There were other ways, if the Laird was cooler than he seemed. An introduction to a cousin. Or a friend.

So he would try. Send his arrow high and see what it brought down. A letter. Aye. A letter was the way to do it.

When Annie heard that Andrew was gone away with the Laird, she told herself that she was glad to be free of him, she would no longer have to wrestle with him or slap away his pawing hands, and she could forget all about him, and look forward to a future with some proper gentleman who would court her openly and honestly and chastely, instead of sneaking around behind folk's backs. And all the time she told herself that, she knew that it was the biggest lie, underneath it all she was in a tight panic at the thought of him, miles away, hating her and forgetting her, and she ached for him, and had no appetite.

She could make nothing of why her mother thought it was such a great joke, 'Dinna fret, Agnes, feed yourself up so you're nae a skeleton. I was lucky wi your father, nae many men like just skin and bones!' She would grunt, and obediently finish the broth that had no taste now that Andrew was gone and did not want her any more, skeleton or no. He had said so himself. Only if she was honest, that wasn't exactly it, she was lying to herself, because it was her tocher, and not her, that he did not care for, that was what he had said. But it amounted to the same thing in the end anyway, how could she think of a future without it, it was her share in her father's inheritance after all, and it would be a terrible thing to be disinherited. He would split it between Jane and Bessie, and that would put a smirk on their faces that they would never wipe off, and every time they saw her eating pease meal because she could not afford to buy oats on the servant's fee her husband brought her, well they would let her know what a foolish choice she had made, whether they said it with words or in the other ways they had.

And whenever her parents started on about the grand match they would make for her, it was enough to make her want to scream in their faces, 'I dinna want some stupid Laird and his fortune, it's my Andrew I want,' which was the truth, although it took her a time to admit it to herself.

She went about her daily tasks in a slow, automatic manner, stepping around the other members of the household with barely a word. Towards the end of October, she counted back the Sabbath days and realised that it was more than a month since she had seen or spoken with Andrew. She bent over the tub where she was washing the dinner bowls, and her head fell forward as she fought to prevent her tears. It was then that Young Will pushed past her and she felt a sharp pain in her side as he rammed his elbow into her ribcage. Her head whipped around in anger and she exclaimed in protest, 'Will! Dinna!' His eyes slid away from her and he mumbled, 'Och, sorry, Agnes, I didna see you there,' and she smiled at him tightly and did not pursue it further. But she had recognised the pleased, vicious look in his eyes that he had quickly hidden when she had turned to glare at him.

It was a look that she had seen often enough, but he had not hurt her for many years. She remembered well enough the last time he had hurt her. It was not long before he had gone to work in the mill, years ago, she must have been no more than nine years old. They had been playing, all four of them, with Grizel and her brother, in the Tifty burn just before it reached the mill, where the lade began. There the stream of water fell a short way into a pool that was just wide enough for a bairn with slim hips to sit in. While the others played on the bank, she hoisted her skirts and waded into the pool, welcoming the cold shock of the water as it lapped up to her knees. Through the water her feet were magnified, and pale. The day was hot, too hot for her, and she let her foot slip on a rock so that she kind-of-by-accident fell *plump-splash* into the pool on her backside. She pushed her back against the wee waterfall, enjoying the pressure of the water on her back. It lifted her skirt and apron as it bubbled up between her knees, trying to push her out of its way as it hurried off downstream. You could confuse it if you liked, making a barrier with your feet or hands at the edge of the little sill where it flowed out, holding it back and frustrating it until at last it overflowed and rushed on to meet the river.

She heard her father's voice, distant, coming up from the direction of the mill, 'Get out of that burn, Nannie. Now!'

She stayed where she was, and whispered to herself, 'Na', and leaned back, splashing her legs up and down in the little pool, one-two one-two, sending an arc of water droplets from the tips of her toes.

'Naaa-nn*ie*!' Jane, using her name the way she hated, telling her she had done wrong. 'Stop splashing Bessie yon way.'

She pretended she had not heard, but after a while she stopped the splashing and lay back to turn her face upwards to where the sun blazed from the heart of a deep blue sky. The light shone through her eyelids, filling her head with a rosy pink glow. The warmth on her face and shoulders counteracted the chill of the water as it slipped past her skin. She liked to stay in as long as possible, until the skin of her fingers and toes was shrivelled and pale like stored apples in January. It was when you got out that you felt coldest, when your clothes clung to you as you wrung out your hair, and then you would run past the mill and up the steps to the house as fast as you could, and the warmth in your core would spread outwards to the rest of your body. But still your fingertips would be wizened for hours after, to remind you of how the burn had stolen the heat from you.

'Now what nonsense is she up to?'

'Looking at the sun yon way, she'll go blind.'

'I winna guide her by the hand if she does.'

Annie opened her eyes a slit and saw Jane and Bessie standing on the bank, watching her. They were right next to each other. They did not have to be so loud. Pointed. They were looking over towards her to see if she was listening. Grizel and her brother were not to be seen. Maybe they had got bored and gone home.

Again, her father's voice from a distance, 'Will! Tell that lassie she's to get up to the house and get dried off this minute!'

Will was sitting on a rock on the burn's other bank. He had taken off his shoes and stockings and his shirt, and his breeches were rolled up above the knee so that he could dangle his feet in the water. He called out to her.

'You heard father. Get out.'

She closed her eyes and hummed.

Quietly, Will waded into the water and came across to where she lay. His shadow fell across her eyes. He cut at the water with his hand and sent a cold spray into her face.

She sat up, startled.

'Will, na!' Whining.

'Get out.'

'Why?'

'Father says.'

'Na.'

'You have to do what father says.'

'Na. I dinna.'

'Aye you do.' He bent down towards her, leaning his face close to hers. She shut her eyes again. 'Get out, you thrawn wee bitch.' Another cold spray of water dashed her in the face, making her eyes startle open. He leaned close to her, his lips twisted in a smile, and started chopping at the water with his hands and forearms, sending a heavy rain spattering into her face. She craned her neck from one side to another in an effort to avoid the blinding spray. Through the chaos of water she could hear Jane's voice, 'Move, Nan.'

And Bessie, 'Now she kens what like it is.'

Suddenly it stopped. She shook the water from her eyes. The sun was behind Will's head, and she squinted up at him as he stood over her. He had soaked himself as well as her, and his hair, plastered down chaotically across his scalp, was made even darker than usual by the wet. For the first time, she noticed a sparse growth of dark hairs sprouting from the white goose-pimpled skin of his chest. Under the water his feet and shins rippled, paler still.

'Shift.'

'Na.'

She returned his stare without blinking. A tremor crossed his face. She spoke too late, her voice sounding high and whiny, 'Will, na!' as his hand flashed out and grabbed her ankle, twisted and tugged, and he dragged her out of the pool. She yelled as her backbone bumped over the rocky sill.

He released his grip on her ankle, and she staggered to the shore, feet slipping on the rocks. There was a pain in her knee where it had twisted as he pulled her, and she limped down the path. As she rounded the corner of the mill, she looked back over her shoulder. Her brother was watching her, his eyes pleased, triumphant, and his face was twisted into an expression that looked like laughter. She would not cry in front of him. But when she was out of his sight, at the other side of the mill, she pulled herself up to sit on the old millstone that leaned against the wall, and cradled her shins. She lowered her head to her knees, and cried, and shivered while the hot sun dried her clothes.

It was the last time that she remembered them all playing together. Later that summer, Will's work at the mill had begun in earnest, and he spent less time with his three young sisters, preferring the company of men, and she had been glad of it. She had finally learned to step around him, to hide from his noticing her, and so that had been the last time he had hurt her. Now, ten years later, she had made him notice her again.

XIV

The days grew thin with the coming of autumn, and the nights arrived early and unheralded by any trumpet blast from the Castle, and Halloween approached. In the evenings, there was spinning and sewing, songs and stories by the kitchen hearth.

Some nights, Annie would go to the nook by the fire and shoo off the chickens roosting there, and pull out a pile of wee folded chapbooks. She would dust off the loose feathers and sort through them, she knew them all by the woodcuts on their fronts, and she would make her choice and pass it to her father to read out. There was a night when she chose a chapbook with a crude skull and cross bones and a noose on the front, and her father read out the story of a man who in the English time, not long before she was born, had killed his wife with an ox bone and how he was only found out at the wake when he went to pay his respects to the departed. There he was, standing by the corpse, the deceitful murdering sinner, piously praying to God for the soul of the dead, with his hand resting on his dead wife's forehead. And slowly through the linen shroud the blood had come seeping up between his fingers, and it was the mark of his guilt, for he could not wash it off, and that was how he was known to be the murderer of her. Her father's voice rose to a pitch as he read out the sentence of death, and woke the cockerel, who had been sleeping sound on a shelf by the fire, with his head tucked under his wing. All of a sudden he leapt off the shelf into the middle of the floor between their feet, crowing and strutting. William Smith sprang from his chair, circling the bird and waving the others out of the way with his arms. 'Gie him room to fight, for he fights with a spirit!' he cried,

'God will it that he wins.' The audience watched transfixed as the cockerel circled and bowed and jumped with spurs flashing as he fought his unseen enemy, and the great black wings of his shadow leapt against the walls. Every member of the household held their breath, wondering whose spirit it was that had returned with an ill will against them.

The battle stopped as suddenly as it had started, and the cockerel crowed, throwing his head back with comb erect and bristling, chest puffed out in pride, and then he began to peck at some motes on the floor as if he was feeding peacefully in the yard.

'He's won!'

'Aye, praise God!'

Before they settled again to their tasks, they drew their seats into a tight ring before the fire, and it was a long time before anyone went to their bed that night. They stayed up for many hours, talking in low intense voices of other strange happenings, of ghosts and witches and the fair folk. There was a time some years back when a witch had drawn off the milk from the kye at Cardonwell, every morning their udders had been dry, and the witch had been found out, it was a neighbour would you believe, an old woman who used to live in Camalouns, you used to see her muttering away to herself, casting spells as it now seemed. The Presbytery Court in Turriff had called in a witch-pricker and he had pricked her body with his long pins until he found the devil's mark on her and then he had got the confession from her soon enough, wailing and crying she had admitted to the deed. But it had not gone to a trial, for she had died in the Tollbooth and gone straight to burn in Hell before the law court could be summoned. The guard at the Tollbooth had sworn that he heard the death-knock the night she died, and that reminded Gibb of the time his uncle had seen a dead-candle moving up the road in the night, blue and wavering along the path ahead of him all the way to his house, and then he had opened the door and found his wife lying cold and stiff and dead on the floor.

Her father told of the time his grandfather had forgotten to brake the miln one night, and in the morning he had gone down to find it still turning, and an odd kind of flour coming down the chute. Though no one was about, there were voices like music in the air, and so his grandfather had said aloud, 'You're welcome to use my mill,' for only a fool would risk offending the fair folk. He had carefully gathered up the flour for them and put it aside in a wee bag, and when he had looked a day or two later, the bag was gone. But, he said, for the rest of his life, his grandfather had always been careful to brake the miln at night.

Then Grizel asked if it was true that the fair folk could be seen riding the roads at Halloween, and Helen said, 'Aye, but it's nae just the fair folk you must watch out for, if you're on the road late at night.' And then she began to tell how her cousin had known a man who had met with a great wild black horse, away up near the head of the Ythan, and it had barred his way no matter how he tried to get past it. 'He went this way and that and the horse was aye in front of him, it circled around him and it wouldna let him pass, and at last it knocked him to the ground wi one butt frae its big head. My cousin used to say that his friend sat on the ground wi the big wild horse running around him, wi its nostrils flaring and its ears pinned back, angry-like, and he looked up at it and said, "Well what is it you want wi me?" And aa of a sudden it gentled, and it came right up to him and stood quiet as anything, waiting for him to mount. Now, he still thought it was just a horse, you see, and he knew it was wrong to steal a body's horse. But it was getting late and there was no one else on the road, and he had a long way to go. And so he said to himself, "Ocht, I can ride it hame and send it on its way the morn's morn, and it would be a hard man who would cry me a thief for it." Well, he put one hand on its neck and another on its back and he got ready to mount, and just when he was about to jump on its back it turned its head and looked him right in the eye, and God's honest truth but that man always swore that it lifted its lip and laughed at him. And right then he felt that its flesh where he touched it wi his hands wasna warm like a living thing, but cold, like the water of a river. So he knew it for what it was, a kelpie, and he knew what it would do to him if he was to ride it, and so he turned tail and streaked like a hare wi the kelpie's breath on his shoulder aa the way back to where he had come frae. He slammed the door shut, and my cousin and his wife were gey surprised to see him again so soon. They could hear the kelpie's breathing through the door, but it wouldna come further. And the next morning there were hoofprints right up to the door and aa around the house. And hear my words, there were no hoofprints leading awa frae the house, but there was nae sign of the horse either. And the ground aa around was sodden wet, as if a river had flowed there.'

Helen's listeners shivered, and Annie drew her creepie stool in closer to the fire, while her father lit more candles to keep the dark at bay, for they knew then that it had been a kelpie for sure, and that the man had been wise not to mount, for it would have galloped to the Ythan and taken him to its lair at the bottom of the river and there he would have been drowned.

That night, Annie, Jane and Bessie climbed the stair all together and slept huddled close in their bed, and woke each other often when the house creaked or the tree branches in the orchard moved in the wind. But by the time the light was fading the following day, the everyday tasks had pushed the fair folk and dead-candles and kelpies to the back of Annie's mind. Her arm ached as she turned the paddle of the butter churn, waiting for the moment when the rapid *splish-sploosh* would be replaced by a slow *dunk-dunk* as the cream thickened. Her mind ran idly along a well-known track, planning how she would carry on after it thickened until it would no longer turn, and then she would pour off the whey, and wash the butter again and again until the water ran clear. Then she would pat the butter between two wooden paddles until the moisture was squeezed right out of it and she could press it into its mould, ready for the table.

She changed hands as she felt the paddle just beginning to resist her, and wondered whether she should light the cruisie lamp now, or leave it until the butter had set, when she heard, distant but clear from the direction of Fyvie Castle, the notes of a trumpet. Her head jerked up and she went to the door, stepped out into the yard and listened as the last clear notes danced across the rigs and up the hill from the Castle.

She returned to the kitchen and rattled the paddle around in the churn, humming Hind Horn.

She looked up to see her mother watching her from the window where she sat to catch the light for her sewing. Helen gave her a thin smile. 'That'll be the Laird back frae Beauly, Agnes, do you think?'

And Annie tossed her head and lifted her chin, 'Aye, it will be, he's been awa mair than five weeks.'

Her mother smiled a satisfied smile, and replied, 'So you've been counting the days, Agnes, til the Laird comes back.'

At dinner, Helen told her husband just what their daughter had done and said, loading her words with wee hints and nods. Annie had no interest in fathoming their meaning, although her sisters' jealous glances might have told her enough if she had bothered to pay them any attention. Her father smiled and nodded slowly, narrowing his eyes, and thinking, thinking.

His knife hovered over the butter as he paused to examine the impression she had stamped into it, the flared tube of a trumpet with a pennant hanging from it.

XV

On the last Sabbath of October, in the Kirk's dim light, a row of bogfir candles sputtered and hissed in brackets along the wall, above the pews. The first arrivals shuffled along the pews to catch what little heat fell down from them. William Smith ushered his family into their customary places near the front of the Kirk, and the other folk of Tifty took their seats nearby. Jess shuffled along the pew in front of them, leaning on Grizel's arm, and sat down heavily. Margaret Urquhart, huge now with only a week or two to go, perched on the end of a pew. The Kirk bell, that had been tolling since they crossed the Brig of Skeugh, still rang out from the belfry above them. Its sound came slightly muffled by the thatch. Annie resisted the impulse to look over her shoulder every time she heard the door open and close at the back of the Kirk, knowing that one time it would be the Laird, closely followed by Andrew. She listened with little interest to the murmur of voices around her, the quiet Sabbath greetings exchanged between neighbours, but she became alert when a sudden hush fell at the opening of the door. She heard the Laird's familiar toneless voice in the hush – 'Ah, Ironsyde, a good Sabbath to you and your family; Good morning and good Sabbath to you, Cardonwell' – and his tenants' brief replies as he passed along the aisle, and then he was at her shoulder, addressing her father, 'Good Sabbath, Tifty,' and she looked around to nod politely to him and then quickly looked straight ahead again, holding her breath. Out of the corner of her eye she was aware of Andrew Lammie's tall figure following his Laird to the high carved pew at the front of the Kirk. He waited for the Laird to be seated and then stood to attention in his usual place, beside the pew. He did not look at her, but fixed his gaze on the side of the pulpit.

The Kirk bell stopped its ringing. There was the sound of the door opening and closing at the back of the Kirk, and then the Precentor passed down the aisle in his sombre black robe. He took a splinter of bogfir and lit it from the last candle before the pulpit. It sputtered before flaring into life. The light it gave was pale and worn, and struggled to shift the dimness aside as he ascended to the pulpit. The Good Book creaked open and its pages fluttered as he searched back and forth. Then he found what he was looking for, and ran his fingers down between the pages to open the book fully, before he started to read. His index finger moved slowly along the lines, as he spoke out to the congregation in a thin voice the words that passed beneath his fingertips. A few stragglers came in, glad that Mr Jaffray was not yet arrived. The reading continued above the greetings that were exchanged between neighbours, and then a hush fell as once more the door clicked open and shut, and Mr Jaffray advanced along the aisle, clothed in deep black robes as if he were in mourning for the sins of the world. The Precentor stumbled to a halt.

'Thank you, Precentor, you may now commence the service wi the singing of the Psalms.' Mr Jaffray took his seat by the side of the pulpit, while the Precentor opened the Psalter, his pale round worried face gleaming like the moon in the half dark of the Kirk. When he spoke, Annie could see the mist of his breath in the light from the candle.

'Let us sing in praise to the Lord. Let us sing Psalm Fifty One.'

The congregation rose. The Precentor closed his eyes, concentrated, and took aim at a note. His face fell as he missed the mark by some distance, but he carried on giving out the line, and waited while the congregation gave it back to him, in a pitch so low that they had to scrape beneath the soles of their feet to match him. He gave out the next line, and the following ones, and Annie heard

Jess in the row ahead of her trying to lift it, but the congregation went with the Precentor each time, repeating his words and pitch but adding their own grace notes to give it a more comely shape. As they ended each line, the Precentor sang the next one and they took it up and moulded it. Sometimes the Precentor leapt in before they had finished, and at others he held back a bit too long. With this, and with the way that some folk liked to rush through it while others preferred to linger and draw the notes out, or ornament them with high quavers, and with the length of the Kirk, it was not long before the front pews were half a line ahead of those at the back, and a full tone and a half above them.

At last, the Precentor sang the final phrases, and the congregation punished the psalm until it gave up the ghost. The folk in the front pews waited with downcast eyes for those at the rear to finish putting the psalm out of its misery.

'Amen.'

A volley of coughs and energetic throat-clearing followed. The Precentor pursed his lips and waited for silence.

'Let us now sing once again to the Lord's praise. Let us lift our voices for God's glory in Psalm One Hundred and Seven.'

This time, Annie breathed a sigh of relief as he hit a good note smack between the eyes. The startled congregation followed in better voice. She sang out clear and loud, singing the verses that told of the good Lord's help to those in trouble. He who could raise a storm could also quiet it, and bring it to safe harbour through the wildest tempest. As they sang on, and the waves of song swelled through the Kirk, Annie saw the Precentor open his eyes. Sure of his territory, he had closed the Psalter after the first verse or two, but now his fingers fiddled through the book uncertainly, and his eyes shifted uneasily in their sockets, while lines of worry flickered across his brow. Still, he continued with the song, and the congregation followed. She noticed that just in front of her, Jess's shoulders were shaking gently up and down, and Andrew, as he stood beside the Laird, was singing with quivering lips, as if on the edge of laughter. As she watched him uncertainly, he caught her eye for just a second, then looked up to the Precentor and back at her, before staring ahead fixedly with that same strange expression on his face as if he were trying not to laugh. She turned her attention to what the Precentor was singing, instead of thoughtlessly repeating his words, and then she smiled broadly as she sang the rest of the song, enjoying the old story, for somewhere in the middle of it, the Precentor had abandoned the text and slipped without realising into the old song of Sir Patrick Spens, who was drowned at sea with all his men, with its slow sad tune so like that of the psalm. And so instead of singing the right words that King David had written when he was nothing but a herd boy, after 'They mount to heaven, then to the depths they do go down again', the Precentor had given them 'And the waves came o'er the broken ship, till aa her sides were torn,' and now Sir Patrick Spens and all his men were drowning once more in Fyvie Kirk, when they might have been better left to rest in the green quiet at the bottom of the sea, fifty fathoms deep off the coast of Aberdeen.

XVI

As night fell on Halloween, the clouded sky grew dark-grey, nearly black, all the way from the eastern horizon to the west, where the far hills were outlined by a thin golden band of sunset. It had rained most of the day, but now a change was on the way. A chill wind blew in from the north-east over the hill of Tifty. The stiff ends of the stubble bent and broke under the feet of the people of Tifty, as they walked slow and stumbling in the gloom up along the rigs towards the top of the hill. Annie pulled her plaid close to her and cuddled her hands together for warmth. Close around her the folk of Tifty walked in whispering groups. Annie turned her head and saw behind her Jess's daughter-in-law, Mary, carrying her youngest bairn on her hip and dragging her oldest by the hand, as he stared around him into the gathering darkness with wide, unblinking eyes. His cheeks, chin and forehead, like those of all the other folk, were streaked with black fingers of soot. Annie waited for them to draw level with her.

'You're nae feart of ghosts, are you, Davey?'

'Na, I'm nae,' the boy replied, but when a gust of wind moaned over the hill, he took her extended hand anyway. He walked on boldly between Annie and Mary, tripping over the hem of the dress that he wore.

'Dinna fret, Davey, the ghosts winna ken you in your granny's clothes.'

Annie herself hoisted up the breeches that she had borrowed from Gibb. They were too large for her by far, and the crotch swung uncomfortably between her thighs. The rough wool of her father's tunic itched her oxters. She drew her plaid closer around her against the wind as they breasted the top of the hill.

In the last light of Halloween, on the very highest point of the hill she could see a mound of brushwood – whin and gorse – stacked in a pile that reached away above her head. They gathered around it, waiting for the stragglers, until all the folk of Tifty were there.

The two Reid boys came over towards them and Davey immediately dropped the two women's hands. Annie addressed the three of them with genuine admiration.

'You lads have been busy right enough.'

'It took us three weeks! '

'I found the most wood!'

'I carried it farthest!'

'I found the biggest bit!'

'It'll go up like a candle,' she said.

'Aye, like a hundred candles!'

'Na, a thousand!'

And the ghosts were forgotten as the boys vied for glory.

'I'm going to light it,' said the eldest Reid lad, asserting his right.

'Nae one of you lads is to touch it.' Peter's voice, coming loud and sure of itself from over the far side, where a pile of larger logs waited to be thrown on once the blaze was established. 'Now wi this wind,' he continued, 'we must tak tent. Everybody come over this side or you'll go up with it.'

The Tifty folk saw the sense in that, and stumbled through the stubble to gather in a horseshoe with their backs to the wind. They huddled together, family groups merging into each other. William Smith stood a little to one side, arms crossed over his chest, feet planted squarely, looking on as, with James Reid assisting him, Peter bent to the foot of the pile of brushwood and worked to light a virgin flame with sawdust and the rubbing together of sticks. You could not take a light from a lantern, for the flame had to be new-born to cleanse the evil away.

Other men in the gathered crowd shouted out to them: 'Gie it mair shelter!' 'Na, let the wind at it!' 'Na, na, dinna blaw on it, it needs less wind, nae mair!' Meanwhile, the women's voices could be heard muttering: 'Every year it's aye the same.' 'How is it they never bring enough tinder?'

At last a yellow flame was born and grew in the shelter of Peter's hands. It spread among the thin dry twigs, at first reluctant but then, with the breeze behind it, licking along them hungrily and making them hiss and whimper. Within minutes a core of brilliant orange was burning in the middle of the pile, and then a sudden gust of wind blew around the gathered folk and with a roar the fire leapt up through the piled brush. The folk gave a raw, open-throated cheer as a whirling column of sparks and smoke spiralled up into the sky.

For a while, the pile of brush kept its shape, and the fire seemed caged within it, locked in behind the fretwork of spindly twigs. But as the fire grew hotter – so hot that you could hardly look at it directly, and the people stepped back from the heat – finally the flames took the outer shell of brush. As it collapsed into the embers, the Tifty folk cheered once more, and then as if a spell had been broken, there was laughter and talk and jugs of ale going round, and the bairns chasing each other in and out between the legs of the adults. James Reid and Peter began to load the bigger logs onto the fire. Then Mary took Annie's hand, and Annie took Jess's beside her, and all the folk linked themselves together in a ring that circled the fire. And they raised their voices to sing against the evil that hovered around them, the spirits that might mean harm to them and would hurt them if they could over the coming year.

As they went around and around the fire, Annie turned her head over her shoulder, and one side of her face was bright and hot, the skin tight and her eye half blinded by the fire, and the other was cold in the wind and dark. She could see the shape of the fire at Cardonwell, and saw, or imagined she saw, the tiny shadows passing in front of it as the folk there danced around it; and all around on the hills of Fyvie, there were points of light glowing in the dark, where the folk were gathered to dance and sing around their own fires that burned for their protection on the highest place in every farmtoun. Scores of fires, diminishing into the distance until they were no bigger than the stars that began to appear, shining huge and brilliant and close overhead, as the wind cleared the sky from the east.

A light began to show on the eastern horizon, making the sky pale and dimming the stars, and as the dancers still circled the fire and their voices chanted the psalms, the silver moon floated upwards, making faint shadows of the stubble on the rigs.

Then at last the dancers stopped to gather their things, the half-empty kegs of ale and the cast-off plaids. The flames had died back but the embers still glowed hot. The heads of the five households of Tifty each took a log from the fire to carry back to his own home, where he would relight the hearth with the protective fire. And together they all took the way across the stubbled rigs, with long moon-shadows walking ahead of them, to the bend in the path that led to the miller's yard, where hospitality might have been offered, if William Smith had not walked on to his door with nothing but a 'Good night to you aa, and God see you safe hame.'

Peter cleared his throat and filled the thick silence with his own invitation. 'Aye, well, you'll all maybe be wanting a drap mair ale and a bannock or two afore you go to your beds. Once you've been hame to light your own hearths, come awa down to mine. There's nae as much room as there is in some big houses, but you'll find a warm welcome.'

Annie heard the mutters as the folk headed off down the path in small groups: 'cold and that wife of his is nae better' – 'enough silver but nae a mug or two ale to spare' – 'bairns are turning out just the same,' and she was glad of the dark to hide her burning cheeks. She dithered in the cold, before following Jane, Bessie and Will in to the mill house.

When they had relit the fire, her mother opened the door and ushered her three girls outside, saying, 'It's off to the kailyard for the three of you, you ken what to do.'

After the light of the kitchen, Annie's eyes took a while to adjust to the darkness. She stumbled out of the front door blindly, stooping, with her hands outstretched until her fingers met with a bundle of thick leathery leaves and she pulled the stem of kail from the ground. The earth was well-turned and moist, and gave little resistance. There was the clean smell of rain-soaked earth, and behind her from the door her mother's voice, 'Have you got one? You must tak the first one you find. Nae choosing!'

'Aye, I've got one now.'

'Bring it in and we'll see what kind of a husband is waiting for you.'

She left the fresh night air reluctantly, and stepped over the threshold back to the warmth of fire and family. Putting her own runt of kail next to the two already lying by the hearth, she saw that the root was straight and clean.

'Och Annie, it's a poor man for you! You must have shaken it.' Jane turned towards Bessie in delight. 'We'll be marrying rich men, look at the mud on our two.'

'A poor man for Annie?' Her father's voice came from the other side of the room. 'I dinna think so – nae if we play our cards right!'

'Aye it is, Father,' Jane's voice was strident, 'She's shaken every wee bit of earth off of it.'

'I didna shake it, it's how it came. At least mine's tall and straight. Look at yours, Jane, aa fat and crooked, he'll be a stupid fat old bodach like the Factor.'

'Mine's a funny shape,' said Bessie, and young Will sniggered. Their father's eyes shot over to him and he said, 'Dinna you say a word there, Will, you tak care of your sisters' innocence,' but you could tell he thought it was funny too. Annie knew what they were on about, well she had half an idea at least, if not a whole one. Men were aye being coorse like that, and she was aye overhearing bits of conversations she was not supposed to understand.

'Now aa of you, haud your wheesht,' said their mother, 'and I'll tell you what your man will be like that you will marry.'

The sisters stopped their bickering and waited for Helen to say her piece.

'Now Jane, you're right, aa that mud clinging to the root is a good sign, he'll be wealthy. You winna have to worry about food for your bairns and you'll aye have fuel for the fire. He's maybe a miller like your father, and he'll be strong too, you can see that from the bulges on it, that's his muscles, see?'

Helen's voice was quiet, she was making it up although she believed every word as she spoke it, it was her own hopes for her daughter that she was giving her.

'And yours, Bessie, well...' The shape of the root was familiar enough for a married woman, but what could she say to a maid? 'He mightna be aa that bonnie, but you can be sure he'll keep you happy and well contented.' Young Will snorted from the corner, and a conspiratorial look passed between Helen and her husband. She pressed her lips together to control a smile.

'What about mine, mother?'

'Ach now, Agnes, see, there's nae earth clinging to the root. Jane was right, that maks it a poor man wi nae land and nae silver either. Go and get another and see if you can do better.'

'Na, I want this one. Nae choosing, you said.'

'Och, you were aye thrawn. Well, this would mean he's nae rich, but he's bonnie for sure, look how even and straight the stem's grown, and the colour of the leaves, they're still good and fresh, he's young still. But see how the leaves just at the top are turning yellow at the edges, I'd say he's got yellow hair! So this one is fair, and young, and bonnie – but poor. Go and pull another stem, Agnes.'

'Na, I winna. You said it yourself – tak the first one you find.'

She took herself off to sit on the creepie stool that she always like to sit in, leaving Jane and Bessie to discuss – too loudly, she thought, and for too long – their rich rich husbands and how they would be well looked after. So she sat on the stool, and she watched the dancing flames of the fire throw their flickering shadows on the walls of the ingle, and smiled to herself, as she thought how her mother would curse herself if she knew what she had said. The only thing she had got wrong was the colour of his hair.

And then she stood up, threw her plaid around her shoulders, and went out the door to pick her way down the path in the moonlight to Peter and Jess's cottage.

Inside, they were all dooking for apples in a pail of water, and taking the chance to wash the soot from their faces at the same time. Jess saw Annie as she entered and came across the room to her, 'Welcome to you, Mistress Agnes – now you just dook for an apple and peel it, and then the skin will tell us what kind of a man you'll marry.'

'Dinna worry yourself, Jess,' she answered, 'my mother's told me already.'

'Has she now? And tell me – did she say he'll have curly hair?' Jess held her gaze, waiting for an answer, while Annie stared, and swallowed, and her cheeks grew hot. Then she gave a loud, abrupt laugh, as she answered, 'Och Jess, I never liked curly hair on a man!' And Jess gave a wee nod and smiled away into herself, and then she lifted her old hand and gave Annie's forearm a wee squeeze and a pat before turning away and sitting heavily down on the box-bed.

Jess clapped her hands and addressed the assembled folk, 'Now. Who'll gie us a tune? John Scott – you were playing at your stock-and-horn aa summer when you should have been herding the kye – surely you'll gie us a tune?' And so John took out his stock-and-horn and others brought out whistles or jaw harps or meat bones to rattle together and they made a whole load of fine tunes while the folk clapped and stamped and jigged in time.

There was a call for a song, and the songs went round the company, and the voices of the tounsfolk joined together, the rough and the sweet and the strong and the quavering. Annie looked around the circle of faces, she knew every one of them, and thought how each one hid its stories and its secrets behind it, young or old, there were things hidden behind there and you couldn't get at them, buried beneath the skin. Her own face was like that too, behind it the love and the fear and the fretting and if you chose, as she did, it stayed inside and no one knew, like Jess they could guess but they could not know for sure, and even with Andrew, if he still wanted her, he would know only what she chose to tell him. But you could only ever say a tiny piece of all your thoughts, you chose which bits to let out, one at a time, while the others milled around unsuspected. You chose the words and polished them to give them the right shine for others to see, because if you said everything that came to your mind they would call you mad. But, she thought, the closest you can get is with a song, when you sing you let the words carry something of yourself with them, and you're saying this is me, this is what moves me, these are my things that I hold close to my heart.

Jess's youngest grandchild, a tiny lad no more than three years old, and still swamped by his big sister's dress, had crept onto the bed and snuggled his head on to Jess's lap, and the black soot on his face was rubbing off on to the apron spread across her thighs. Jess started to sing now, and she stroked her wrinkled hand over his hair with the rhythm of her song. It was the story of Jeannie of Saltoun, that was a true story that happened long ago and not so far from Fyvie. And her voice had a scratch in it, and it was a wee bit thin on the high notes, her voice had been stronger a few years ago. But Annie thought the song came through strong and true, and it was like Jess wasn't there at all, she was wrapped up in the song and the story and far away from them all, like she was there watching the whole thing while it happened, and she could see the faces of Jeannie and her father and her loon, Gordon of Annachie, and you could see the anger in the face of the father who was forcing her to marry Lord Saltoun, and it was a terrible thing.

But not far into the song, the two Reid lads started nudging and pushing each other, and Jess snapped her eyes open and broke the spell, she looked straight towards the lads, and she said, 'You shush now, lads, gie some respect to the ballad. It's nae just any song you see, it's a true story that happened and it tells about a terrible thing that was done. And because it's true, when you hear it you must gie it due respect, and when someone gies you a ballad you must listen, because it's nae just you that's listening, it's the ghosts too.' That quieted the boys, the mention of ghosts, and Jess nodded to them, glad of their understanding. 'Aye, that's right. The ghosts come to hear it and to see that you're telling their story right, as it should be. And even mair, this night of Halloween, when aa the ghosts are close by.'

Then the whole room was still, and the Reid lads looked down at their hands. Jess closed her eyes and began again her singing of the old story, and the song filled the room as it grew and grew, until they were all inside of it. Young bonnie Gordon coming back from the sea too late and the maidens leading him to Jeannie's bedside and him kissing her dead, cold lips, and then him dying himself, because he couldn't bear the grief. And it was Halloween and she knew their ghosts were there, listening, from the quiet of the room, time had somehow shifted so that through the whole spell of the song they were there among them, and there was a spirit of quietness and keen expectant listening, you couldn't deny it. It was always like that with the old ballads, not like the other songs, even the sad ones, they didn't carry the same quality.

And there was something in Jess's singing, not just in the story she sang, but in the way she sang it, that all of a sudden could make listeners feel a sharp hot pain in their chests and tears burning their eyes, as if the song had cut inside them, quietly without their noticing, and opened up a deep well of sadness that they did not even know was there. And Annie wondered why it was that the ballads were often so sad, they told such sad tales, and often it was a woman who got the worst of it, for loving or not loving or being loved wrong. She wondered who they were and what their lives had been, only one or two words came down to tell you the whole sad tale of their lives that had been full, entire, like hers, or Andrew's, or anyone's.

Then the ballad came to an end, and the last words were left ringing in the air, and then they fell slowly to the ground and settled in amongst the hard-packed earth, and the spell was lifted. The gathered listeners came back to the room, 'Aye, well done, Jess,' 'Lovely', and there was scattered clapping before Peter started up a bawdy song and they all joined in, except for Annie and one or two others maybe who held the old ballad still within them. Whenever she heard that song it went straight to her heart and set a bell ringing there, and she hugged it close and knew it would be one of her songs when it was her place in some future time when attention turned to her and they would say, 'Will you gie us a song, Mistress Agnes?' And she would, but for now when it came around to her she just gave them Eppie Morrie and they said, 'Well sung, Mistress, how is it you dinna sing for us mair?' and she nodded and smiled, a wee bit shy at the compliment, and she was sure they all thought she was having a fine time.

And she was having a fine time, in a way, but in another way she was nowhere near fine. Because she was reminded of another time when she had sneaked away to Jess's place, on Fastern's eve after the Fyvie Fair. With Grizel and Bessie she had squeezed in amongst the rest of the folk of Tifty, who had given them a nod or two in welcome, while carrying on with their songs and their din. Someone had piled far too much peat on the fire, as usual, and she and Grizel and Bessie squeezed all three of them together onto a kist at the far end of the room from the hearth, where the heat was nearly bearable. Young Jamie Buchan from Cardonwell came in with a laugh and a bounce, short and broad and beaming, bringing laughter with him although the Lord knew when he had had a drink you could hardly make out a word he said, but still he was funny somehow. Jamie and Peter put their arms around the neck of Bella, just as well she was such a placid beast, who chewed the cud contentedly while they sang to her a psalm tune, but with words that you would never hear in the Kirk. Every time Annie or Grizel or Bessie shifted a bit on the kist, whichever one of them that was sitting on the end started to fall off, so they would be singing along with the crowd and then there would be a squeal and a laugh and the shuffling of backsides as they clung together, trying to hold on. But then the one in the middle would give a shuffle, deliberate now, and off the end the other would go, almost into her neighbour's lap. If it was one of the older men he would throw his arms wide and make a joke of it, how she was welcome any time, she had only to ask. There were times of year when you could do that kind of thing, few enough of them, Halloween and Hogmanay and today, though the rest of the year half of the same folk would be solemn and serious and would be horrified at the terrible goings on in the parish when they had some news of the scandalous carriage of a young couple found walking together, perhaps holding hands, or worse. So anyway, that had been their game that night, and they did not bother too much about the three men from the Laird's service who were gathered at the far end of the room, by the hearth, though of course they had noticed them, it wasn't so often you saw the Laird's men in a cottar's house. But Jess's cottage was like that, it drew people to it on a night like this, or on any night, so there they were. There were two that she had seen before and then the new laddie, just a few years older than she was herself, maybe. The word went round the room that Alexander Seton had brought him from Edinburgh to fill the post of the old Laird's trumpeter. Word was he had been in the service of some other Laird who had visited Seton in the big house in Edinburgh, and that Seton had taken such a liking to him that he had brought him home to Fyvie Castle, and it wasn't just Seton who liked him, there was a kitchen maid or two who was a good bit gayer about her duties since he had arrived. Annie didn't bother with that gossip, it was nothing to her. Then someone had shouted out above the din, 'Get yon Laird's trumpeter to gie us one of his Edinburgh songs,' and so he had pushed himself away from the wall where he had been leaning, and stood there straight, with the sweat from the heat of the fire glistening on his brow, and his eyes closed like he was dreaming. He had not sung an Edinburgh song, though, but Hind Horn, which they all had heard since they were bairns, and loved. When he was finished, he had opened his eyes and by chance it seemed he had looked straight across all the heads in the room right into her own eyes, and then a look had come over his face, like surprise, and for her own part, she felt there was something about him that she recognised, although she knew that she had never seen his face in the world before.

That had been in February. But eight months later, at Halloween, no Laird's trumpeter had come from the castle.

There were songs, and more songs, and then without warning the door banged open, letting in a blast of wind and five figures, robed and masked in sheep's skins, and carrying lanterns. The first of them leapt across the threshold, holding a short sword high in the air, and strode about the room, yelling above the din of the crowd, 'Stir up the fire, and gie us light! For in this room there'll be a fight!'

She shrank away back because, just for a minute, she thought it was the Hielan men come to carry them all away. Then someone shouted out, 'Guisers!' And there was an uproar.

XVII

Jess's grandson woke, lifted his head from her lap, and began to bawl and scream in terror at the sight of the masked figures parading around the room. But Jess only cuddled him close and comforted him, saying 'Dinna be feart, my hinnie, it's only the guisers,' and so he watched with wide eyes as they went through their play, bashing each other with the flats of their swords and falling to the ground. They were well fed and watered when they finished, but still they never took off their masks, despite the heat, leaving the company to guess at who they might be.

Annie left Jess and Peter's cott and headed towards the mill house an hour before the dawn. The weather had changed again, and the day would be wet. She stopped for a while by the willows, where the Tifty burn emerged from the ravine on its way to join the Ythan. As she watched the rolling cloud masses skimming the tops of the hills on the far side of Tifty's meadowlands, she thought of the burn passing beneath the Brig of Skeugh, and the path from there to where their tree trunk lay, and she began to feel uneasy and uncertain. In the few days since she had seen Andrew in the Kirk, when he had looked to her to share the great joke that the Precentor had unwittingly given them, she had been making it the way it was before, forgetting and forgetting the way it had been between them when they parted. And she had convinced herself that he would come up the road for Halloween. But now she was thinking of what had passed between them at their last parting, and how long he had been away, and how he might still be angry over the words she had said. Or, worse, he might be thinking of some other lass, from Beauly. She turned her feet towards the mill house. Now that the night of burning fires and celebrations was over, she felt ash-grey with tiredness.

As she stumbled half asleep past the byre, a hissing sound cut through her. She looked around in confusion for the source of the sound, and then looking towards the byre she saw that the door was open, and framed in it was a man. She almost shouted out for help, and then she saw that it was her Andrew, wearing a guiser's sheepskin, with the masked hood thrown back. His face was white, like a ghost's, in the gloom. She was so surprised and confused that she did not think to whisper. 'Andrew!' And then she slapped her hand over her mouth and looked around in case anyone was there to hear, and stepped hurriedly into the byre, closing the door behind her.

There was no awkwardness or hesitation as they enclosed each other in their arms. It was enough that he was there.

He pressed her head into his chest and kissed her hair.

Hanging from a peg, the clyack sheaf, dressed in its plaid and skirt and apron, seemed to watch in mute approval.

After a while, he stirred and spoke, 'Did you no ken me, Annie, in my guising?'

'Na! Naebody kenned who you aa were. You never took your masks off, or your cloaks. Didna you hear us guessing at who you might have been?'

'Aye, I did.'

'So how was it you didna speak to me?'

'I was guising, I had a part to play.'

'You played it right well, swinging your sword around. It was you that got killed, was it nae?'

'Aye, I was the corpse.'

'You made a good job of the dying. And the doctor made us laugh, wi his speeches. What was it he gave you to drink?'

'Whisky!'

'That would put the life back into any body.'

'And it did. Did you see how quick I jumped to my feet?'

'Aye. Like a – a –. Andrew. How was it you didna speak to me?'

She hugged him close and looked up into his face, searching for the answer.

'Ocht, Annie. I thought maybe you'd have gone and found another lad to tak my place. I thought I'd watch and hold my peace until I was sure of you.'

'Na. Na, aa I thought of was you, the whole time you were awa. And there was me thinking you must have forgotten me, and found a lass in Beauly, I was that cruel to you.'

He shook his head slowly, and pressed the back of his hand gently to her cheek, 'The Beauly lasses couldny hold a candle to you, my Annie.'

'But dinna you hate me, for what I said?'

'Ocht Annie, I could never hate you. I shouldny have said those things, I was angry, I thought you didny want me.'

'I aye wanted you. Naebody but you.'

She took his face between her hands and kissed him, fiercely, deep on the mouth, to show him that she wanted him, just him and no one else, and no land or money or gold or kye. But she did not say it. It was not the time to start talking about tochers again, or to bring back the memory of how it had been the last time they had spoken with each other.

They stood there in the gloom, surrounded by the huffing of the kye and the oxen, and she leaned against him, nestling her head against his shoulder, and breathing in the smell of him, for as long as she dared. But soon the house would be wakening, and before long she stirred and spoke.

'Let me go out first. I'll gie you a wave if there's naebody in the yard.'

'When will I see you? It's no the weather to be meeting like we used to.'

'We must, Andrew. Whenever we can. Whatever the weather.'

'It's still no enough.'

'We've naethin else for now. But listen – they say Ironsyde has only the roof to put on his byre, and the Factor's working like an ant at his fiddle. There'll maybe be a dance come Hogmanay.'

'Then I'll dance wi you the whole night.'

There was no one in the yard, so with a quick tender kiss they parted, and Andrew ran from the byre and across the yard. He dived into the shelter of the orchard, passing quickly out of sight as he went down the slope between the trees. Before she went into the house she leaned back against the cracked millstone that stood by the door, and closed her eyes, and smiled and smiled. Then she went inside and floated up the stairs and got into bed as quietly as possible. As she crawled under the cover, Bessie stirred and turned towards Jane, but did not waken. She counted the times that she and Andrew had been together, just the two of them, in the last year. Some few times when she was gathering reeds; another three or four times walking back from Kirk when she had slowed her steps and fallen behind the rest of the party from Tifty; every evening through the week of the Laird's shearing. Some other times when she had got away, and they had crawled in under the log, or walked up the glen. And one time, very precious to her, when they had sat on the Deer's Hill when the flax flowers were blooming. But all told it came to hardly more times than she could count on her fingers. And the time they had argued, and this last time in the byre, and that was all, and it was not enough, nowhere near enough, she wanted to have all of him, and for him to have all of her. So then her choice was made, and it was an easy one, in the end.

She lay without sleep for the brief half-hour until the rest of the household stirred, listening to an owl hooting intermittently not far from the window. She was thinking not just of Andrew, but of Jess and Peter, and of how they were like each other somehow, not just in the set of the shoulders and the gait when they walked, but as if they had grown together over the years to make a pair. Like trees that stood in the same wood with their roots entwined, so they looked like two things but they were really just the one. Peter's hair was silvered grey now but still plentiful. She remembered him from when she was a bairn, when the grey was only just coming at the temples, and she thought of Andrew, how she had found once a single grey hair and teased him about it, how he was old and he would be grey by the time he was twenty-five, and he had not liked it one bit, even when she said she did not care, he could lose every hair on his head and he would still be her bonnie Andrew. She wondered really what he would look like when he was Peter's age, sixty maybe, she thought he would still stand straight but his hair would be grey and there would be two lines between his brows because they were there now, fine lines that formed when worry or anger came over his face, like when they had argued about her tocher. There would be deep lines in the skin around the corners of his eyes, radiating like sunbeams, you could see how they would be when his face leapt into a grin. She wondered what she would look like herself, and if he would still love her, of course he would, he would care for her just like Peter cared for Jess. And maybe they would go deaf together and they would shout at each other, 'Is there peat for the fire?' 'Aye, plenty heat,' and all that kind of thing. It would annoy them and it would make them laugh, they would still make each other laugh all those years later.

XVIII

William Smith got a good price for his cattle at the Martinmas market. He went down to Woodhead with John Scott herding them ahead of him, and he admired their rumps, still good and solid and fat from the grazing on his pastures, and they were fine black kye and sold well to men whose lands were less rich than his and who would slaughter and salt them for their winter meat. Good money he made that day, plenty good silver to store in the kist, and that got him thinking on the subject of his daughters' tochers, and the letter he would send to the Laird. Still he had not put pen to paper. Or rather, he had made a start once or twice, but had put the paper away unmarked. But no matter. He would do it soon. Today, he felt good with the silver in his pocket. Solid. A man of consequence. A man who could make an offer to an Earl, with good hopes of being accepted. He would write that letter, maybe this evening.

As he picked his way between cowpats, he came across his neighbour from Meikle Gourdas, Ironsyde. Ironsyde he admired. A man of consequence, like himself. They stood for a while, exchanging news of the day's trading, not far from the door of the Woodhead merchant's house. The merchant was another man like them, a man who knew how to turn one penny into two, as Gervase Markham himself might say. The merchant's wife did good business by opening their home as an ale-house. Tifty felt the weight of the silver in his pocket, and extended an invitation to Ironsyde to take a draft or two of ale with him.

'Come awa in, Mr Ironsyde, and tell me how the kye will be housed in the new byre.'

As always, Ironsyde was eager to talk, and after a few rounds, the miller's thoughts found voice.

'Hey hey, Gourdas, you'll have time for another?'

'No, no, Tifty, I've business I must see to.'

'Ocht and awa, I thought you'd be wanting to raise a glass wi me.'

'For what, Tifty? It's a gey long time since you had anything to raise a glass to. Three daughters to find husbands for and a son mair interested in dramming than milling, tell me, you've never found much to drink to in that afore now.'

'Three daughters to find husbands for, you say? And there was me thinking it was just the two.' Tifty's eyebrows danced a suggestive jig across his forehead.

'What's that you're telling me, Tifty?'

'Aye, well, you've nae heard then how the Laird of Fyvie has made a habit of coming by Tifty? He's aye happy to have a wee word wi my Agnes.'

It was maybe not strictly true – when was the last time the Laird had come by? The shearing-time, maybe. But still. It carried enough of the truth to make Ironsyde stare, blink, and cogitate. Tifty could see his mind was turning slowly, like the big wheel of the mill when the burn ran low in summer. Clunk. Clunk. Ironsyde slowly ground this new information into a usable form. And then, as the flour of enlightenment dropped down the chute, his mouth fell open in surprise.

'Agnes! My God man! Agnes and the Laird of Fyvie, eh? That's worth a toast after aa!'

'Then we'll mak it a dram of good whisky.'

In the gloom of the ale-house, they drank a toast. 'To unmarried daughters!' William Smith sat chuckling over his drink, his great belly jiggling up and down, his face pink and the bulbous nose snorting now and then with mirth. Smith bought a round for the other five or six drinkers in the house – a rare event, but a

Gentleman Miller could afford it. After the third dram, he became loquacious.

'Ho-ho, Ironsyde, you see I'm no such an unlucky man after aa. I may not have my father's land or title – to be the last of four brothers, I took that as a curse. But the Laird of Fyvie! It's about time he married, see, a thirty-year-old man at that, it'll be on his mind now his parents are gone. And he's looking for a bonnie wife to gie him an heir. And who's the bonniest lass for miles around, Ironsyde? Who is it? Whose daughter is it?' Ironsyde was now half-asleep with drink and made no response. The smile dropped off Smith's drink-flushed face and the punch he gave to Ironsyde's upper arm was harder than it needed to be.

'What's that, Tifty?'

'Whose daughter is it that's the bonniest lass in the whole parish?'

'Yours, Tifty, your Agnes.'

Tifty stared at him a moment longer, before his face relaxed once more into a broad smile. 'Aye. That's right. My wee Agnes.'

That evening, he sent Grizel up to light a fire in his bedroom hearth, and he mounted the stairs early. He hung his cruisie lamp over the small writing desk that stood in the corner, and pulled up a padded leather chair. He prepared pen, ink, paper, blotter and sealing wax. Then he balanced the pen between his thumb and the stump of his right index finger, and began to write, blotting the wet ink as he went. When he had covered a page, he looked back over what he had written. Damn it, writing had become a slow and tedious affair since he lost his finger. And it made his handwriting look rude and untutored, like that of a plain working man, instead of a gentleman, just when he needed to remind the Laird that the Miller of Tifty was far more than the good miller that he had seen when he came to see his harvest being ground, when Tifty was dusted head to toe in the colourless powder and the good earth smell of ground oats. As he pictured himself like this, his jaw tightened as he heard the Laird laughing his high-pitched laugh, and he saw him passing the letter round to his companions as the wine went round: 'A miller's daughter? His father and his grandfather were millers, too, ye ken, at Rothiebirsben so I'm told. And his brother has the tack of the Mill of Ardoyne. A family of millers. If I were to marry sic a lass, I would be well served wi pigmeat!'

He screwed the page up into a ball and crushed it between his palms. There was a pain in his tooth. He moved his jaw from side to side, deliberately, trying to loosen it off. He pushed the chair back from the bureau, and sat staring at the wall, stabbing at the pain in his jaw with the stub of his finger. And he began to regret how the drink had loosened his tongue with Ironsyde.

He hoped that Ironsyde would not gossip. He could hear the voices of the Fyvie folk, if they got wind of it.

'Have you heard of the wedding there's to be up at Fyvie Castle?'

'Na! What's this you've been hearing?'

'It seems there's to be a wedding soon, two dozen lairds and two dozen ladies are to be the guests. A grand wedding at the Kirk, and then the Miller of Tifty and his wife and aa will be invited to the high table at Fyvie Castle, and they'll dine on a big stuffed goose served on silver ashets, and the candles on the table –'

'Hold on, did you say Tifty and his wife are to be there?'

'I did, aye.'

'And how's that then?'

'Och, can you no guess? They're the proud parents of the bride. Agnes Smith herself.'

'Agnes Smith and the Laird of Fyvie! Well, they say yon William Smith is a gentleman's son, after aa. Nae lands, but good blood. So Seton plans to marry at last. I never thought he'd get round to it.'

'Ah now, nae so fast. I didna say the Laird was planning to be married. I said there was a wedding planned nonetheless.'

'How's that? How can there be a wedding planned when the groom knows naethin about it himself?'

And they would laugh, long and loud.

He slammed the bureau shut. He would do it another time, when he could think straight.

XIX

Margaret Urquhart's bairn was born not long after Martinmas, before November was out. A long, skinny, weak girl-child, that made Helen Black exclaim, 'She minds me of Agnes when she was born, before I took her to the Shargar Stane!' The bairn was christened in the Kirk and, despite Helen's misgivings, began to grow fat, while the few kye that had survived Martinmas grew skinny, as if the wind that blew over the hill stripped the flesh from their bones as they sought, stumbling amongst the stubble, for nourishment. Christmas drew near and in the Kirk Mr Jaffray railed longer and harder each week, like the winds that swept down from the sea away in the north-east, and trembled with righteous rage as he preached against those who would bring popery back by swearing off work on Christmas Day. And yet on Christmas morning the only work that was done at Tifty was when the women-folk crossed the yard to the byre and undressed the clyack sheaf and shared it between the hungry kye and the oxen and the pony, and when they lit a small fire of sharp-scented juniper to purify the air. And in the mill house they prepared and ate a big fish brought specially from the coast, and drank toasts, and had gifts of new clothes, new-spun by the womenfolk and woven by Peter and cut and sewn together by his son James.

Grizel had a gift of Annie's old skirt and apron from the year just ending, and she had Helen's old things to take to her mother, who would have a job opening up the seams and sewing them back together with the narrowest possible hem, and the clean unworn cloth would show in a line down her sides all through the next year.

There was little work done in all of Fyvie for another three-four days, and visiting and singing and laughter passed between the farmtouns when the weather allowed it. And the visitors brought news that the Factor's fiddle was made, and he was ready to bring down the roof at Meikle Gourdas if Ironsyde would risk it, and so all the Fyvie folk readied themselves to dance the New Year in.

But none of the stour and grime of the old year was to be taken into the new one, so at the end of that week there was a sudden fury of cleaning from before dawn to day's end, with all the women polishing and wiping and scrubbing until every flagstone, timber, bowl, pot, cruisie, spoon and barrel in the Miller's house was free of the old year's dirt. When it was done, there was barely a minute to rest before making the supper, and then in the evenings they would pull their seats around the fire and breathe easier, and set their spindles thrumming.

The night before the dance, Grizel excused herself – 'I'm awa down to see my mother and father' – and Gibb shuffled out to make his annual visit to the alehouse, leaving the Smith family to sit just themselves for the first time in a long while. When Grizel and Gibb were well away, Annie went to her nook by the fire and pulled out an old thumbed chapbook. Her father took it from her and when he saw the cover, he did not open it up but instead, as she had hoped, said, 'We had this from that Gavin Sinckler. Do you remember the trouble we had wi him, Helen?'

Young Will folded his arms. Annie and her sisters looked expectantly at their mother, but they kept their fingers busy in the twirling of their spindles. Helen drew herself up in her chair and straightened her mutch, and the miller closed over his copy of Markham and sat with a thumb holding his place between the pages. As Helen began the story that was for the ears of the family and none else, her eyes looked into the fire as if the past was found there, but her hands carried on spinning the flax of their own will.

'Ocht well, let me see, it was about a year and a half afore you were born, Bessie. Agnes wasnae even thought of. Will was just a wee lad, he was just starting to speak and to get into everything, and I must have been carrying Jane. And the kye were aa falling sick, gey sick wi the quarter-evil. They would go lame in the one leg, and then they would swell up, aa hard, and by the time night fell that same day they would be dead. And we had lost some beautiful beasts, I mind them well, every one of them, and their names. Half the herd we lost that year, and there were other touns in Fyvie stricken just the same. Well, this mannie frae Ireland – he was a travelling man, ken, a chapman, he used to go about aa over the country wi nae place to call hame – well this Gavin came into the yard there just as if he knew he was wanted, and he says – now I canna speak his Irish way, but he says, "Well Mistress if you gie me broth and meal and a bed for a night or two, I can cure your cattle." And I says to him, "Ocht and awa wi you, we have bled them, and we have drenched them wi sulphur and garlic, and we have driven them aa atween the needfires, and a hard job it was too, for they wouldna go near the flames, and if that didna cure them then I dinna ken what will." And he says, "But Mistress, I have a magic stane in my breast pocket, and if I but lay it on the threshold of the byre and the kye walk over it when they go out in the morning, then it will cure them right quick. And if you dinna believe my word, then tak the word of the Laird's Chamberlain, for he himself had me cure the Laird's oxen with it." And I had heard of sic a thing, just a week or two before, so I said to him, "Tak a meal and a bed for the night and gie us one or two of your Irish songs by the fire this evening, and I'll speak to my husband and find his will on the matter." So that was what happened, he stayed with us and oh! but his songs they were fine, songs like I had never heard, you ken the Irish dinna sing the same songs nor the same way as we do, wi them it's aa twiddling up and down on one word for it seems like ever, whereas we sing the notes straight and true, but anyway he was a fine singer and we had a rare night, and your father and this Gavin took a wee bit mair to drink than they should have.

'Well so anyway, in the morning he was up and about and your father speired at him what was the business wi the stane, and this Gavin told him about it, and your father says, "Aye, do it then," and so he lays the stane down on the byre door-stane and aa the kye step over it on their way out to the field, and there was three-four looked like they were beginning to sicken, they had a wee bit lameness and we kenned well what that meant. When they had aa gone out this Irishman taks up the stane – it was flat and round and kind of a greeny colour, and it fitted in the palm of his hand – and he cradles it in his hands and speaks to it, I tried to hear what it was, but he turned awa so I couldna hear, and then he washes it three times wi water frae a jug, and dries it off and puts it in a pouch that's hanging at his breast, inside his sark. Then he goes off to do the work your father has given him, as if naethin has happened at aa.

'But do you ken what happened that night, when the herd brought in the kye for the milking?'

'Na, tell me.' She did know, she knew fine, she had heard the story plenty times, but still she said na, to make her mother carry on with it.

'Well. They were kicking up their heels, every one of them, like young calves.'

Her father cleared his throat, 'Now it wasna quite how your mother tells it, it was a day or two before they were well. But we never lost a single one mair that whole year, except a month or two later one of the fair folk shot one and she dropped dead in the field, just like that. So that was the end of the quarter-evil. But it wasna the end of the trouble, it was the start of it, because your mother was that pleased wi Gavin Sinckler she went about telling everyone she met, and so she brought the Kirk Session down on us.'

'It's true, I was full of it, and what would you think but next thing five-six of the elders come along wi Mr Sharpe – he was the minister then, a fine man he was – aa solemn and saying, "What's this we hear about witchcraft at Tifty?" And I says, "Witchcraft? Never here, please God." But it comes out that folk have been saying we've used witchcraft to cure the kye.'

Shaking her head, she gave out a sigh, and as she continued, her spindle slowed and stuttered to a stop, and her voice dropped low and lower still, until she was speaking in a whisper.

'Witchcraft, they said. *Witchcraft*. And that was when the fear came on us. Neither I nor your father had a wink of sleep, hardly, for weeks, until the business was settled. And if we did sleep, we would dream, terrible dreams they were, full of smoke and flames and the witch-pricker's pins, and the terrors of – that place below.'

She stopped entirely, and sat staring, intense and strained, into the fire. At last she shook her head and started her spindle twirling again, and continued.

'Well. They sent me and your father up to stand before the Presbytery Court in Turriff. And they sore bothered us with aa kinds of questions, us and the Laird's Chamberlain and his wife and Thomas Mill and aa, and Thomas and Isabel had a hard time, for they denied everything, "Na na na" they said, "We've never heard of this Irish charmer or a magic stane and nane of our kye has been sick for oh! we dinna ken how long," and of course the Presbytery men couldna believe that they were there for naethin at aa and gave them a gey hard time.

'But your father and I, though the fear was on us, we kenned what to do, and we took a different line, instead of "Na na na," we said "Aye aye aye, everything you say except" – except, mind – "except that Irishman never used a charm. We let him sleep in the byre and he fed the cattle up for his keep and looked after them and that was how they got better. And we never paid him a penny, but he bought a part firlot of meal frae us and we let him keep the rest of it for his pains." That was it. Nae that one bad thing you say we did, but aye to the rest of it, and that went down easy wi the

Presbytery men, it didna stick in their throats like it had wi Thomas Mill, and so they were easy on us. But even so, it set folk against us for a gey long time, and your father took it hard that his good name was dirtied. For there were plenty that thought the Presbytery men had ill done their job, and they werenae afraid to say it, except to your father's face. But it shows that the Kirk and the law dinna ken aa there is to ken about what's right, for if it wasnae the Lord's will that those kye got better, then I dinna ken whose will it was.'

'But mother, wasnae it wrong to tell a lie? To the minister, like?' It was the question she always asked at this point in the story, since she was a bairn she had asked it, and still she asked it now, and her mother gave the answer that Annie knew would come.

'Well, Agnes, the Good Book says it's wrong so of course that's true, but it would have been a far greater wrong for them to send us to be strangled and burnt, and that Gavin too, aa for the sake of a wee bit charming.

'Remember that, my bairns, if you're in trouble for a thing. Aye, aye, aye, and then na, and they'll tak it frae you.'

The five listeners nodded, and carried on with their work, and Helen turned her attention back to her distaff.

XX

On the last afternoon of the year, there was nothing left to clean in the house except the people that lived in it, and so they set to, taking turns to fetch water from the burn in a pair of buckets carried from a yoke across their shoulders, and boiling it up in the great cauldron over the fire until the kitchen filled with clouds of steam, and water streamed down the windows.

The girls were banished upstairs while the men took their turns to bathe in a great tub pulled up close to the fire, the Miller first while the water was still good and hot, his wife pouring water down his back and scrubbing away the long year's dirt from his broad shoulders. Then Will and Gibb were left to clean themselves, and Gibb, being the last in line, had to make do with grey, lukewarm water with a scum of soap and grime floating around on it.

When the men had finished, Annie and Grizel hefted the tub out the door and tipped the filthy water into the midden, where it steamed in the crisp air. There was a pale rosy glow in the sky beyond the orchard, the sun setting, so early in the day, for the last time that year, and already the yard and the house were grey with shadows. Annie found herself already longing for the spring, when at this time of day it would still be light, and the ploughmen would be out on the rigs with their teams of oxen, slow and heavy and surefooted in the sodden soil, six pair to a plough to drag it through the thick earth, followed by the birds that hopped behind with bright eyes, waiting to see a blind worm turn in the unfamiliar light. Then you would hear the whistles of the ploughmen as they urged their oxen on, and from far off see them creeping slow as maggots up the slopes. But just now, though the year had turned, the dark was close on them, and she returned to the house, where the drops of water inside the kitchen windows sparkled like jewels in the firelight.

More water was soon set to boiling for the bathing of the women, and the clouds of steam grew so thick that you could hardly see across the room, and they had to take care in their bare feet on the slippery floor. They moved leisurely about, taking it in turns to pour water or use the brush to help each other clean wherever they could not reach themselves.

It came to Annie's turn, and she got out from her clothes and for an instant stood naked, with the air cool on her skin. Helen, Jane and Bessie, already bathed, sat on wooden chairs around the tub, bending their heads over to one side or the other so that the long skeins of their hair would dry in the fire's heat. Her mother, with an unaccustomed colour in her cheeks, looked up and smiled to see her standing there, 'The water's good and warm, Agnes. You tak your time, now, because this is the one time in the year when we're all queens.' And it was true, there was not an hour of any other day when they could sit and do nothing for as long as they liked, without even a spindle in their hands.

As she stepped into the tub, Helen said, 'Just look at you, to think you were a wee girl not so long ago. My youngest, too.' Then a twinkle came into her eye, as she started a song, *John, come kiss me now*, and all the others joined in happily, glad that they had had their turns already. Annie shook her head, saying 'Ocht, awa with you,' but she knew that she did not blush as much as her sisters had, and not near as much as she had a year ago, as she lowered herself to sit and the water swooshed in waves and splashed over the sides.

She closed her eyes, loving the warmth of the water and the way it caressed her skin, for it was the only time in a long year that she would bathe her whole body at once. When she opened them again, through the steam the faces and figures of the other women were softened and indistinct. Only her own body was clearly defined, very white and smooth, with fine red hairs on her arms and legs. Grizel set to scrubbing away at her back, and she sat with her arms holding her bent knees. Curled in on herself like that, all she could see were the shifting shadows and curves of her body as the firelight fell across her, and she heard the steady beat of her heart, and the *swoosh* of blood in her ears. Grizel ran the brush up and down her back and along her limbs, lifting away the grime. She was a queen, or a priestess, in a far-off land, and her maidens were preparing her, purifying and making her ready in a bath of sweet calves' milk. Her hair fell forward around her down-turned face, like a veil.

When she rose from the tub, her whole body felt new, clean and fresh and tingling, alive inside and out, readied for the New Year to come, and for the night that lay ahead.

She sat on the creepie stool and joined her voice with the others while her hair dried and Grizel had her turn to bathe. Then, when they were all dry, the three sisters took the stairs to their room, still singing. There were clean new clothes to be worn to the dance, hair to be combed and ribbons to be tied, and so Annie found herself passing a comb through Jane's hair in long even strokes and handing a tin mirror to Bessie, and herself asking to borrow a ribbon from one or the other, and feeling a space open up between her two sisters that she stepped into, as if she had always belonged there.

Maybe the bathing had made them all new and young again, because there was a playful spirit about her father too when they came down the stairs, and he greeted them by clapping his hands together with a loud, 'Oh-hoh! Would you look at those three bonny lassies, Helen!' and with a flourish he lifted a glass to toast them all.

As they filed out into the yard, Annie found herself right next to her father as he pulled the door closed behind him. He paused, and looking down at her, lifted a hand and very gently chucked her under the chin, as he used to do when she was just wee.

'Your mother's aye said you were queens on this day, Agnes. And this time I can almost believe it.'

His eycs rested long on her face, and then with a wee shake of his head he winked, 'Now let's go and dance the New Year in, and we'll see what it brings, eh?'

When the mill-house folk at last took the path around the bottom of the Tifty hill towards Gourdas, Annie walked abreast with Jane and Bessie as if they had never done anything else. They passed through the yard at Meikle Gourdas, and on to where the new byre, stone-walled all the way up to the thatch, stood alone on the top of a low rise, bursting with music and light that leaked out into the night through the window slits. When they opened the door, a blast of fiddle music greeted them. Lit by the candles and cruisies that hung everywhere from pegs, hooks and beams, and just visible through the shifting gaps in the dancing crowd, was the Factor. He was seated on a low stool, opposite the door, and already sweat was pouring from his face, as his elbow jigged and dived with the bow above his great belly, and he beat out the rhythm with his wide-planted feet. The stubby fingers of his left hand leapt and sprang from string to string, while he grinned and winked and nodded at the dancers as they circled past with stamping feet and clapping hands, and the stool beneath him creaked and strained beneath his weight.

The party from Tifty headed towards one end of the byre, where Ironsyde presided over a row of ale-kegs. As they jostled their way through the crowd, they reached out to shake the hands that were stretched out in greeting and returned the smiles of welcome. When Ironsyde saw them coming, he raised a hand, and shouted over the heads of the dancers, 'Hey, hey, Tifty! Come and have some ale wi me and we'll drink to the new byre!' Annie's father clasped Ironsyde's hand and drinks were poured for them all from the kegs.

Someone snatched Grizel for a dance, and Annie was left with Jane and Bessie. An assortment of stools, benches and kists lined the walls, and they edged their way along until they found a place to sit at the far end of the byre. Annie searched the crowd for Andrew, and at last she caught sight of his curly head bobbing as he danced with one of the Ironsyde lasses. He looked fine to her, and they would have their dance together soon enough, and then maybe they would give the Fyvie folk something to talk about. She didn't want people to talk, of course not, how could she with her father and mother right there? Only she did, deep down she did, she wanted the folk to see them dancing, the pair of them looking so bonnie together, and to whisper away behind their backs, 'There'll be a wedding coming soon – Did you see yon pair, the miller's daughter and the Laird's trumpeter, they were gey bonnie thegither – Aye, a fine pair they would make.'

She hovered on the edge of her sisters' conversation.

'There's David Baillie, do you think he'll ask you for a dance? He's aye looking at you when you're nae watching,' Jane was saying to Bessie.

'I hope so, he's braw.'

'I heard he's winching a lass frae Cardonwell.'

'He's nae!'

'Na, he's nae, but dinna you like him?'

Bessie shifted on her buttocks and gave her older sister a shy grin. 'Aye, I do that, he's braw. Jane, I wish he'd speak wi me.'

'Maybe the drink will gie him some courage the night.' Jane pulled a hip flask from her apron pocket. 'And maybe we aa need a wee bit courage ourselves.' She took a swig herself and passed it to Bessie, who glanced quickly around the room before handing it on to Annie, 'Dinna let father or mother see. Or Will.'

As Annie let the drops of whisky burn their way down her throat, she had a thought that her sisters were maybe not so different from herself, and she asked, 'Do you really like him, Bessie? I think he likes you, you should smile at him when he looks over.'

'It's Jamie Buchan I like,' said Jane, 'he aye maks me laugh when he comes by the mill.'

'He maks everybody laugh,' said Bessie, 'even mother.'

They all three laughed at that, and the flask came round again, and Annie took a deeper pull at it.

'Do you think he'll ask me to dance?' continued Jane.

'Aye,' Annie said, 'you look gey bonnie the night, aa the loons'll be after you.'

It was true, Annie thought her sister looked grand, and Jane gave her one of her infrequent open smiles. Then she asked, 'Do you really like the Laird?' and it made Annie nearly choke on the dram she was swallowing. She had to be patted on the back, and her voice squeaked an answer, 'Na, how could I like him? He's an old man, he's thirty! And he's aa tall and thin and pale, like a plant that hasna ever seen the light.' Her sisters grinned at her description of the Laird.

'Dinna you like him, then? I thought you were meant to marry him. You'd best like him if you're going to be wed.' Bessie, earnest.

'Wed?' Annie gasped with a surprise that quickly faded, as with a jolt of understanding, she saw what her parents' game was these last few months. She must have known it all along somehow, she thought, how could she have missed it? All the hints and nods and the looks that passed between them whenever the Laird was mentioned.

'Och Bessie, she doesna need to like him, she'll have plenty room in the Castle to get awa frae him.'

'You be quiet, Jane, I want an answer frae Agnes.'

'Wed? Na! Na, how could I wed wi him? And what would he want wi me anyway, what am I, a greyhound?' Because the Laird liked only his dogs, she thought, more than anything else, and that made Jane and Bessie laugh, they thought just the same.

'But you'll maybe have to marry him anyway, dinna you think, if father and him are both for it?'

She shook her head, it was not a thing she could even begin to think of, 'Na. Na, I winna. I winna. I'll marry the man I like.'

'Who's that then, Agnes? Who is it you do like?'

She threw her head back to let another gulp of whisky burn its way down to her belly. She had had enough of pretending there was nothing, putting on a face of stone, if all it did was make them think it was the Laird of Fyvie she was after, she had never heard of such a ridiculous thing in all her life. For once she wanted to be like all the other lasses, saying nothing and letting her face tell everything. She wanted to say his name, but she dared not, but she did not do her usual trick of closing her face up. She was enjoying too much her rare inclusion in the conspiracy of sisters. So she bit her lower lip and gave a shake of her head, and though her tone said 'There is someone', her words denied it, 'I didna say I like anyone.'

'Aye you do!'

'Agnes has got a loon!'

'Shush, shush, dinna let anybody hear.'

'Who is it? Who?'

'I didna say I've got a loon. I just said I wanted to marry the man I like.'

'But what man is that, Agnes?'

'I winna say another word on it.' But she left the game open, because she was enjoying it and it was a small release of the pressure that had been building inside her for months.

'Very well, Agnes, if you dinna want to tell, we winna mak you. But I bet he's here, and I bet we can find out.'

The game went on for some time, and as the drink went down, more facts came out, maybe she met someone sometimes when she went to the woods, maybe she didn't, maybe he was in the Laird's service at the Castle, maybe he wasn't, maybe he didn't exist, but now the game was getting dangerous, and she knew that they could do it, pull the whole story out of her bit by bit, until a sober voice inside her said, *Keep safe.* And suddenly, without warning, she ended the game by erecting the barriers behind her eyes, 'There's naebody, you're just being daft, the pair of you.' She turned away, ignoring their hurt and rejected expressions, why should she care, they had done it to her often enough. And although she had tried to keep her tone light, so as not to make enemies of them, she knew that she had failed from the glances they gave to each other, *We're the sisters, she's nae one of us*, and she was alone again, with the pressure building in her chest, and she wished there was someone she could safely tell, when not even her mother or her sisters would understand her. But there was only her, Annie, and Andrew Lammie, and it was Annie who would share her life with Andrew and would give herself to him, every bit of her, whether they wanted Agnes Smith to marry a laird or a gentleman or not.

She turned her attention away from her whispering sisters, and concentrated instead on the crowd surrounding her. She was careful now not to spend too long looking over at Andrew. And every time he looked over to catch her eye, look at me dancing Annie, it's for you really, she looked right through him so that they would not think anything of it. He danced with one of Ironsyde's daughters, and then with another, and then – and here he really wanted her to see – with each of her sisters in turn. She played her own part, swinging around with her arm crooked through the arm of a tenant or a cottar, her hair spinning out behind her in a long copper fan, she had to keep stopping to tie it back, running her fingers across her scalp that was damp but hot as coals from the dancing.

Then at last he came over to her, all proper and pretending to be polite, like the servant he spent his life masquerading as, but underneath it all he was cocky as hell, one side of his mouth curling into half a grin as he finished the question, 'Would you care for a dance wi me, Mistress Agnes?' And she had to say aye, there in front of them all, so she let him lead her by the hand, on this one occasion it was allowed, and they danced. They danced to the tunes of *The Bonnie Brow* and *The Gypsy's Lilt*, and when the Factor struck up another, a reel that went by the name of *I Love My Love in Secret*, they could not help grinning at each other and it did not matter, everyone else was doing the same, stamping and turning and spinning and reeling and letting out great 'heeuchs' as the fiddle sawed away like mad. Then it was over, four dances would be too many, and she headed back to her seat on the kist, but as she squeezed her way between the press of bodies, she felt the light pressure of his hand on her upper back, between the shoulder blades, and he gave a lock of her hair a secret gentle tug and she heard his voice, lowered, for her only, 'I'll wait outside.' Then he pushed past her as if they were strangers and headed for the door. Her seat on the kist was taken anyway and Jane and Bessie were up dancing, so she bumped and jostled her way through the boiling heaving sweating drunken mass of bodies that made the dance, and stepped through the door into the cold biting dark where the night of the New Year waited to be let in.

Her eyes were blind for half a minute or so, and she took a few uncertain steps forward. Away from the light, her eyes started to adjust and she saw him waiting for her, his head and shoulders making a hole amongst the stars on the horizon, and she breathed his name out, she could see it take on the light of the stars as it floated on the night air, 'Andrew'. The shape of his head turned towards the sound and he stepped forward and his arms went around her, 'It's been too long, Annie.'

The music of the fiddle came to them, muffled by the walls, and he danced her around in the dark, reckless. They could hardly keep their feet and they had to stifle their laughter. He had been dramming, too, with the lads from the servants' hall, and she was glad that it made him cheery, not brooding and bitter like her brother Will. Then abruptly the reel came to an end as her back bumped into the wall of an outhouse, and she felt his weight as he leaned against her. They were breathing hard already with the effort of the dance, and hot although the night was cold and the thousands of stars glittered like steel through the naked branches. Her head was spinning with the dance and the malt and Andrew's face laughing down at her, and there was nothing else but the two of them, no father or mother or Laird or tocher, and no Cat Campbell either, only Annie and Andrew and the wheeling stars in the new-born year's sky, and the hunger that had had enough of being not quite satisfied. They had to scramble inside the outhouse to get away from the cold, and they lay down together on a pile of sacks, and then they were quick, and as quiet as they could be, each with one hand over the other's mouth. There was some pain, as she had heard there would be. But she didn't care, she was proud, she had given herself for love alone and nothing else, not land or silver or even the promise of his modest fee for the rest of her life. And she was proud too of the power of her body and what it did to him, she knew then the power of a woman and it was no wonder the Kirk took pains to deny it. Afterwards they cleaned themselves shyly, and then they lay down again and clung together in the dark. But it was too cold to stay there and before long she sat up and began to check over the arrangement of her clothing.

'Dinny forget to tie your hair back. It's come loose.'

He helped her with it, or he pretended to, getting his fingers tangled up in the ribbons and stopping to nuzzle her neck, and when it was almost done he gathered it all together and rolled it up at the nape of her neck, and he said in a low voice, 'You'll have to wear a mutch, now, my Annie,' meaning the cloth cap that married women wore. And she gave a tut and shook her hair free again, and carried on tying it the way she knew he liked, while he slipped his hands around under her arms to cup her breasts and run his fingers over the nipples that stood proud through the cloth. But the world was returning slowly, they felt the bite of frost on ears and noses, and the noises coming through the wall from the byre. As they stood up, their bodies were reluctant to be separated, and she wanted to lie down with him again right there among the sacks and the straw, and she could tell he felt the same by his pressure against her. But there was no time, some other pair might come in as they had, or her sisters might notice that both of them were missing, and come to their own conclusions.

He said, 'You'd better go in first, Annie,' and she slipped her hand down before she answered, 'Aye, you canna go in like that, can you?'

He gave a wee groan and pulled away, his breath short, 'God, that's no fair,' and as they giggled she felt again that pride in her body's power. She went to leave him, but he drew her back by the hand, and all he was in the dark was a warm hand holding hers and a dark shadow and a voice, suddenly serious.

'You'll marry me, Annie.' Not a question.

'Aye. I will.'

'Tocher or no?'

'Aye. Tocher or no.'

She squeezed his hand, and then she stepped away from him.

As she headed back to the byre alone, she could hear that the fiddle had stopped its frenzy and was playing a sweet slow air that came drifting through the door as it opened and closed. It pulled at your heart so that you wanted it never to stop but to go on for ever, like youth and love and springtime. And then it was over.

XXI

She followed close behind a group of three of the other Fyvie folk, hoping that they would make her entrance less obvious. As the door swung open there was a blast of music and warmth, and the light from the candles and the cruisies dazzled her for a moment, while the odour of the gathered bodies filled her nostrils. She went over to take a seat on the kist near her sisters. Jane was sitting this one out, but she was rosy pink up to her yellow hair and there were beads of sweat on her forehead, she must have been dancing like a mad thing, good, she would not have noticed. Bessie came and sat down beside them when she had finished her dance.

Bessie asked, 'Where have you been, Agnes? You've missed the last umpteen dances.'

And Jane joined in, 'You look cold. Have you been outside?'

They were not questions. They were challenges.

'I went out to tak a look at the stars.' Guarded.

'Nae alone. You werenae alone.'

Annie's head jerked up, 'What maks you think yon way?'

'Och naethin, just a guess,' but the set of Jane's mouth said otherwise.

'I just went out for a wee bit air. It's too hot in here.'

And the rest of the night, she danced with Andrew, or Ironsyde, or Peter, or any man that asked, until there wasn't a man left on his feet, and they groaned with fatigue when she pulled them up for another whirl.

At last the Factor put away his fiddle, and the few who were left bid each other a Good New Year, and weaved away to their homes, just as the first light touched the eastern sky.

In their bedroom at Tifty, the three sisters crawled under the covers without bothering to undress. On the edge of sleep, it seemed to Annie that Andrew pressed his lips to hers, and his name slipped out between her lips, very quietly, 'Andrew'. Jane, lying next to her, rolled towards her and mumbled 'What's that?' but Annie was already asleep and gave no answer.

On the first morning of the New Year, no one stirred at Tifty until almost midday. Annie woke to the sound of voices coming from the kitchen. The bed was empty: Jane and Bessie had risen already, without waking her. She went down to take her sowans with the rest of the household, with the sleep still scratching at her eyelids. Already, she was making plans, thinking on the road to Edinburgh. The roads would be bad for months yet, and sleet and wind and hail were cruel companions for travellers, so it would only be in the spring that they could go. There would be no asking her father. With his mind set on the Laird, what point would there be in that? Only to anger him. She could well imagine what he would say, she could almost hear him now, 'I'll no gie the hand of a granddaughter of Inveramsay to some landless servant boy frae Edinburgh.' So there would be no asking, and no tocher, but there was no other future she would take now. The future she would share with Andrew, where they loved each other and cared for each other, was clear and firm in her mind. When she tried to imagine any other thing for herself she rejected it, the vision of herself sitting an old lonely lady in that grand old castle, greyed and dulled and tired by all the laughterless years with a man she could never love. She would not accept that, she would throw it back in the face of anyone who offered it to her.

So they would wait, and in the spring they would go to Mr Jaffray, just the two of them, and persuade him that they should be wed. There would be no staying in her father's house after that, and so Edinburgh it would have to be however things fell out. But for now she would meet with Andrew as she always had, secretly. And then she wondered if she was blushing, as she lingered over the memory of their secret touching in the outhouse only hours ago, and thought, *Will it happen again, next time we meet? And how can it not?*

While the other members of the household rose one by one from the table and began the tasks of the day, she scraped up the last spoonfuls of her breakfast, gazing unfocused out the window and humming the tune of a reel. Soon only she and Will were left at the table, and after a while she became aware that her brother was watching her intently. Feeling his unspoken challenge, she returned his gaze uncomfortably, until with disbelief she saw him push his tongue out between his teeth, and run its upturned tip against the inside of his upper lip. Disgust prickled her skin and she could feel the blood rushing into her face. She averted her gaze, but still out of the corner of her eye she saw Will's half-snort, and the way he looked deliberately away as if he had seen a repulsive thing. And she remembered how, after she had come in from the outhouse, she had seen Andrew coming in a few minutes after, and Will following. Her brother's eyes had slid slowly over to the back of Andrew's head, and slowly back again to hold her gaze, and his nostrils and upper lip had been raised, just slightly, as if there was a smell of sick or shit. A knot of fear clenched in her stomach. He must have been outside, taking a piss maybe against the wall of the byre, while they had been together in the shed. Maybe they had not been quiet enough. Or maybe worse, maybe he had waited and watched as they came out in turn. She felt as if he could see right through her clothes to her skin, and it was the skin of a dirty hoor, and there was a sick quaking in her belly, what if he told their father? Or what if there was a bairn?

In the following days, Annie steered clear of her brother, and her tongue lay quiet in her head, blocking the way to her sisters, stopping them from reaching towards her again and feeling about blindly for her secret. In the house, the air was stifling. In the evenings, Jane and Bessie's whispered conversations had always been a common thing, but since the night she had lain in the outhouse with Andrew, it seemed to Annie that they looked over at her as they spoke, watching her with quick sideways glances, while they sat and spun their linen and their plans. She knew from the way they carried themselves, united, cutting her with their eyes, the way they turned inwards, towards each other, that they were punishing her for her failure to let them into her confidence. Punishing her, and warning her too, and she hated it, hated them, the way they were two and she was one, alone. She had never known why, how it had started or how to stop it. But she knew that they wanted her to give them entry to the secret spaces inside her, and that if she did that, they would wound her, so she kept quiet, and kept them out. But that night of Hogmanay she had nearly give them what they wanted, and now she could feel their resentment, their hostility, and their will to punish her. She tried to ignore it, nodding absently as she let her mother take the reins of a conversation, but by the third day her skin prickled in anticipation all day and when she came to sit down with them in the evening she was stiff, awkward, and the skin of her face was tight. She knew that they would bring it to an end some way or another. It would be Jane who did it, she was sure of it, but not how or when, or exactly what she would say.

But it was Bessie who delivered the first wound, with a knife so sharp that she did not feel it. It was the fourth of January, and the air had crackled throughout the day. Aware of their attention on her, Annie tossed her head to show she didn't care as she left the room to go and feed the chickens before it got dark. As she crossed the floor, she heard her sister's voice, raised pointedly so that the question she seemed to direct to Jane rang clearly in their mother's ears, *Where's Agnes awa to?* Her mother looked up at Bessie in surprise at the question that they all knew the answer to, the question that did not need to be asked because the answer was the same as it had been every morning and evening for the last fourteen years. The door closed behind Annie, so that she did not witness how quickly her mother got out of her two other daughters the things they appeared so reluctant to divulge, 'Och I dinna think she would want us to say it, mother, but...' Annie did not see how Helen's face changed as everything she had guessed at and hoped for over the last year was turned on its head. Nor was she there when her father came in through the door and the three women turned to him. But when she came back in from feeding the chooks she felt the weight of the silence filling the room, and the latch dropping, *snick*, into its place was loud, intrusive. Her mother and sisters had been sent up the stairs. Only her father waited for her. With her back to the door, she looked across the room at her father's face and thought, instantly, *He kens*. Time slowed, slowed and stopped as they faced each other, and in the space between heartbeats, before her father spoke, she felt a strange calm. Her shoulders dropped, imperceptibly, and her throat softened. It was a kind of relief. She did not need to hold the secret to herself any more.

'What's this about you and some servant from Fyvie Castle?'

The way he said it, *sair*-vant, the emphasis on the first syllable, as if it were two separate words, filthy ones. She could not answer. She had nothing to do with a sair-vant, she had to do with a fine man, Andrew.

'Answer me, Agnes. Who is it?'

Afterwards, she went over the whole thing many times, constructing different answers, 'I dinna tak your meaning, father' or 'Who is what?' or 'It's the Laird of Fyvie himself.' She wondered what he would have answered to *that*. But right then, when she was standing before him, only the truth was possible. Not solely because he demanded it, and not because of the fifth commandment – it was too late for that – but because she had made her choice already, three nights ago and eight months ago and all the days in between, and she had had enough of evasions and deceptions and sneaking about, and it was simply the time.

She told him the name.

He grasped her by the arm, and shoved her against the dresser. Her tail-bone bumped painfully against the hard edge of the dresser's top board, forcing an involuntary cry from her, and there was pain in her upper arm where he gripped it, it would bruise later. He was taller than her, broad and deep, for a moment her face was pressed against his chest and she could smell him, the old male sweat and oatmeal dust clinging to his shirt and jacket, and she felt his rib cage heaving against her with rage. Suddenly he released his grip on her arm and threw himself away from her. He crossed the room in three paces, his shoulder brushing a cruisie lamp and rattling it in its bracket on the wall, and stood with his back to her, pummelling his temples with the heels of his hands. Then he whirled on one heel and brought his fists crashing down onto the dining table, and it seemed to her that he filled the room. A purple vein throbbed in each temple. There was a yellow rheum in the corners of the bloodshot eyes that bored into her face. He leaned heavily on the table, his scarlet face contorted, and drops of spittle discoloured the wood as he spat out the words.

'The whole of Fyvie must know. Laughing at me. Bitch. Aa this time I'm planning a good match for you, and you, you – awa in the woods – with a *sair*-vant. A penniless loon. You could have the Laird himself and you choose that – that –. Nae even one of our own folk. The shame of it. Bitch. By God, he'll be keeping his hands off you frae now on.'

It went on and on, there was no stopping it, and there was nothing in the world except her father's brutal words hammering at her, and the roar of blood in her ears. Hot tears and anger were burning her cheeks, a tight band around her chest hindered her breathing, and words were spilling out of her mouth, 'Dinna talk of him yon way, he's nae a sair-vant, he's mine, I want him, I dinna want the Laird, or money.' But her father carried on, as if he could not see her, only her shame, and as if he could hear nothing but the taunts of his neighbours.

She did not know how long it went on for, but suddenly it stopped. She leaned against the dresser, exhausted. Her voice was ragged with pain, and her body was shaking. Then suddenly a cool detachment came over her, as she realised she truly did not care what her father thought of her Andrew, or what he thought of her, or whether she had her share of his wealth or not. She felt a strange kind of pity for the old man who stood before her, staring at his hands, which were still clenched on the table between them.

'I'll wed wi him, father, whether you gie us your blessing or no.'

'By God, you'll never have him.'

'I will, father, you canna stop us. You canna stop a marriage if the Session approves it. We'll go and tell them, and they'll read the banns, and you winna have any way to stop us.'

He looked up to meet her eyes. His Adam's apple moved up and down as he swallowed, twice, three times, and his eyes drilled at her face.

'You wouldna. You wouldna do that.'

'Aye, father, I would. As long as we're both willing we can be married in the Kirk, and there's naethin you or mother can do about it.'

She had won. She had won, she had nothing to be afraid of, why had she been feart? As her words came to an end, she jerked her head up, defiant, thinking *You canna touch me now, you're beaten.*

She could hear her father's breathing, irregular short breaths that went in with a jerk of jaw and chest, and whistled out through clenched teeth. It occurred to her that he might drop dead with the anger of it, and to her disgust that thought made her want to laugh. She imagined the thud he would make as he hit the floor, lifeless, the screams of her mother and sisters as they ran down the stair to help him. She tried to appear unconcerned, *That's it settled, there's nae need to bother yourself about it*, and looked away, but her heart was beating and her hands were cold and shook as she turned and opened the door of the press to take up the dishes for the table.

Then William Smith moved his bulk around the table to stand close behind her, with his face lowered to speak straight to her ear, and his voice was hard-edged, and controlled.

'Woman. You have the sin of rebellion in you. The witch's sin.'

She froze. His hand – a hand that hefted sacks of meal each day and lifted the millstone for dressing – gripped her upper arm, biting into the flesh.

'Who has bewitched you, eh?'

She swallowed. 'Naebody, father.'

'Na. It canna be by your own will. Na. It canna be. You only do this by the will of another. Who has gien you the spirit of rebellion?'

'Na, father. I'll go to the minister wi him freely. It's by my own will that I'll marry him.'

She heard his intake of breath as the grip on her upper arm tightened.

'You can only go to the minister if you can leave this house. You stay at home frae now on. You dinna go out. It winna be for long. You winna have to worry about your wee sair-vant lad for long. Now get out of my sight.'

She turned on her heel and walked across the kitchen and up the stairs, trying to make it look as if she had been planning to do that all along, and hoping that he did not notice her trembling hands.

In the yellow light of the rush lamp, the miller of Tifty leaned in to the table. Slow now, the nib of the pen dipped into the ink well, and was set at an angle to the page. Slow the black words crawled on to the paper. From time to time the miller paused, laid the pen down, and stabbed the stub of his index finger into the side of his jaw, working the chin from side to side. Then he would pick up the pen once more, balance it carefully against the stub, and lift it to the well to gather the next load of ink that his will would shape to its purpose.

The flame guttered as the dogfish oil ran low in the lamp, but still the words crept onto the page, slithering their coils around one name, and an accusation. Finished. Blot. Fold. Drip of wax. Roll the seal. The seal of a lesser son of Inveramsay. Call Grizel? No, Gibb. Voice loud, harsh, 'Tak this to the Laird of Fyvie right awa.' Loosen jaw. Hand it over.

Not the letter he had been intending to write, the one he had been planning these last months. Still, enough for the present time, to clear the way. Not a name, either, that he had expected to write. But a name he would not be hearing for long.

Lammie. Andrew Lammie, the servant.

True? True enough, for him, for his purpose. Enough to do the job.

Andrew Lammie.

Tempter.

Witch.

Later, through the door of her room, Annie heard his voice, 'Dinna worry, Agnes, I've sent a letter to the Laird. He kens how to deal with aa this kind of business. It's terrible things that some folk are saying. It would chill your blood if you heard it. Nae that I like to believe it myself, but you never can tell wi these foreign folk. And it's my duty to tell the Laird straight, gie him a fair chance to deal wi the laddie before they start saying he's part of the business himself. You'll be safe too, frae his black art charms. Andrew Lammie? We winna be hearing that name around here again. What do you think, Agnes? Is it a good plan? Eh?'

She heard his tight laughter coming muffled through the door, but she made no answer.

XXII

'His Lordship wants you, Lammie, in the Charter Room.'

Andrew Lammie lifted his head in surprise and looked down the servants' hall to where the messenger-boy stood in the doorway.

'What for? Do you ken?'

The boy shrugged. 'Na. He just said to go up right awa.'

Andrew laid down the rag that he had been using to polish his trumpet and pushed himself up from where he sat on the edge of his straw pallet. Hastily, he adjusted his jerkin and walked the length of the hall, returning the quizzical stares of the other off-duty men with a shrug and a wryly raised eyebrow. He went out into the courtyard, and turning left he broke into a head-down, shoulders-lifted trot to protect himself against the freezing rain. Quickly, he passed along the wall of the Castle and in through another door in the corner of the courtyard. He shook his head dry, and as the raindrops soaked into his jacket, he juked into the larder to beg a handful of raisins from the larder man, who dropped a smattering of the dry black pellets into his palm.

'I've to go up the stair for a word wi his Lordship.'

'That's good news, then.'

'Do you think?'

'Aye. Either that, or it's bad news.'

'That's what I thought.'

'Good luck.'

He finished the raisins as he made his way up the narrow spiral staircase to the first floor, where the Laird had his apartments. *Tung tung tung* his boots sounded loud on the stone, and echoed back from the walls. There was a small landing on the first floor, and he paused there outside the door of the Charter Room. As he used a fingernail to pick out the sticky remains of the raisins from between his teeth, he contemplated the ornate figures carved into the almost-black wood of the door. From amongst the bunches of grapes, pomegranates and the like, one of the fair folk grinned at him slyly. He wondered if it knew why he was here, standing before the Laird's private quarters, for the first time. He surely didn't know himself. As far as he was aware, Seton had no complaints about his service, although once or twice he had nearly been late to blow the fanfare for dinner, and had arrived in the Great Hall still fastening his jacket. Maybe that was it. The old laird might have let him go for such an offence, but the son had softer hands, or so he had come to think. Still, he had no option but to go through to whatever waited for him on the other side, and to put on a good face for whichever Laird it was that Alexander Seton had decided to be today. He winked back at the fairy face, and for good measure, imagined the contorted features of Alexander Seton squatting on the privy. Then he took two steady, deliberate breaths, as he did to focus himself before playing the trumpet, lifted his curled hand, deliberately relaxed the fingers, and knocked.

The Laird's voice answered his knock immediately.

'Enter!'

He pushed the door open, entered smartly, and closed it behind him. He was in a small, square, wood-panelled room with an arching ceiling of white plaster. In the same wall as the door, a small but hot fire crackled at the heart of a broad fireplace. A pair of dozing greyhounds basked in the fire's warmth, and Andrew himself was glad of the heat after the chill of the courtyard and the lower floor. Windows looked out to the west and the south. Alexander Seton was seated at a desk with his back to Andrew, looking out of the window that gave onto the south. The downpour obscured the view beyond the castle gardens, but on a fine day you would be able to see down into the notch of the glen where the

Ythan ran, and the Highland hills in the distance. Seton continued to stare out the window as Andrew waited.

'Who is it?'

He cleared his throat. 'It's Andrew Lamb, my Lord. You sent for me.'

'Ah, Lamb, good, good.'

Still Seton contemplated the dark banners of clouds as they hurried themselves across the sky. Andrew stood in his place, with his eyes fixed on the Laird's back, waiting. The desk the Laird sat at was covered with a mass of papers, rolls of parchment, pens, an inkstand. The Laird himself was wearing a voluminous silken dressing gown of pale lilac and a nightcap, also of silk, that had slipped to one side a little and exposed the pale, grey, shaven skin of the scalp. The Laird seldom wore a wig around his house unless he had guests. There was a dark line of hairs on his neck that started abruptly where the barber had stopped his shaving, and led down below the collar of the dressing gown.

Finally, when Andrew felt that every single hair on the Laird's neck had become a personal friend, the Laird spoke again.

'I'm minded to send you to Edinburgh right awa, Lamb.'

'How long will I be awa, my Lord?'

'How long? I canna say. I'm giving you on loan to the Earl of Balcarres. He has need of a trumpeter in his household there.'

'Balcarres, my Lord?'

'You remember him, surely? A handsome young lord. He visited me in the harvest time. You sang Otterburn for him. He was right taken wi you.'

'Very well, my Lord. But I'll return to Fyvie soon enough?'

The Laird coughed into his hand, and carried on staring out the window.

'I think it likely he'll want to keep you in his service for good.'

Andrew had to bite his lips together as he took this news in.

'But, my Lord, do you never mean for me to come back?' His voice was louder and more indignant than he had intended, and it made the Laird swivel around in his chair to face him at last. As the Laird turned towards him, Andrew noticed the lines of tension around his mouth and the depth of the lines across his brow, and the thought came to him that he must have had a bad night.

'Na, Lamb, na. But you like Edinburgh well enough?'

'Edinburgh I like fine, my Lord. But Fyvie I like more. Are there no trumpeters in Edinburgh better suited to it?'

The Laird's voice was sharp in reply. 'It's nae right for a servant to question his master's orders, Lamb. My father wouldna have stood for it. You're lucky your fee depends on a mair patient man.'

Their eyes locked together for the briefest of moments. Then Andrew dropped his eyes to the floor in a pretence of humility and examined the weave of the rug.

'I'm sorry, my Lord. I shouldny have spoken.' So today it was the Commanding Laird. The Masterful Laird. This Laird of Fyvie he had not met with before.

Andrew continued to glare interminably at the floor. At the edge of his field of vision, he was aware of the Laird's hand tightly gripped on the arm of the chair as he sat stiffly upright. A peat settled in the fire and a spark landed on the rug where it burnt itself out with a hiss. One of the greyhounds whimpered in its dreaming, and its paws twitched as if it was following a hare over the rigs. Seton leaned back with a sigh and a weak smile.

'Aye, very well, Lamb, I'll leave it. And you're lucky I have a good idea how it is you want to bide. She's a fine lass, after aa. But I'm afraid her father winna have it.'

Andrew's head jerked up to look at the Laird in shock. The world inside his head spun silently apart. He could feel the colour rising in his cheeks and he had to snap his mouth shut when he realised it was hanging open. The Laird seemed to be struggling to repress a smile, and he continued to speak as Andrew pulled his scattered thoughts back together.

'So it's true then, Lamb? You've been winching Agnes Smith? '

Seton turned to the table to pick up a piece of paper, giving Andrew time to take his two breaths, slow and deep, to settle back into the centre of himself, and to still the whirl in his mind, before the Laird faced him again.

He hesitated. Where were the words to hold it? Winching? That was a poor word for the thing there was between them. He searched around for some words that were big enough to do it justice. But there were few words that he knew that would suit it, and so he used a common enough expression to give his answer.

'Aye, my Lord, I've been courting Agnes Smith since the spring. She's gien me her word and we're to wed.' As if it was a plain, ordinary, workaday thing, but nevertheless as he said it, he felt as if he was breathing for the first time in months, and the words lifted his chest and made him stand taller. For the first time he had dared to say aloud that he had courted and won his Annie, and that she was proud and glad to have him. The Laird watched him intently.

'So it's nae true, then, that you used the black arts to bewitch her? Be careful in your answer.'

Again, the world in Andrew's head began to spin, and his mind lurched sickeningly.

'The black arts, my Lord?' There was a tremor in his voice, and he paused to control it before going on more calmly. 'I ken naethin of them, my Lord. A man can win a lass fair and square if he puts his mind to it, and if he's kind.' He hesitated, and then carried on, 'My Lord, it's an evil thing I'm accused of. Do I no have a right to ken who has said sic a thing?'

'It's in her father's letter here.' The Laird turned to pick up a closely-written piece of paper from the desk, and held it out. 'Here, read it yourself.'

Andrew took the page, and read the few words that condemned him. His hands shook as he handed the letter back, and he had to resist the impulse to spit in disgust before he spoke.

'These are nothin' but lies, my Lord. He wilny let her have me. A trumpeter's no good to him. I've no land. Nothin' but my fee. She's told me as much herself. But I'm no a witch for aa that.'

'I didna think so,' said the Laird, in a gentler tone, 'but the Kirk Session may tak a different view.'

'I'm no afraid, my Lord, I'll go before them and persuade them like I've persuaded you.'

The Laird watched him for a short while, considering.

'Na, Lamb.' He sighed his breath out, and sank a little as he did so. 'This is worse than I thought. Plenty other men your age would be happy to lie a lass down in Fyvie and go off to the brothels of Edinburgh without a backward glance. But still, you'll be better off in Edinburgh until the father cools down. If you're awa frae here, I dinna think he'll care to tak it further. But if you stay, I can see him taking it before the Session, and they winna let it lie. You ken that well enough. So it's off to Edinburgh wi you.'

Andrew sagged, defeated. 'When, my Lord?'

'The morn's morn, Lamb, that's best, do you nae think?'

He nodded, wordlessly, and extended his arm to hand the letter back. The Laird reached out to take it and then seemed to be struck by a thought.

'Read the postscript again, Lamb, will you? Does it mak any kind of sense to you at aa?'

Andrew read the postscript. The handwriting was in a worse scrawl than the body of the letter, as if it had been added quickly, as an afterthought. *My Lord, for some time I have wished to speak wi you on a matter of importance to both our families. Pray gie me the honour of coming by Tifty when this ill matter is well behind us.*

'No, my Lord, I canny guess the meaning of it.'

'Well then. You'll be on your way.'

Andrew clicked his heels together, left the room and ran down the spiral staircase with the boom of the closing door still echoing behind him.

In the servants' hall, he pulled out the small store of paper and ink that he used to write to his parents in Edinburgh, and quickly scribbled a short note:

Dearest Annie,

I've to go to Edinburgh the morn. For good. Meet me now at the Brig of Skeugh.

He began to sign it Andrew Lamb, the big L of his surname curling up gracefully and finishing with a flamboyant flourish – and ruefully he thought of the Miller of Tifty's clumsy script – and then he wrote not Lamb but Lammie instead, she would like that, and then cursed himself and his stupidity because it did not matter whether he signed Lamb or Lammie or the Laird of Fyvie or any other name, she could never read. And so he dashed out into the courtyard and found the boy who had brought the Laird's message to him and gave him the letter anyway and begged him to go up to Tifty and find Mistress Agnes – he would know her easily enough, she would be the bonnie one – and tell her to come to the Brig of Skeugh right away, he was leaving and had to see her.

Then he threw his few things into a box, ran over to the stable to give instructions for his horse to be got ready, and paced the servants' hall until the boy would have had time to go up to Tifty and come back.

XXIII

Grizel went to answer a quiet knock at the door, and Annie in the kitchen heard a young lad's 'Peace be here' and then him asking for her by name. She and Grizel were the only ones in the house, the other women being busy at work in the brewhouse, and the menfolk still down at the mill.

The boy came shyly a few steps into the kitchen and gave her his message, and she turned to Grizel, 'I'll have to go. Dinna say a word to them about it.'

'You'll be sorry.'

'It canna be helped.'

She went to the door. Looking out, she saw that no one was in the yard, and she and the boy went quickly past the kailyard and steeply down through the orchard. When they got to the main path, she told him to go ahead to the Castle quickly and tell Andrew she was coming, and the boy held out the letter to her, saying. 'I near forgot.'

She took it from him and ran her finger over the marks that Andrew had made with his pen, and then folded it up and held it tightly in her hand as she picked her way between the puddles on the way to the Brig of Skeugh, in the dimness of an overcast January afternoon.

The bridge was deserted when Annie reached it, and she stood looking over the rail remembering the dappled light in the spring, and how together they had watched the young salmon holding their places in the stream, facing intently into the current on the lookout for a meal. Now the waters churned brown with silt and the cobbles grated like millstones as they turned unseen in the streambed. In the strange after-rain calm of the late afternoon, Annie watched the waters as they twisted below her, here and gone, off and away like her time with Andrew.

In the distance, she heard a horse's hooves and thought with alarm, *Is it him, or a kelpie?* She stared rigidly along the dim path that led beneath the trees, getting ready to run, if she had to, and only breathed easy when she saw that the horse had a rider, and the bridge vibrated underfoot to the rhythm of the chestnut mare's step. Andrew leapt from the saddle and they embraced silently, not knowing how to say the words that would be the only link across the distance that was to come between them.

At last she said, 'How is it you've to go?'

He told her, and she told him her side of the story.

'I thought I would go wi you, next time you went to Edinburgh.'

'You could come wi me.'

'How can I? I'd be a hoor.'

She pressed her face against his chest, shaking her head.

'God, Annie, I canny believe a man could care so little about his own flesh.'

'He thinks that's aa I am, his and naebody else's. Nae mine and for sure nae yours.'

'He's wrong, Annie. I'll mak you mine, I will. I'll come back frae Edinburgh. And I'll bring you your bridal gown and we'll be wed in the Kirk, you'll see.'

'But when can that be, Andrew? When will you be back at aa?'

'I dinny ken, Annie, maybe Balcarres will visit come the spring, or the summer... but I'll tell you this, I'll come back for you some way, if you promise you'll wait for me, I'll find a way, whether it's this year, or next year, or –'

He stopped as she pulled herself violently away from him. Her voice strained, 'Andrew. What if there's a bairn?' She gazed at him hopelessly, waiting for an answer that she knew he did not have.

'Then... then...' He pressed his palms against his eye sockets, and stood stiff, immobile, while she waited for him to breathe. Then with a great sigh he let his arms fall by his sides, helpless, pleading with her, 'Ach, there canny be a bairn, Annie, it was just the once.'

Then she felt her face, that had been held in a stiff mask, crumple in on itself, and sobs started to shake her, because he believed what he said and he did not understand, no man could understand, and she was alone now entirely, even as he took her face in his hands and tipped it up to kiss away with gentle lips the tears that would not stop wetting her cheeks and her lips and her chin.

'Och, Annie, Annie, I canny thole it when you cry like this.' She looked up then, because of the catch in his voice, and saw the tears that he would not let flow from his own sad eyes. He bent to kiss her cheek again, and then he said, 'You'll have to stop crying, my Annie, I canny drink any mair of this salt water.'

That made her laugh, although the laughter was much the same as the sobs, but less desperate.

'That's better,' he said, and gave her upper arms a squeeze. The pain where her father had gripped her made her wince, and he frowned and looked intently at her.

'What is it? Dinna tell me he's hurt you.'

She turned her face away, neither denying nor confirming. His eyes widened in disbelief and anger, before he turned his back to her and stood rocking from toe to heel as he gripped the rail of the bridge and made his plans.

'No. Oh God. No, he canny do that. I wilny let him. He hasny the right. You'll have to come awa wi me. We can get on that horse right now if you want, and we'll ride aa night, we'll ride as far as we can get, and we'll get married before they catch us, and then there's nothin' they can do, we'll belong to each other and we can come back and be thegither, man and wife.'

She wanted to do it, to leap up behind him and ride and ride south and away from Fyvie. But what good was there in it, when the Kirk would be waiting for them wherever they went?

She shook her head from side to side as she answered him. 'We canna, Andrew. We canna. He's only told the Laird now. But if we go, hc'll tell the Kirk, and Mr Jaffray will send word to every parish in Scotland, and they'll be looking for two witches frae Fyvie wherever we go. And we canna settle *anywhere* without a letter frae the minister.'

'Then we wilny settle, we'll ride to the coast the night and we'll get in any boat that will tak us, and you'll see the sea like you wanted. How would that be, my Annie?' He was gripping her shoulders with both hands, almost shaking her in his excitement. Still she shook her head.

'Na, think. It would be proof of your witchcraft. Do you nae see? My father would tell the Kirk you'd bewitched me, stolen me. Whether we were married or no. And when they found us, they would tak you. And you ken what the witch-pricker would do to you. And the courts.'

'Do you mean I have to just go? Just leave you here? I canny leave you here. No like this. No alone, wi *him*.'

'Aye you can. You must. The Laird's sending you to Edinburgh, and my father winna touch you there, as lang as I'm nae wi you. You'll be safe.'

'Aye, maybe I will – but how about you?'

'It's you that has to worry. Go, and be safe, and wed wi me when you come back.' She made herself believe it, so that he would believe it too. Gradually some of the tension left his body, and they held onto each other, pressing themselves together tightly to exclude the world. As they stood together on the bridge, the sun slipped out from a blanket of cloud. Its last rays dazzled them for a moment, before it fell away to the other side of the world.

'It's time, Andrew.'

'Aye. Well, if you wilny let me tak you to Edinburgh, or awa to sea, at least let me tak you up the road to Tifty. There's no folk about in this weather. And anyway, nobody will see us in the dark.'

He mounted, and pulled her up behind him, and she snuggled her arms under his around his chest, and pulled herself in to his back, resting her cheek in the space between his shoulder blades. They moved together with the slow swaying rhythm of the mare's walking. The warmth and the smell of him came through his clothing to comfort her, but, even so, his jacket was wet with her tears before they got to Tifty.

He reined in the mare at the place where the willows grew. The horse and its riders stood motionless in the dark. Annie, still holding tightly on to Andrew, felt him leaning back against her. Then he made a move as if to dismount, but she stopped him, pulling gently on one of his curls with one hand, and leaning forward to caress his cheek with the other.

'Na, Andrew, just let me go now. Or I'll never be able to say goodbye to you.'

She kissed the back of his neck, drinking in the smell and the taste of him, the touch of his skin on her lips, so that she would remember. Then the mare stamped her foot, and Annie slipped to the ground. She looked up to see his face a last time, but he was only a dark shape against the sky above her, and already his voice sounded distant, 'I'll come back for you, my Annie, I swear it.' He straightened up in the saddle, dug his heels into the mare's sides and whirled about and away. The sound of the horse's hooves faded rapidly into the night.

XXIV

Annie stood in the dark long after the sound of the mare's hoofbeats had faded from hearing. As the minutes passed, she felt diminished, as if a piece of herself had been snagged on the mare's saddle, and she was being spun out, slowly, slowly, until there was nothing left inside. Heavy spatters of rain whipped her face and quickly soaked through her plaid. The night cold gathered around her and sucked the heat from her body, and spread through her fingers and hands, and the numbness inside her spread outwards to meet it, until there was no warmth anywhere in her.

At last she turned, heavily, and took slow, wandering steps up the path to the mill house. She paused before the door. At the thought of opening it, nausea swept through her, and she closed her eyes, leaning a hand on the cracked millstone to support herself. Beneath her fingers the stone was cold and slippery with wet, and its edge dug into her palm. Heavy footsteps sounded on the other side of the door, and it was flung open. Her father was a dark shape silhouetted by the firelight. His fingers dug into her shoulder as he pulled her roughly inside and slammed the door behind her. A sharp jab of his fingers to her breast bone pushed her against the door.

'Where have you been, you?'

'Out.'

'I ken that well enough, woman. I ask again. Where?'

He was standing very close. She could hear his breath going in and out through his nostrils. A chicken shifted in the inglenook, the ruffling of its feathers loud in the waiting silence.

Her brother's sly voice sounded from a corner of the room, 'Tell father, Nan. Do what he says.'

Her father nodded in approval. 'Aye, Will, that's right. Now tell me. *Where*.'

'The Brig.'

'Wi him?'

'Aye.'

He gave a quick intake of breath and his hand flew towards her face and took hold of her lower jaw, squeezing the soft flesh of her cheeks against her teeth. A grunt of pain escaped her lips, and she heard her mother's voice, raised in protest, 'William!'

He barked over his shoulder, 'I will have order in this house, Helen. I will have order in this house if I have to thrash the lot of you, and get Will there to help me. Do you understand?'

Her mother muttered, 'Aye, William.'

'Good. Now.'

He turned his attention back to Annie, punctuating his speech with staccato shakes of his hand that rattled the back of her head against the door.

'You – *dinna* – leave – the yard. Understand?'

She stared up at him, and nodded, dumb. He nodded back, slow, thoughtful.

'Aye. You dinna leave. Nae until you repent. And the witchcraft leaves you. And you beg to be forgiven.'

The thin line of his mouth tightened, then relaxed just a little as he loosened his grip on her jaw. Her heels dropped back to the ground as he released her.

'Now get out of my sight.'

He turned his back on her, and went to take his seat by the fire.

She went straight up the stair without a word, shaking from nerves and shivering with cold, and the stares of her family chilled her further as they watched her go. In the bedroom, she peeled the sodden clothing from her goose-pimpled skin, and dried herself as best she could. She crept in under the blanket, and hugged herself and the memory of Andrew's back, but the cold lingered, and sleep would not come.

As she lay in the chill of her loss, the fitful wind brought the sound of Andrew's trumpet in short bursts, distorted by the distance. It carried on a long time, because high in the castle's turrets, Andrew Lammie was playing every tune that he knew, facing into the northeast and sending the notes to her through the wind and rain.

Her father, too, wished to make himself heard. From the kitchen, where the fire crackled, he raised his voice for her ears. 'You hear that, Agnes? That's your cow lowing for you!'

Under her breath, she gave him her answer. 'Aye, but I'd rather hear that one cow than aa the kye in Fyvie.' But he did not hear.

The next day, no morning trumpet sounded from the castle, and she knew that Andrew was gone, and that she was alone. She kept to the house – there was no reason to do otherwise – and spoke to no one, doing her tasks wordlessly. Only Grizel would meet her eye. Purple bruises blossomed on her jaw line, and faded to black and yellow, and she stayed home from Kirk on the Sabbath. Anyone who asked after her heard that she was poorly and had to rest.

At mealtimes and in the evenings, there was the weight of silence, and she could feel her father's will pressing upon her as he waited for her to show some sign of repentance, to admit her guilt. When she could not stand it any longer, she would retire to bed early, and lie listening to the sounds of the house, still aware of his will directed towards her.

She wished for some change to break the mood of anger that hung over the house. It seemed she was not the only one, because after a week or so, Gibb begged a few days off, saying he had urgently to visit his only kin, an elderly cousin in Inveramsay, who was ailing. Her father let him go, because the miln was needing repair and there was no great hurry to fix it. Then the Miller was about the house all day, and she invented tasks to do on the upper floor, but still she had to join the rest of the household for supper.

At the table she felt his eyes boring into her as he ate slowly, only looking away to scoop up his next spoonful. No one spoke a word, as if Gibb had been the heart and soul of the household, until at last Helen broke the silence, her voice shrill and brittle with false cheer, 'I didna ken Gibb had a cousin, did you, William?'

He shook his head minutely.

'Na,' Helen continued, 'I thought he'd nae family left at aa.'

'He doesnae.' Annie broke in, and every eye turned to her, she had barely spoken in a week. Will, seated next to her, shook his head, a warning, but one loaded with sly delight.

'Aye, he does, Agnes, did you nae hear him?' Helen's voice was shriller still.

'Well, it's the first I heard of any cousin, that's aa. More like he just wanted to get awa frae this house.'

She heard her father swallowing a mouthful before he spoke. 'And why do you think that would be?'

For the first time, she met his eye, but though she could not hold it, and looked instead at the butter dish, her voice was sullen, 'I dinna ken, father, maybe you can tell us.'

Out of the corner of her eye, she saw his pointing finger, raised in admonition.

'The sin of rebellion is in you still, woman. I see it in you.'

In the past days, she had clamped her jaws tight and refused to answer when he had started on at her. But she had had enough of holding her tongue.

'Have I done wrong?'

'You ken you have.'

'What evil is it I've done, father?'

'You ken what it is!' His fist banging down on the table made the cups and bowls rattle. Then he reined himself and his voice was calmer in the asking: 'The only thing I want to hear from you, lass, if you saying sorry for the evil you've done your family.'

And she thought, *But will I get forgiveness if I ask for it? Even if I crawl like Will's dog there?*

She reached a decision, looked straight at him, and the line of her mouth was set. 'I'm sorry, father. I'm awful sorry.'

An ugly look came over his face then, ugly, and pleased, the twist of the lips like Will's when he had elbowed her aside. He sat back in his chair, arms folded across his belly, 'Go on, then, Agnes, let us all hear it.'

She took care to keep her voice low and even, though she wanted to yell the words, to spit them at him, at all of them, 'Aye, I'm sorry. I'm sorry you sent that letter. I'm sorry I love a man who's so far awa, I'm sorry I didna go wi him to Edinburgh. I'm sorry you've never loved my mother the way Andrew –'

'Will! Shut that girl up!'

A stinging blow landed on her ear. Beside her, Will's expression echoed the look on her father's face, his mouth contorted with some cruel pleasure, and his eyes penetrating her. Then Will shifted in his seat, curving towards her as he leaned on his elbow, and whispered behind his hand, very quietly so that only she could hear, 'I ken what you are, Agnes. Will I tell them?'

She swallowed thickly, and held her peace.

'Good lad, Will. If she starts up again, you ken what to do.'

Will grinned, and nodded, 'Aye, father.'

'I winna suffer the name of that *sair*-vant to be said in my presence.'

Throughout the rest of their supper, the only sounds to be heard were Grizel and Bessie's snuffling as they fought back their tears.

Unmoving, she sat where she was, staring into the remains of her food. She did not finish her supper, thinking only that there was no way to make oats again, once the meal was ground.

The next day, and the days after that, she stayed within the confines of the house. The winds battering the rain against the walls and windows seemed worse now than they ever had, and when they let up she could hear the burn churning angrily down in its glen. It was a far cry from the narrow stream it had been in summer. And she tried to hold on to the summer, to remember the days of sun and the hours she and Andrew had spent together.

Often she would think of the one high summer's evening when he had dragged her, laughing, protesting, the both of them tripping over the tussocks of moor-grass, all the way to the burn's source on the Deer's Hill. Amongst a sea of wild grasses that tossed under the bare blue of the sky, they had stepped carefully between the peewits' nests, while the frantic birds screamed and dived around them. They had sat down side by side, looking west to where the high mountains rose above the rolling hills they knew, and all the way to the mountains, here and there between the green rigs, stretched lines of the flax flowers, that bloomed the same brilliant blue as the sky.

'Do you see the flax in bloom there, aa the way to the hills?' she had said. 'Do you ken that the flowers last just the one day?'

'No. And what happens to them then?'

'They die and they fall to the ground.'

Andrew had been quiet for a bit, looking into the distance at the lines of flowers stretching away, and his mouth had a sorrowful set about it.

'Do they?' he said. 'Now that seems a gey sad thing.'

They thought about it in silence, while they sat with the comfort of their arms around each other's shoulders.

At last she stirred, and said, 'But Andrew, they're only flowers.'

'Aye.'

'And do you ken another thing? They're bonnier for that one day than aa the other flowers thegither.'

Then he turned to look at her, deep into her eyes, saying earnestly, 'Maybe they are the bonniest flower. But they'll never be as bonny as –'

She waited for him to say it, 'never as bonny as you, Annie', but he saw her waiting for it, and the corners of his eyes crinkled up with mischief as he finished, '– as me!'

So she cuffed him, the way he liked, and he pretended that it hurt, and then she kissed him, so many, many kisses, while all about them, skylarks rose singing into the deeps of the summer sky and their song tumbled down through the air.

The featureless days crawled past. For much of the time she could think of neither future nor past, only close immediate things, her fingernails and the dirt under them, and the grain of the wooden bowl from which she ate. And hardly able to breathe, she counted the days since Hogmanay, twelve, thirteen, fourteen days, and still she waited for the sign that there would be no bairn. When she thought of the months passing and her belly swelling and the gloating eyes of the whole congregation, she would go into the storeroom and pummel herself in the stomach, gasping dry sobs. Then, her mind would fill with frantic thoughts of escape, elopement, messages she could try to send to Andrew. Briefly, she would think that these were things she would try, but then she started to feel flat and dull and she must have a good long sleep first, and then it would seem of little concern to her, as if it were someone else who was confined to the house, and she was watching from outside, a curious and politely concerned observer. She watched with little interest the trivial scenes of Agnes sitting in a chair, Agnes eating her bere porridge at night and morning, Agnes lying in bed, Agnes squatting over the chamber pot, and she wondered why the girl did not speak or go out, and then she would remember, there was a lad, what was his face like again?

XXV

'Ah, Tifty, I was wondering how things are wi yon wayward daughter of yours. She'll have forgotten my trumpeter by now, I'm guessing?'

'The witchcraft winna wear off just like that, my Lord.'

It was not long before nightfall and Annie listened from where she lay curled, immobile, on the bed. Above Grizel's clatter in the kitchen, there had been the jingle of harness and the muffled voices of her parents welcoming the Laird of Fyvie to their home. An unusual event, she thought it must be her doing, hers and Andrew's, and her father's through his letter. Now a snatch of conversation came to her as he mounted the stairs. The Laird's voice was familiar enough to her, loud with false joviality, and she could imagine her father's sour face, the nostrils flaring in disdain as he answered, one side of the mouth pulled down to make a deep line in the grey stubble on his chin.

Then her father seemed to think better of it, for she heard him say in an altered tone, 'But I've nae doubt she'll see sense soon enough, my Lord, now that you're taking an interest in the matter yourself.'

As they moved into her parents' bedroom, she strained to hear, and caught little more than the tones and cadences of their voices. The Laird's jovial tone seemed to take on a sharper edge after a while, and her father spoke in a sullen monotone, and then she heard her mother's foot on the landing and the door swung open, and Helen Black was on the threshold with dull, hostile eyes.

'So this is where you've hid yourself. The Laird of Fyvie's here. He wants to see you. Clean yourself up and come through-by.'

She sat up and carelessly passed a comb through her hair, and then she tied it back the way Andrew liked, the way she had worn it for Hogmanay. She did not bother to change her skirt or apron, for what would she do that? Only her wedding. So it did not take her long to get ready, and then she went across the landing and stopped short before the open bedroom door. Directly in front of her and at the far end of the room, Alexander Seton was sitting in the best chair with his legs stretched out in front of him and his ankles crossed. His forearms lay on the armrests with the pale hands hanging loosely off the ends.

'Well, well, Agnes, will you nae come in? You were never afraid of me afore now.'

She stepped forward into the room where her parents sat to entertain their Laird. Her sisters, polite and upright, sat side by side on the bed. Every face in the room looked up at her sharply as she entered.

'Now what's this I hear about you nae being well? We canna have a bonnie lass like you stuck in the house for much longer – there's a lad or two in my servants' hall who wouldna want to hear of that.'

Stupid man, thought Annie. *Can you nae see I dinna care about any lad that's left in your Castle?*

'I'm nae sick, my Lord.'

He looked directly at her father as he gave her his reply. 'Oh are you nae? Your father's told me wrong, then. Well, my trumpeter would be glad to hear that. You ken my trumpeter Andrew Lamb, dinna you?'

He did not wait for a response, and his eyes did not turn to her but remained attached to the rigid face of William Smith, in which the only sign of movement was a throbbing purple vein at each temple.

'And do you ken he's off to Edinburgh to tak up a place wi the Earl of Balcarres?'

'Aye, my Lord.' Her eyes flicked between the Laird's face and her father's, and her heart beat three, four, five times in the silence.

Then the head of Alexander Seton swivelled towards her, and his eyes slowly followed as if they were reluctant to leave William Smith alone. But when he spoke to her, it was as if there was no one else in the room, and his look was gentle.

'And do you nae have something to say about that, Agnes?' he said, soft, like when he talked to the hound pups when they were weaning.

It seemed then as if her heart and her breath stopped for a long minute, and when her heart started again, it came stronger with each beat, and she spoke straight to Seton, ignoring the fixed glare that her father directed at her.

'Aye, I do, my Lord, I ken you've sent him to be safe, because he's nae the witch they say he is, like my father said in that letter he sent you. And I wish you would send for him to come back to Fyvie, so he can wed wi me, because it's naethin wrong we've done, and I winna wed with anyone else. No matter what they – ' here her accusing eyes pointed out both parents, 'try and mak me do.'

The Laird slapped one hand to his leg and held out the other towards her as if he was celebrating a very fine wine he held up to the light, and turning to her father with a broad grin his voice was glad as he said, 'Tifty, Tifty, surely you can see now they must be married? The lad spoke to me just the same way, they're a pair without a doubt! Gie your blessing for God's sake and let's have a wedding.'

But there was no reflection of his delight in the miller's face. William Smith ground out his words with some effort, as if his tongue was a quern-stone being slowly turned by hand. With intense eyes he held his Laird's gaze steady, handing his thoughts over slowly, like sacks of meal to be taken home and digested at his leisure.

'Na, my Lord. Na.' He shook his head heavily without dropping his gaze. 'It's nae the *trumpeter* of Fyvie I would be letting my daughter marry. Nae the *trumpeter*.' He paused. 'It would need to be a man of a far higher degree than that.'

'Well now, Tifty, it seems it's a gentleman husband you're wanting for your lass. The thing is, she winna have one. She's made her choice plain enough, and if I were you I would let her have her way. It'll be ill luck to you if you control her.'

'I was thinking you might tak another view, seeing as you've yet to marry yourself.'

The Laird sat back in his chair, and blinked. He gave a short, light, surprised laugh.

'Ha! Ha! Tifty, now you're speaking plain, I understand you. Is that what you meant in your letter?'

Her father leaned forward, eager, lips stretched in a grin.

'Well, well, Tifty. Ha!' The Laird shifted and twitched in his chair as if it had suddenly become unpleasantly hot. 'Of course she's a bonnie lass. A fine lass. I winna deny that I've –. I mean, any man would –.' He paused, searching for words. 'The thing is, Tifty. Ha! Maybe last year. If my brother had lived. But, Tifty –' He sat back, shaking his head slowly and ruefully, 'Tifty, I'm the Earl of Dunfermline.' He lifted his hands and let them fall into his lap, helpless.

Her father leaned further forward, speaking urgently. 'She has a tocher, my Lord. A good tocher, amounting to –'

'I dinna care, father, I'll only tak Andrew. I winna have any other man. I winna gie him up for any lands or gold. Keep your tocher. I dinna want it.' Annie did not know she had spoken until the words were out of her mouth.

'You be silent, woman!' Her father whipped around towards her and his face was scarlet, distorted. Then, remembering himself, he grasped the arms of his chair as he struggled to bring his breathing back under control.

The Laird stood up very quickly.

'There you are, Tifty. You've heard it frae her own mouth. Now, if you'll see me to the door, I'll leave you aa in peace. It's been dark for some time and they'll be wondering at the Castle where I am. Damn, the rain's come on. Goodnight Helen, Agnes, girls. I look forward to hearing the banns read in the Kirk.'

He left.

The Miller rose abruptly and followed the Laird down the stairs. While the head of the household stiffly exchanged parting words with the Laird at the door, the four women of the family were left alone together.

'He'll never tak you now,' said her mother, and Bessie suppressed a nervous laugh, while Jane bit her lips together.

Annie looked at her mother's thin, rigid face, and wondered how it was she could have so little understanding of one of her own.

'He'd never tak me anyway, mother. Did you nae hear him? He said it himself. The Earl of Dunfermline. He doesna want the likes of us. All folk ken a trumpeter's closer to us than an Earl. All folk, but you and father, you think you're above them aa.'

'God knows we've tried our best wi you, Agnes. But you've aye liked to play wi dirt.'

Her jaw began to tighten, 'Dinna you talk about my Andrew sic a way, mother. Dinna you dare.'

Helen began an answer, but at the same time there came the sound of footsteps leaping up the stair, two at a time. Her father's voice, right behind her back, 'You'll say you're sorry for this, my lass.'

She wondered then if that one simple word would come, if she could make herself say it, but her jaw remained tightly clamped. The rain drove at the window. The fire crackled in the grate. There was a clatter in the room below, Young Will home from the alehouse, drunk, from the sound of it. Still she waited, and still no word of apology formed on her lips. And somewhere deep inside her the last kernel of a daughter's love for her father crumbled to dust, crushed at last by the grinding of his will against hers, stone on stone.

She felt a freedom then, she could say anything and it did not matter, how could he hurt her when she no longer cared for him? And she felt a contempt for him, for them all, their clumsy attempts to court the Laird on her behalf, a fool could see it was an impossible match, only their pride and stupidity could have blinded them to it. And she wanted to laugh at them, trying to force her into a marriage with a man so far above her, who would see her married to Andrew himself. And she said so, keeping her back to him to anger him more. She could feel the contempt and the anger and the laughter fighting for control of her face, the silent shocked stares of her mother and sisters, maybe they too thought she was bewitched, why not? Maybe she was. And she could feel the heat of her father's rage building up behind her, she gloried in the thought of those pulsing veins and imagined his nostrils flaring, and when he said, 'Another word from you, my lass, and I'll –' then she turned to look up into his face which was just as she knew it would be, and she laughed and laughed, at his stupid stupid face and his stupid stupid dreams, and she said 'Do you think I would gie up Andrew, my Andrew, because you say so? Gie up my Andrew, for you? For you? Dinna you ken every soul in Fyvie would laugh at you, if they knew?'

There was a moment of blackness, nothingness, followed by a high-pitched whine that seemed to come from all around, or from inside her head. There was a sharp pain in her wrist, and she wondered why she was sitting on the floor with her back against the Laird's overturned chair. One side of her face was stinging, and she shook her head and blinked until her vision came clear. Her father was towering over her, his face obscured in his own shadow, which pitched and tossed around the room as a cruisie lamp swung crazily on its chain. The only other light in the room came from the settling embers of the fire. Her mother and Jane had jerked to their feet and were standing, immobile, with mouths half open. Bessie, still seated on the bed, was emitting a gasping, desperate laugh.

'Get to your feet.'

She pulled herself up, using the chair for support and wincing as she leaned on her hurt wrist. The room seemed to be turning slowly around her, and a wave of nausea passed through her. Rain battered the window and the wind howled fitfully in the thatch.

'What do you say now, Agnes?'

'About what, father?'

'About your filthy witch, yon bastard Lamb.'

The fight had not died in her yet. 'You're the witch, father. You and mother. Get Gavin Sinckler and ask him. He kens the truth.'

She felt the blow the second time, an open-handed slap delivered with the full force of the miller's long right arm. She had time to anticipate it, to brace her legs and to turn her head away as the blow landed. Though she was not quite knocked from her feet, her neck wrenched as if the muscles would rip away, and her vision dimmed momentarily. The nausea engulfed her briefly, then subsided. Her chest and belly were shaking with rapid sobs, but her face was dry. Perhaps it was laughter then instead of tears, why not, Bessie was laughing too just the same. Her father was glaring at her, though she could not meet his eye now, she was looking down at the floor timbers, red from the firelight, her own feet, bare, and his in their leather shoes. Out of the corner of her eye, she saw her father begin to raise his hand again, but then it was her mother pushing her to one side out of his way, over towards the fireplace, and peppering one side of her face with sharp stinging slaps as she directed towards her a hail of accusation.

'Witch, you wee witch, what have you done wi my sweet lass, you lying lustful devil, going in the woods wi that witch man, you lustful, carnal woman, how could you do it, what have you done wi my Agnes, you'll gie him up, you'll say you're sorry, you talk back to your father like that, you know what's coming, how is it you canna be like your sisters, good lasses, waiting for good husbands, nae lustful, lustful, dinna look at me like that, you did, you did, of course you did, I can see it in your eyes, how could you nae think what if there was a bairn?' On and on, slap after painful slap, words on hurtful words, and on the edge of hearing, the whispers of her sisters, as indistinguishable from each other as they had always been, 'Couldna she do better than a servant, and her so bonnie too? Did you hear what she said to father, I wouldna dare. A witch, she called him, and mother too, would you credit it?'

Eventually, Helen stopped her tirade, and her hand was wet with Annie's tears. Annie was crying and shaking now, and the only other sounds were the guttering of the cruisie lamps and the storm outside. With her face close to her mother's, Annie waited without knowing it for her father's next move. But it was Young Will's voice that came from the dark at the top of the stair, so soft she could hardly hear it.

'I dinna ken why you're gieing her such an easy time.'

XXVI

The light of the fire and the lamps flickered across her brother's face, with its high cheekbones so like her own, and the lips that were subtly twisted in the look she had seen so often as a bairn. He walked across the room straight up to her, but the steps he took seemed to her very deliberate, as if he had to concentrate on making each foot fall exactly where he planned, and once his toe dragged a little and caught on the raised edge of a timber, nearly tripping him. When finally he leaned heavily against the mantle close beside her, she could smell the malt on his breath and his skin, dram after dram must have gone down his gullet and was now distilling back out of him into the air.

'What are you staring at, you?'

She looked quickly away. 'Naethin, Will.'

'Aye, it's nae me that's shamed this family, is it, Agnes? Nae this time, na.'

His voice was soft, not quite a whisper, and only slightly slurred. She leaned away from him a fraction of an inch as his hand casually took hold of a handful of her hair, as if they were bairns again, and he gave it a playful tug, 'Your sins will find you out, eh, Agnes?' She could feel his breath as he whispered into her ear, and his quiet deliberate voice set a panic fluttering in her ribcage.

'Dinna, Will, please.' Her voice came out in a whine, like a bairnie, she thought, don't play his game, but she could not help it.

The head of the household signalled for the rest of the family to leave. 'You'll maybe have better luck wi her, Will. The spirit of rebellion's in her, still. She winna listen to your mother or me.'

Young Will looked away from her as the rest of the family filed out of the room, cocking his head to listen to the receding voices.

'Na, Helen, we'll gie the lad his chance to keep order in the house. He's as much right as any.'

When they were gone, she felt his attention settle on her once more. He looked into her eyes, and smiled, as if they shared a special secret together, something dark and shameful, that no one else knew. Then his hand slipped around the back of her neck to take a firmer grip on the hair close to the scalp.

'What's wrong, you witch's hoor? Has he got a bairn on you?' His words came in bursts of warm whisky breath on her face, and he rocked her head from side to side to punctuate his speech, gently it might have seemed if anyone had been watching, but with each word his fingers tightened and twisted in her hair. She pulled away, but this was a man who hoisted sacks for a living, and she could not resist as he drew her head in towards him, until her forehead rested against his.

'Has he? Answer me, hoor.'

Her answer came after a moment's hesitation, 'Na,' hardly a word, a whispered breath.

He hooked the fingers of his free hand around her jawbone and jerked her head up, forcing her to look him straight in the eye.

'Dinna lie, hoor. Ye've aye been thrawn. Answer me right, has he gien you a bairn?'

This time she spat the word at him, defiant, 'Na!'

A tremor crossed his face, like a small earthquake.

'Aye, he has. Dinna worry, Agnes. Your brother'll help you.'

There was an explosion in her belly as he rammed his fist inwards and upwards under the ribs, three times, fast. It lifted her off her feet and she passed out as he released his grip on her hair and let her fall to the floor. A moment later she was on her hands and knees, retching, her spread fingers sliding in a yellow pool of vomit. Will was crouched beside her, his face wild with delight at the violence and the filthy words that he was letting fly out of it.

'Hoor, you witch's hoor. Lying deceitful slut, you scarlet woman you, spreading your legs for witches and warlocks, you filthy fucking hoor.'

Then the kicking started.

'Look at you wi your dirty filthy eyes of a hoor, look at you, you shameless bitch, going wi that witch, animals the both of you, I heard you, I saw you, you dirty whore bitch. Filthy fucking hoor, you filthy fucking hoor, I'll mak sure your stinking bastard bairn never sees the light of day.'

She bore blow on blow, and then as he circled away to take a run at her, suddenly she was on her feet down the stair through the hall and out the door into the night. She was blinded by the dark and a squall of rain that slashed across her face. He was right behind her and two or three paces into the yard he caught her, grabbed her by the hair and the arm and spun her around to face him, throwing her over against the millstone. He lifted his fist and her nose broke with a sickening crunch – 'You'll find it harder to tempt the laddies now, bitch' — and vicious blows landed on her breasts and cunt and the belly where no bairn would ever grow. The edge of the millstone dug into her back as he bent her over it, ramming her shoulders back towards the wall. There was a loud crack and a jolt and a buzzing feeling all through her legs and back, and then nothing.

XXVII

She came halfway to consciousness as they carried her up the stair. She could feel the strong grip of hands holding her under the oxters and her head flopped back into someone's belly. She was shivering, and she felt her soaking clothes sticking to her arms and chest. There was a metallic taste in her mouth. She heard her father barking out a terse instruction, 'Dinna let her legs drop.' With difficulty, she opened her eyelids a slit and saw a skirt and apron bundled around her waist and her bare calves with Will's hands gripping them. She saw him shift his grip, but she did not feel it. Will too was wet through, and his dark hair was plastered down on his head. Behind him, her mother, sisters, Grizel, standing at the foot of the stair, their faces tense and worried. It was too much effort to keep her eyes open and her eyelids fell shut again. They laid her on the bed and she felt women's hands gently loosening her bodice and sponging her face and arms. She started to cough, and she spat out red gobs of blood. Then she slept.

There was darkness and light and her mother coming in and out with a cruisie lamp. Once, when it was dark, she was disturbed by the high-pitched yelping of her brother's dog, and her father shouting, 'Nae mair of that!' and the dog quieted.

'Will you nae go up and see her, William?'

He shook his head, but made no other reply. Continued scooping the sloppy sowans from his bowl while his wife hesitated.

'She's asking for you.'

He finished the remnants of his breakfast, looked across the table at Gibb, and gave him an order, 'Go down to the mill. I'll be there in a minute.'

Once the door clicked to behind Gibb, he continued for some time scraping at the bowl until the grain of the wood became dry and began to feather. Then he splayed his hands flat on the table, pushing against the wood, one on either side of the bowl, and he hung slumped over it as if feeling for the first time the weight of every sack he had carried in nearly thirty years of mill-work. He stared into the depths of the bowl as if it could give him an answer, or an absolution. When he heard Helen's intake of breath, he knew that she would press him again, and he spoke first to forestall her, saying in a voice that was barely audible, 'Dinna mak me do it, Helen.'

Helen's reply was slow in coming. When it did, her voice was shrill and desperate. 'You must go, William. Your daughter's asking for you.'

Then a warmth of anger rushed through him, and gave him the strength to rise. He slapped his open palms down onto the table with force. 'Dinna you be telling me what I must and must not do, wife. I'll go down to the mill as I aye do. You go to her. It's woman's work to tend the sick.'

The house door quivered in its frame as he slammed it behind him.

The flats of his hands were still stinging as he entered the mill. The dust filled his nostrils. The runner stone lay on its back, belly upwards, exposing the pattern of grooves on its underside. Gibb had already put himself to work dressing the stone, deepening the grooves and sharpening their edges, carefully scraping and tapping away with a pick and chisel. Smith stood for some time, looking dully around at the dismembered parts of the miln laid out for replacement or repair, until Gibb, made uncomfortable by the eyes watching over him, stopped his methodical tapping at the stone and straightened up. His one good eye swam with tears.

'And how is your lass, Mr Smith?'

Tifty shrugged and hardened the line of his mouth. 'Nae better.'

Gibb looked down at his hands. 'It's a terrible thing, Mr Smith, terrible. Is there anything I can do to help?'

'You can pray, Gibb. Just pray.'

'Aye sir, prayer is a great healer. Only –'

'What, Gibb? Only what?'

He watched Gibb's Adam's apple dip up and down nervously.

'It's just, sir, well I dinna ken because I'm nae the minister, but they say that those who try to tak their own lives are beyond the help of prayer.'

Smith closed on Gibb until he could feel the unpleasant warmth of Gibb's breath against his cheeks. He fixed Gibb's good eye with an unblinking stare.

'I winna have any body – *any* body, mind – saying yon about my lass. Do you understand me? Do you?'

Gibb lowered his gaze and mumbled, 'Aye, sir, you're right, you're right.'

'And I winna have you spreading that kind of talk in the parish, either. If I hear one word from anyone about *my* lass doing *yon* to herself –' He stopped himself abruptly because the shaking of his diaphragm was causing his words to quaver. Gibb stood round-shouldered before him, with fidgeting hands. Smith snorted a burst of air in through his nostrils, and loosened his jaw off from side to side.

'Just you be careful you tell folk what you ken, and just what you ken, nae what you've heard from outside this house. They werenae there to see it, and you werenae there either, so dinna be making up stories or telling them. Now get back to your work.'

He set to himself, fixing the cogs of the trundle. There would be more work for him and Gibb for a while. He could not stand the sight of Young Will and had ordered him to keep away from the mill. When Gibb had returned from his visit to Inveramsay, or wherever it was he had been, they had taken care to let him think that Young Will was sick with worry about his sister. Gibb had little to say to Grizel at the best of times, and in any case Tifty had made sure of her before Gibb got back.

There was no grinding to be done that day. Plenty water in the burn, but it would take them all day to dress the stones and replace the broken cogs. Gibb helped him to unfix the trundle, place it on the workbench and coax the snapped cogs out of their sockets. In his deep concentration on the work, Smith managed to push aside the other thoughts that fought to invade his mind. The two men laboured without words, grunting a bit with the effort of the work. By mid-afternoon, the pieces of the miln were ready to be fixed back in place. They put them into position, tested the movement and the balance of the wheel, readjusted, stepped back in satisfaction. When it was done, he let Gibb go early, with a brusque dismissal. But as Gibb hurried towards the door, Tifty made sure of him with a few well-chosen words.

'It's near thirty years you've been wi me, Gibb. There's nae many millers would keep on a man of your age. But that was good work the day. There's a place here for men who know how to work. And to hold their tongues.'

With the day's work done, his thoughts turned back to the house and what lay in it. There would be the hum of the spindles, the hiss of the peat in the hearth, the creaks as the house shifted, everything as normal except for the sound of Helen's feet going up and down the stairs, up and down the stairs, up and down, and the broken rhythm of Agnes's breathing from the room above. It was barely audible, and yet it filled the house. A long slow gasp in, a pause, and then a quick juddering release as the lungs collapsed, and another terrible wait for the next struggling intake, filling the house with and adding to the smothering weight of their collective guilt. He had no mind to return to the house just yet, and he did not follow Gibb through the door. His gaze fell on the spokes of an old broken trundle, still lying on the workbench before him, and he picked up a tool and set to fixing it.

The chisel turned awkwardly and the sharp metal edge dug into the flesh at the base of his thumb, and with the pain and the sight of the blood welling slowly to the surface there came a deluge of curses, a torrent of filthy words, directing hatred at himself and his son, at his wife and at the obstinate unmanageable woman who had replaced the daughter who had adored him. And then in mid-flow he bit back the curses, and he pressed his thumb down onto the wound to keep the blood and the anger inside him. He was glad of the pain, glad that he could feel that at least, and he closed his eyes and clenched his teeth and stood waiting for the flow of blood to stop, and as he did so a memory came back to him, long-forgotten but as strong and warm as the sunlight that had come through the window maybe a dozen years ago, summer afternoon sunlight falling across the workbench.

'What you doing, father?'

She looks up at him with her eyes shining. She stretches up on tiptoe to see over the top of the workbench where his hands are working. Her red hair is shining in the rays of sun that are streaming through the narrow window. The air smells of the dust of oats and freshly sawn wood. The miln is still, there has been no rain for weeks. He knows she misses the spray of water around the wheel as it turns. She loves to sit and watch it, perched on her own rock by the side of the burn, the rock with the white lines on it, the one that's different from all the others, and to see the wheel turning and the spray flying up and around, and the rainbows that come sometimes when the sun shines. The sun is shining now and it lights up his own hair as well as hers. He knows she likes it that they have the same colour hair, almost the same, his is a bit darker with silver streaks above the ears, but it's the same.

He looks down at her, smiling as he bends down towards her and whispers conspiratorially.

'You just wait and see, wee Nan. It'll be a surprise.'

'What is it, what is it?'

'Never you mind, you'll see soon enough.'

And he drops the gentle weight of his big hand on the top of her head, stroking her hair with a long firm stroke. Her hair the colour of his, and the soft gentle stroke of his hand reassuring her, running over the crown and down the back of her head, once, twice, three times, and he feels strong, and protective. Then he takes the hand back to its work on the bench, and he laughs to himself because still she can't see and it's driving her mad. She shifts from foot to foot while he ignores her and concentrates on his work, paring and sawing. He likes it that instead of going away to play outside she stays because she wants to be here with him, in the dusty quiet of the mill, the flecks of dust dancing in the beams of sunshine. Out of the corner of his eye, he watches her start to dance in the sunlight, stretching out her arms and hopping from foot to foot. It's a game she often plays. She has to stay in the sunbeam or she'll disappear like a speck of dust, pffft! *gone and she won't come back. He hums a jig tune for her, and he carries on cutting and sawing and paring and fixing and then he puts down the tools with a dramatic flourish and she is over to him like a flash. So he picks her up under the oxters and she flies through the air and lands with a bump on the workbench beside a tiny wooden mill, a foot high only.*

'What's that, father?'

'It's a mill, Nan, for you.'

She puts out her finger, the smooth pink nail still fresh and clear. The finger touches the paddles of the wheel and it turns, and inside, the miln turns too.

'Is it a real stane?'

'Na, it's wood.'

'Oh.' For a moment she sounds disappointed, but then she starts to spin the wheel. She spins it and inside her mill the miln turns and turns, she is grinding oats for the Laird, or maybe bere barley and peas that the tenants have grown for their supper.

'Do you like it, Nan?'

She nods, mute, hypnotised by the wheel going round and round, and her feet swing like pendulums.

'You can take it to the burn and see how it goes in the water. That way you'll aye have a wheel to watch even when the miln's nae at work.'

Then her smile like sunshine, two teeth missing in the middle, but they'll grow back in, 'Can I? Can I can I?'

'Aye, off you go.'

He lifts her down, holding the wee mill tight to her chest. Her feet land shuush *in the soft pile of sawdust and oat dust, and she is out of the door, running, while he watches after her before he goes back to his work.*

The soft thud of the tabby cat landing on the bench disturbed him and his eyes jerked open. The blood had stopped flowing from his wound. Night had long since crept in through the windows of the mill, and the cat's eyes glinted at him in the darkness. The limp body of a dead mouse sagged between her jaws.

Absentmindedly, he extended a hand to stroke her, but her back sank away from his touch and she slunk into a corner to dismember the mouse in peace. He shivered. A chill had come into his bones from the dark outside, but he did not bother to light a lamp. He needed no light to guide him along the path he had trod four times each day for the last twenty-four years. When he returned to the house, Agnes's breathing met him at the door.

Helen Black moved into the dark of the landing at the top of the stairs, where the sound of Agnes's laboured breathing seemed louder than it was in the room where the girl lay. Her face was dimly lit by the flickering yellow light of the cruisie lamp that she held in one hand. Her other hand reached towards the handle of the door and then pulled back to form a white-knuckled fist that she pressed, trembling, to the one soft place in her body, just above the belly and beneath the ribcage and breastbone that enclosed her heart. She clamped her eyes tight shut until the trembling ceased. Then she reached up to push a strand of hair under the edge of her mutch, and opened the door.

She hung the cruisie on its bracket and then advanced towards Jane and Bessie, who sat beside the bed. Neither turned her head towards her. Grizel sat in a corner apart. Helen had refused to let any of the other women of Tifty in.

'Has she spoken?'

'Na. She's just the same.'

'Aye. Maybe tomorrow.'

Helen did not sit down for some time, but stood watching Agnes's face. In the dim light, the bruises seemed like shadows, so that almost she looked unhurt. Agnes's mouth hung open, and Helen's gaze fixed on a thick string of saliva that was stretched between the teeth and vibrated in and out with each slow breath. Both of the front teeth were badly chipped.

'You winna like that, Nan, na, you winna,' and Helen's face began to crumple, before she rescued herself, pressing her lips together and sweeping her skirts aside with a brisk movement in order to sit down on a low stool. Then she sat in silence, and from time to time she prayed, with hands clasped and lips fluttering, and between prayers she lifted her eyes to look around the room. After an hour or two, or three, Agnes gave a low moan, barely audible, and the women looked towards her face, which showed no signs of change, but had fallen a little to one side. The breathing now was slower than before, and shallower. And then Helen's face began to crumple again, and for the first time in many years she took her daughter's hand in her own and held it and patted it with rapid little taps and strokes.

'Did I ever tell you, Nan, it was in this room you were born? Aye, it was, and I had a good bit trouble wi you, too, nae like the other three. They say it's the first that gives the worst pain, but Young Will, he was nae bother to me at aa.'

She lowered her head, and bit her bottom lip, and then she looked up again, and continued.

'Na, he was nae bother to me when he was born, but when I was brought to my bed wi you, my youngest, that was when I had my worst time. It was two days I was laid there wi the birth pains, and for a week after you came into the world I hadna my strength, and I thought I would lose you, because you wouldna suckle, and I had barely any milk for you even if you had. I could hardly sleep, and when I did, I would wake up and hear you screaming in the night, your wee bonnie face aa screwed up tight and red. And Nan,' – her voice cracked – 'it pulled at my heart not being able to do a thing for you, and you so wee and helpless. But it was your father – your father, mind, you mustna forget – he says, "*You and Nannie will have to go down to the Shargar Stane, there's naethin else for it*." And it was true, we had crossed you with iron, and killed a pigeon in half, and still you wouldna feed. And so your father – we hadna even a pony in those days – he just picked me up and carried me, wi you tucked in at my breast, and he carried us aa the way down the miles past the Castle and the Kirk to the clearing where the Shargar Stane stands. I swear it, I could hear the fair folk laughing at us aa the way, like they were mocking us, and it was dead of night wi the moon awa high up in the sky, and the clouds fleeing across its face, and the wind in the tops of the trees. But it was warm, because it was June. And when we got there, your father put me down on my feet at the edge of the clearing, but he wouldna go into it. He just turned his back, and said, "*You're on your own now, lass, this is women's business*."

'Then I took you in my arms, and it was the first time you had been quiet.' Helen's face and hands were still and calm with the remembering of it. 'And I thought for a minute that I had lost you then, that you had been smothered as I carried you. But you were only sleeping. And I walked on into the clearing, out of the shadow of the trees to where the moonlight was falling on the top of the three stanes. You ken how they are set up like a doorway, two standing and then the Shargar Stane like a lintel across the top. And the light of the moon was making it almost shine, it was like silver wi wee flecks in it that glittered like a hard frost. And when I was there, standing before it, I thought *But I dinna ken what to do*. But I prayed to God, and I held you out before me wi your head cradled in my two hands and your wee thin body lying on my forearms. You were light, so light. And I knelt down on the grass so I could see through the gap between the stanes, and I offered you through them. I passed you through that stane, and then I brought you back. Three times I did that, and I prayed as I did it, I said, "*If it's your will, Lord, tak her, but I'm asking you to gie me my wee Nannie for just a bit longer*." '

Helen's shoulders bent over and began to shake.

'And then I stood up, just holding you, and looking down at your wee crumpled face, and your wee bit hand sticking out of the bundle, curled tight into a fist wi the nails showing pink, just perfect as God made you. And as I looked down at you, you opened your eyes and looked up at me and you put your hand out to reach for me and I gave you my pap, and when you took it there was milk, as much as you wanted.'

The hand that Helen held did not twitch. She let it go and sank back on the stool, looking towards Annie's face.

'And when you'd had your fill, Agnes, your father took you and held you, his big hand cradling your wee head on his shoulder. And all the way home, he held you, and he wouldna gie you back to me.'

For some time she sat, watching the motionless face. And then she half stood, clutching at Annie's forearm with both hands, leaning her face in close towards her daughter's, and her expression was fierce.

'It was your father, Agnes, your father that took us to the Shargar Stane. Do you hear me? He carried me and you aa the way in the night. Dinna forget that.'

The eyelids did not flicker, and only the slow, faint breathing answered her.

XXVIII

A thin layer of snow covered the yard outside Jess's cottage. There was a line of melt holes and dirt where the water dripped from the edge of the thatch. Meltwater trickled down the path past her kailyard. A pair of rooks straddle-hopped along the ridge of the roof, cocking their heads to watch as Jess, hunched over the basket of peats in her arms, made her way along the side of the cottage wall with red, swollen feet slipping in the snow.

From some way off, in the direction of the miller's house, there came the sound of a bell. The rooks flapped away as the ringing came closer, and Jess looked up towards them. When the sound of the bell came to her ears, she leaned one hand to steady herself against the edge of the thatch, dropping a couple of peats. She bent painfully to gather them up, carried them into the cottage and stacked them in the nook by the hearth. Then she went to the door and waited with her grandchildren gathering around her skirts, watching the squat black figure of the Precentor making his way up the path and into her yard. When he took a step forward, he lifted a small handbell to his shoulder, and he let it fall to his side with the next step. The bell had a light, joyful tone that did not suit its purpose. As they waited, Peter came round the corner of the cottage and came to stand by her with his arm around her shoulders. At last the Precentor reached the yard and stood a few feet in front of them, letting the bell hang idle by his side. The lines on his forehead were pinched together with worry.

'Brethren and sisters,' he said, in the voice that he used to read from the Bible, only it was thinner and more strained than it ever was in the Kirk, 'we let you to wit that we have a sister departed at the pleasure of Almighty God yesternight, and you are invited to attend the wake this e'en at the mill house of Tifty.'

The Precentor blinked two or three times when he had finished.

Jess looked into his pale, round face and said, 'So she's awa then.'

The Precentor nodded, and replied in his normal voice, 'Aye. Tifty sent your Grizel down for me at first light. She's still down at the house wi my Mary. She was in a state. But I doubt she'll be long now.'

'I'll see her in good time. The burial's the morn then?'

'Aye, the morn's morn. At first light. There's three men digging the grave.'

'They'll have a job wi the ground sodden with aa this snow. It's nae a good time of year for a funeral.'

'It never is.'

'How's her mother taking it?'

The Precentor shrugged minutely, 'I saw nane but the Miller. The house was quiet like the grave. He just says, "Our Agnes has been called hame by the Lord. Will you ring the mort bell for the wake the night?" And I says, "Aye, I will that." I says, "I'm right sorry for your loss, sir, she was a grand lassie." And then he just stands looking at me, you ken that way he has, and then at last he says, "Did Grizel tell you how it happened like?" And I says, "Aye sir, and a terrible thing it is too," and he nods and then he says, "You'll be on your way wi the mort bell, Precentor, and travel far – we'll need plenty bearers to carry the kist." That was aa there was of it, and I came awa. Now I must be on my way. I've far to go, and the days are short this time of year.'

'Aye,' said Jess, 'I would offer you some drink to sup, but you'll need to be off. We'll see you at the wake, I dinna doubt.'

The Precentor turned his back with a nod, raised the mort bell to his shoulder, and began the plod up the hill towards the other cotts of Tifty and the settlements beyond.

Grizel made her appearance halfway through the morning. There were dark circles under her eyes. When she arrived, the two women held each other, and Jess comforted her daughter's face against her breast, and took comfort herself in the strong grip of Grizel's arms around her back.

'It canna be helped, dearie, it canna be helped.'

'I canna stay there, minnie, I canna thole it.'

Jess stroked her hair gently.

'You must, you must, for now at least. You must wait for the feeing fair, and then you can find another place if you want it. And now – ' she straightened and loosened her embrace, 'I'll be needed at the miller's house. You might as well come up the road wi me.'

And she took from the press a pile of linen wraps which she shook out and re-folded and laid across her arm. Then she tightened her plaid around her and the two women walked arm in arm through the snow up to the mill house, where only a trickle of smoke coming from one chimney betrayed the life within. She knocked at the door, and pushed it open gently. Helen Black and her two living daughters sat in the kitchen, bolt upright with their hands folded in their laps. There was no sign of the miller or his son.

'Peace be here, Mistresses, and I'm sorry for your loss. I've come to attend to the lyke.'

Helen Black turned her head towards them and blinked slowly. Eventually a hollow voice came from her, 'She's there.' She pointed to the end of the room, where a sheet had been thrown over a long narrow object on a trestle table under the stair. 'Do you have aa you need?'

'Aye, I have, and I have Grizel to help me. You needna worry yourselves with it if it's a trial to you.'

Helen nodded, and rose to her feet. Jane and Bessie followed her up the stairs. Jess waited until she heard the sound of the bedroom door closing behind them, and then she lifted the sheet that covered the corpse. The body was cool, and stiff. There were many marks on it. Purple and yellow bruises stood out against the waxy pallid flesh of the limbs and back and belly. The teeth were chipped, and the nose askew.

Grizel dipped some water from the barrel by the door, and heated it on the fire. Tenderly they washed the body and wrapped it in the linen sheets that Jess had brought. When they were done, they set two candles by it, one at the head and one at the foot, and then Grizel went up the stair and knocked softly on the bedroom door.

When Helen Black came down to the kitchen, Jess said to her, 'It must have been a terrible fall she took, Mistress.'

The answer did not come right away. 'Aye. It was that.'

'Grizel tells me she wasna awake for much after.'

'No. Just fits and starts. She was awa in a deep sleep for the most of it.'

'That's a mercy at least.'

Helen nodded, and Jess turned to go.

'I thank you for your service, Jess. You'll be at the wake the night I hope?'

'Aye, we will aa surely come by to pay our respects.'

Jess had no songs to sing at her work that day.

At dusk, she and Peter led their household up the path to the mill house. Folk were coming from the other cotts of Tifty, and from further afield: Gourdas, Cardonwell, Camalouns and beyond.

The house, when they entered, had a darkness about it. The light of the cruisies struggled with the darkness, and the peat in the hearth could muster only a dim orange glow, with little flame. Folk came in and out, murmuring greetings and condolences, taking a seat where they could or standing in close huddled groups. From time to time, a figure would move away from a group, and go over to stand before the corpse where it lay on its table, a white silent thing wrapped head to foot in the bands of linen. The candles burned with a yellow light at its head and feet. They would stand with head bowed, praying and remembering in silence, or speaking to it a few brief words of remembrance – 'I'll miss your bonnie face'; 'You were aye good to me'; 'Who'll sing Eppie Morrie for us now?' – as they patted the hand beneath its linen bands, or reached out to touch the shrouded forehead.

The three womenfolk of the family sat on folding chairs along one wall, near the corpse, and allowed the visitors to press their hands while they nodded numbly, barely hearing the words of sympathy and regret. The brother sat all night by the door, with his hands buried deep in his pockets; Jess did not see him go over to pay his respects to his sister.

The Miller was the only one of the family who had much to say through the night. For the most part he moved between the small knots of people, entering their conversations abruptly.

'Did you hear how it happened?'

'Aye, a terrible thing, she fell down the steps to the mill.'

'How did that come to pass?'

'She was taken with a devilment, Mr Ironsyde, shouting and screaming like she was bewitched.' It was the miller, standing tall, looking slowly around at the faces of those he addressed.

'Bewitched, Mr Smith? Surely na!'

'Aye Mr Ironsyde, I fear it. And she wouldna listen to me, nor her mother, nor her brother. And she wouldna hold her tongue. And so Young Will there, he went to hold her, for she was throwing herself around the room with a terrible strength. Nae the strength of a woman, if you understand me. And he was feart she would do herself a damage. So he went to hold her still, but she ran frae him and out of the house as if he was the devil himself and nae her own brother, and at the head of the steps she tripped.'

Tifty reached out a hand to grip Grizel's shoulder as she passed with a plate of bannocks and cheese for the guests. 'Here, Grizel can tell you as well as I can.'

Grizel spoke her piece in a few short, flat words.

'I was down here, setting the fire. There was shouting and banging up the stair. Mistress Agnes ran down the stair and out the door. Master Will ran after her. I didna ken what the business was about. A wee bit later Mr Smith went out. And then...'

The soft flesh of Grizel's chin began to pucker and tremble, and she pressed her lips together until she could speak firmly again. 'And then a wee bit later Mr Smith and Master Will came back carrying her between them, and she was aa wet and covered in mud frae falling down the steps in the dark, and her dress was aa torn. And she couldna move her legs.'

'Ach, terrible, terrible, Mr Smith, a terrible loss, and a needless one.'

As the murmur of regrets started up, the miller slowly released his hand from Grizel's shoulder. Jess saw him give Grizel a strange look, a momentary thing, the smallest possible nod and the twitch of one corner of his mouth like the beginnings of half a smile, before he turned his attention again to his audience.

'And you say, Mr Smith, it was as if she was bewitched?'

The miller folded his arms, and nodded slowly while the knot of people gathered around him sucked in their breath, tutted anxiously and shook their heads.

'Terrible, terrible.'

'To think there are witches among us again.'

'But who was it that bewitched her?'

'They must be found out.'

'Aye, and brought to justice.'

'And wi haste, sir, for we canna have sic things spreading among us.'

'You must call upon the Laird, Mr Smith, to head up a court to enquire into the matter.'

The Miller's jaw clenched, and the colour rose in his cheeks.

'I fear the Laird winna tak action. He has already sent the man far frae here for his protection.'

'You ken who it is, then?'

'It's a man, you say? Nae an auld wife?'

'You dinna mean to say he's in the Laird's service?'

'Aye, Mr Ironsyde, I do. And one of his favourites. A man you ken as Lammie.'

'The trumpeter?'

'Surely na! He seemed like a decent enough laddie to me.'

'Maybe. But think – what did you ken about him? Naethin. Naethin at aa.'

Uneasy glances passed among the group.

'It aye seemed to me the Laird couldna see past him.'

'You're right there, Mr Ironsyde. For I wrote to the Laird myself to warn him of the danger. And he has done nothing but send the witch back to his own country.'

'I dinna like to say it. But this new Laird's nae a man like his father.'

When the Miller had moved on, the conversation continued for a while in whispers.

'More like she was in love wi the laddie than bewitched by him.'

'Aye, that's so, but it seems she was gone off balance one way or another.'

'It's as well Lammie has gone back where he came frae. The miller would never let it rest if he was still in Fyvie.'

Ironsyde turned to Jess. 'She must have been sore hurt, Jess, for you to swaddle her face like that. I would have liked a last look at her.'

'Aye, but there was nae sense in letting aa the folk see her for the last time like that. Better to remember her bonnie face the way it was.'

At the wake for an old fellow who had had his good share of life, there would be laughter, songs and stories and even dancing sometimes. That was how it would be for her when she passed on herself, and for Peter too. But for a bairn, or for one who had only had the first taste of life and had not yet had their fill of it, the weight of grief was too heavy to be shifted by a thing so light as a song. And so the remainder of the night was passed in murmured prayers and whispered condolences, and from time to time the gathered folk would raise their voices for comfort in the Psalms.

When the dawn was close it came time for the kisting. Men brought the iron kist to the door and laid it across two chairs in the yard. Helen Black and her daughters rose from their seats and went to the corpse. Helen stood at the head, Jane and Bessie by the sides. Jess took the knees, and with Grizel at the feet, very gently they lifted the body. It was not too heavy. The assembled crowd parted and stood with heads bowed as the five women bore Annie's body between them to the open door.

Jess welcomed the chill of the outside air on her face after the closeness of the crowded room. A single star pierced the western horizon above the bare branches of the orchard. It was so early in the day that she could not tell whether the sky above was clear or clouded. One by one, the folk came out of the kitchen and gathered in the yard around the kist. The snow underfoot was soft and turned to mud where the people gathered; she was thankful, for the men would have had a hard job if it had been frozen.

As the women laid the body into the coffin, the back bent unnaturally in the middle, and Jess heard a faint grating. She looked up, and saw that Jane and Bessie's faces were white, and wet with tears. Helen Black sagged over the head of the coffin, and Jess heard her say two muffled words: 'My youngest.'

Jess stepped softly to Helen's side and put her arm around her shoulders, trying to draw her head to her breast. But Helen straightened up and away from her with a quick, audible intake of breath, and turned away to take the mort cloth from the Precentor who stood nearby. As she shook the black sheet out over the kist, her voice was even as she said, 'We need mair womenfolk to tak the first lift.'

Three more women stepped forward from the crowd, and took their place at the handles. William Smith, Young Will, Peter and another five men stood ready and waiting, while the women bent at the knees, and hefted the coffin to shoulder height. Quickly the men stepped in to take the weight, and balanced the coffin between them, shifting it slightly as they braced themselves to move off. It was Young Will who took the handle from Jess, and she saw that there were fresh scabs on his knuckles, as if he had been in a recent fight. Drinking, she thought, at the alehouse in Woodhead. Then the men began to move off through the gathering light. Behind the coffin, other groups of men followed close, ready to bear the weight when their turn came. The women followed only as far as the turn in the path that led down to the meadows, and there they wept together, and watched it go. The mort cloth and the men's funeral clothes stood out stark and black against the white of the snow. Gradually they diminished to a dark line creeping towards Fyvie. And then great white flakes like feathers began to drift down out of the sky, and hid the procession from sight.

'Look,' Jess said, 'They're plucking geese in Orkney.'

XXIX

Grizel took a place at Meikle Gourdas at Whitsun, and Jess saw less of her daughter than she liked after that. But every week, Grizel would come back to Tifty on the Saturday night when her week's work was done, and stay with her parents through the Sabbath. On the Saturday night they would sit around by the fireside and spin, Jess and Grizel and Mary and anyone else who chose to come by.

One time, late in the year, it was just Jess and Grizel sitting up together, and Grizel said quietly, 'There's nae many folk comes here any mair,' and Jess answered, 'Na, na, your father and I havena been in the way of it these last months.' Which was true, for the songs had died in her in the winter's snow, and had not returned with the spring. And they had been feeling their age. She and Peter would lie in their bed at night and laugh at the list of complaints that age had brought to each of them. The shearing this year had been hard on her. She had fallen into her bed each night into an exhausted sleep, and had barely been able to rise in the mornings. Her hip and back had been troubling her ever since, and she had to wonder how many more years of such work she had left in her.

'Minnie, would you sing about Eppie Morrie for me?'

Jess sighed. 'Aye, aa right then, my dearie.'

And she sang, accompanied by the thrum of her spindle, and before she had finished, Grizel's eyes had filled with tears. When the last words were sung, Jess leaned forward and patted her daughter's hand, and said, 'I ken, I ken, it puts you in mind of Mistress Agnes. She liked to hear it, and to sing it herself. I mind her last summer at the shearing, she was aye humming it awa to herself under her breath.'

Jess thought back to the shearing time more than a year ago, when she had sat with her back against an apple tree, and how her eyelids were heavy and scratched with tiredness, and she passed between dreams and waking so that she confused the dreams with the picture before her, and so Andrew Lammie's head bending close to Agnes Smith became her own Peter's, in the long ago summer when he had courted her, and she shook her red hair down her back, although it had never been red but dark brown like nuts in autumn, and she felt again how it was to have the hair falling loose against her neck, instead of bundled under a mutch. She fell further into a half-sleep, and she could feel herself smiling a little as she dreamt of the first kisses Peter had given her, barely remembered through the years of cutting peat and spreading muck and worries over the weather and the harvest and the sicknesses of sheep and kye and bairns. And then she had woken with a start, when a shadow had fallen across her face, and looking up had invited Mistress Agnes to sit next to her. And when she had made a wee dig – just to test – about the Laird's trumpeter, how the light had dimmed in Mistress Agnes's eyes, as if she had put a hand in front of a candle to shield it from the wind.

A mischievous thought came to her. She looked up at Grizel, crinkling her eyes in fun, and said, 'She liked that trumpeter laddie, didna she?'

And Grizel nodded aye, silently. She hesitated, and swallowed, and then the tears started to fall as she said, 'I dinna think she fell.'

Jess was very still, and she took care to keep her voice steady and neutral when she answered.

'And how would that be, dearie?'

Grizel replied, 'Because I ken more than I telled them. Because he said he would put you out, you and father and James and Mary and the bairns.'

'Who did?' Although she knew.

'Mr Smith.'

'Aye. I see.'

Jess laid down her distaff and spindle, and took up a stocking that needed to be darned. She carefully licked the end of a thread and concentrated on passing it through the eye of the needle, while she asked, 'And what was it he didna want you to say?'

Jess listened, saying hardly a word, as Grizel told her the things she had heard, and the things she had seen, that she had held close and locked within her for nearly a year. As she listened, Jess thought of the fight scabs she had seen on Young Will's knuckles, and the miller moving among his guests at the wake, and a tight, hard knot began to form in her belly.

When Grizel had done, Jess nodded, and nodded, and said nothing, and the two women carried on sewing and spinning together. And at the next feeing fair, Jess and Peter took a place with Ironsyde after forty years at Tifty, saying to Tifty that it was more comfortable at Meikle Gourdas, and they would be closer to their daughter in their old age.

And all the time, the anger that had formed in Jess's stomach was growing and taking a shape, circling around within her as she thought of the orchard at the shearing time and the light in her eyes that Agnes had hidden from her, and she was angry and sad both. Sad at the loss, and to think of the trumpeter laddie far away in Edinburgh, maybe not knowing, even, why he had never had a message or a word from his lass. And sad and angry both when she thought of the young body she had wrapped, rotting in the graveyard. The anger and the sadness met together and took on a form and words and a rhythm of their own, that beat within her when she breathed at night.

There came a time when Jess said to Peter, 'Let's have aa the Gourdas folk around for a song or two,' and so the Gourdas folk came and sat by the fire and the songs went around as they used to. Jess sang all the old songs that had come back to her, and then she sang them a new song, a long long sad song, that no one had heard before, and as they listened, and for a long time after, they sat still, and quiet, and wondering.

XXX

It was a week's hard going for Andrew Lammie and the chestnut mare, through sleet and hail and mud, and he was glad to reach Edinburgh at last and to be welcomed into the Earl of Balcarres' house there. He was not expected, having arrived before the post, but he had a letter of introduction for his new master, who remembered him well in any case and was right glad to see him. He was a young man, no older than Andrew, who smiled knowingly as he looked up from the letter and said, 'No to worry, I've been in that kind of trouble myself. I'll no be sending you back any time soon – the father will just have to deal with it as best he can. And he canna be sure it's yours, now, can he?'

For that, Andrew wanted to strike the man hard in the face, but he held his fists clenched by his side instead of raising them, and bit his tongue while Balcarres handed him over to his chamberlain, who showed him to his place in the servants' hall. It was a dim corner with the hardest and thinnest of straw pallets, but nevertheless he slept well that night and for the whole of the week after. But on the Saturday night, he slept badly. In the early hours he woke from a dream. In the dream, he was walking hand-in-hand with Annie by the Tifty burn, passing between the sun and shade of the woodland in spring, and they laughed together as they walked. He could feel the warmth of her hand, the intimacy of their two palms pressing together.

Then they were on a high moor where the cottongrass blew, the white tufts of the seedheads dipping and swaying on a shifting sea of rippling grass. They were standing up to their knees amongst the grey green grass stems. He looked up, and all around them, stretching away into the distance and far over the horizon, there was the sky-bright blue of flax flowers. Skylarks rose singing from the ground and strove towards the sky. Then there was one lark only, showering them with its bubbling song, and the notes became loud and insistent, like hammer blows on ice. He was watching the lark, minute in the arc of blue above, and he had forgotten Annie until he felt her hand tugging at his, three, four times, and as he turned to look at her the song of the lark stopped dead, and he saw nothing in the place where she had been as his eyes snapped open on the shifting blackness of the hall where he lay. He did not know what had woken him. The blanket had slipped from him as he slept, and he shivered as he tried to get back to sleep, while around him the other men snored and mice scratched in the walls. But sleep did not come for a long time. The sudden wrench from the world of high, clear light and lark song into the dark of the servants' hall disoriented and shocked him. He did not know why the dream had disturbed him so much, only that the song of the lark and the tug of Annie's hand in his now filled him with dread as he recalled them. Or, rather, it was the way in which they had been cut off, without warning, leaving him in the chill and the dark. It nauseated him.

He lay awake then for the rest of the night, surrounded by the ebb and flood of snoring. From the feel of the night and the quiet in the street outside the window, he thought that he must have woken at around half past three, the true dead hour of the night. That was when they said the sick departed, he remembered his grandmother telling him that, and she had gone herself around that time, he always thought of that on the rare occasions he found himself awake at such a time. At last, the men in the servants' hall began to stir, and a grey light began to seep in through the windows, which he had watched blankly as his stomach turned and he heard the lark's song stop, and stop, and stop again, and felt the insistent tug of Annie's hand in his.

It was about a week and a half later that a letter came for him, dated the 23rd of January 1673.

It was the hour before dinner, when the men of Balcarres' household in Edinburgh gathered in the ante-room of the dining hall, a time for laughter and gossip. A page handed a thin letter to Andrew Lammie and withdrew. He turned the letter over in his hands several times, examining Fyvie's seal before cracking it open and reading the first sentence. The handwriting was heavily ornamented and erratic. It was a job to decipher.

To Andrew Lamb, trumpeter to the Earl of Balcarres, Edinburgh.

'What's that, Lamb, a love letter?'

He grunted, disturbed, and took the letter into a quieter corner, leaning over it with a frown.

Gradually the phrases emerged from the jumble of words, deafening him to the jovial banter around him.

When he had finished reading, Andrew Lammie leaned forward, retching, and sent a stream of green bile spewing from his mouth onto the floor between his feet, where it spattered his boots. He continued to retch as he stared wide-eyed and desperate into the cooling mess.

He kept that letter a long time, even after it had broken into four along the folds, and he re-read it so often that he could call to mind every sentence at will, and yet he often returned to the grey and grubby piece of paper, running his finger over the familiar fading words, smudging them. They gave him no comfort, but they anchored him during the times when he feared that he would be swept away in a current of madness, those times when he took to thinking that Annie was no more than his own private fantasy, that she had never existed in this material world, and that perhaps he had never even been to Fyvie, that he had never left Edinburgh except in dreams of wood and water. Here, in the city, one hundred and fifty miles away, there was no one who had known her, no one who could confirm her existence to him. His mother and father could say to him, 'Aye, when you came down the road frae Fyvie, it was just your lass you were going to marry and you wouldny speak about a single thing else,' but they had not seen her, had not touched or spoken to her, maybe they thought he had been dreaming all along. It was then that he would pull the letter from his pocket and read it again, proof in another man's hand that, once, they had known each other, and loved.

He could not cry, not even in his mother's arms.

For months after the letter's arrival, he carried a fist of anger with him all day in his stomach, and at night the memory of her tormented him. The long empty space next to him where he lay pulled her name out of him, and he would whisper it to fill the emptiness, 'Annie, my Annie,' and though there were times when the loneliness made him reach down and touch himself until he groaned in release, he never no not once felt her there next to him, there was only empty space and dark, and at last he would sleep. Then the morning would come, and once or twice, just after waking, the day seemed bright ahead until he remembered and the ground beneath him fell away and he closed his face tight like a lid on the anger that grew within him through the day.

But the tears would not come, and dry-eyed he stalked to his duties in the morning, and dry-eyed he stalked back to the servants' hall at night. Sometimes he would impotently swear revenge, but on whom he did not even know, not for sure. Then night would come and he would be alone in his bed without her, once more.

So that was how it was at the start. But after some months he found the fury no longer held him so relentlessly in its grip. The Laird came down the road from Fyvie and told him what little he could, and he persuaded himself that Alexander Seton was a good man, who had sought and found the truth, and it was time that he, Andrew Lammie, take comfort that at least there was no one to blame. So said his rational mind, and it succeeded in dampening his rage despite the suspicion that lay in his gut. After that, he went along smoother, but the space that was left by his subsiding rage was filled by the emptiness of Annie's absence, which crept inside him at night from the space in the bed where his wife should have lain beside him. He went on in life, up at the crack of dawn, blowing in the morning on his trumpet. The previous spring, in Fyvie, as the new day's light rippled over the tops of the trees and the birds joined their sweeter chorus to his own braying notes, and he saw the buds bursting from the grey branches and glistening in the growing light, and he looked towards Tifty and thought of his lass wakening, he had thought that the morning's promise was for him, that the day was holding out a gift that he had only to reach out for and it would be his. Now, his senses were muted and indistinct. And only three years later, he would think back to his youth and think how age dulled the senses, without realising that it was his loss, and not those few years, that had drained the colours from his world.

He thought of her every day. Over time, he found it more difficult to remember her face and her touch, and he would feel a sense of panic that he learned to allay, a little, by forcing himself to remember a handful of times in great detail. The time, when he hardly knew her yet, when they had leaned over the rail of the Skeugh Brig, and he had watched the light of the river's ripples playing over her downturned face. It brought a self-mocking smile to his lips when he thought of how Smith had accused him of being the one who had cast a spell on her. But how else could the miller explain it, how a gentleman's daughter would choose the servant over the master?

Another memory, this time of when he had first spoken to her, when he had seen her coming up through the trees carrying a pair of new shoes. The breeze sending the strands of red hair wandering over her face, and her fingers crooking to comb it away as they talked, and the wind blowing it back again. Her smile as she spoke about the song that he had sung and she had liked. He had thought she had a fine spirit in her, her and her 'It's nae Nan, *Mister* Trumpeter, it's Agnes.'

And the time, nearly a year ago, on Fastern's Eve in the old cottar's home at Tifty, when he had opened his eyes and seen her for the first time, and he had felt just the same as he did those times when he first heard a song, and knew that it would be one of his songs, that he would be singing for the rest of his life.

So he remembered, and he spent his days in the city of Edinburgh, in the bustle and the reek and the stench, and as time went on, his family and friends began to recognise something of his old self. Quieter than before perhaps, but still he would laugh and crack a joke in the company of the coffee house or the tavern, where there were few that noticed the sadness that remained in the lines around the corners of his mouth, and in his reflections on the flavour of coffee.

XXXI

Grizel had left the household the previous May, to go to service with Ironsyde. It was as well she did, from Tifty's point of view. He had aye thought she had a sullen way about her, and in those last few months at Tifty she had got worse. All last year, in fact, from January up until she left. January. Aye. So that was another change there had been in the house. Young Will was still away. From time to time he had news of him, a letter from his brother Patrick in Ardoyne. He seemed happy enough with Will's work, although he complained about him taking a drink, but by the sounds of it, it was only on rare occasions. Another change.

So they were settling down, as much as they could. At first, there had been folk in and out. The Laird amongst them, with his quiet questions. He had seemed gey shaken by the thing. But he had done his duty rightly, investigated as head of the Barony Court, talked to each of them in turn and sought the truth. They gave him what truths they could, 'Aye, aye, aye,' they said, 'this was how it was. But nae that one hard bad thing, na. She just fell.' It was how it had to be. Because a man had a right to rule his own household. And because they would take his lad, if they knew the whole truth. They would take the young William, and hang him high, and they would leave the old William behind, the one who had allowed it. Who had heard from below, and not gone up. Who had let her run. Who had sat, hard-faced, and had not followed. No, he would not have it. No father – and no mother either, because he knew that Helen could bear it no better than himself – should have to lose two bairns. One was enough.

So there were truths and truths, and in the end the Laird had not pressed the matter. Maybe a man who had been less shaken, who had not been so close to the thing, would have had the strength to dig deeper. He had barely been seen in Fyvie this past year. It seemed he had a lot of business that took him away to Edinburgh.

He had not seen hide nor hair of that trumpeter loon, either. Word was the Laird had dismissed him – so he should – and he was in the household of some other Earl in Edinburgh. No doubt he would be riding about Edinburgh much the same as he had here, giving the eye to all the Edinburgh lassies, turning them against their families.

Helen had taken it hard. But she chained the grief away deep inside. It was just every now and then that he would hear it fighting its way to the surface, gasping and sobbing, in the lonely night hours when they lay side by side without touching, and he would wait, with his back to her, unmoving, until she had mastered the grief and forced it back into its place. In the mornings after those nights, her face would be grey and rigid, and they would not meet each other in the eye. There had been never a word between them about it since the day they put her in the ground.

There were times when he heard Jane and Bessie whispering away at night – he could hear them through the wall – he could not stop that. But in the house, when they ate together, or when they sat in the evenings at their spinning, he would not suffer a word on it. Not even at Halloween time, and that had been a gey bad time, with the womenfolk starting up at every slight sound, while even he himself jumped at noises in the dark on the way up from the mill every evening, Gibb ahead of him wondering at his fright. No, they had not spoken of it then, and they had not spoken of it since.

It was the way it had to be. And it had been like that since the day they had put her in the ground, and he and Young Will and Gibb had come back to the house through a foot of snow, and Grizel had called them to table. They had stood by their places to say grace, and then the tears had begun to roll down Grizel's cheeks as she stared at the unneeded place she had laid without thinking. Helen with pursed lips had flown around the table, grabbed the bowl and the spoon in both hands, and rushed them back to the press, where they still sat, gathering dust. He himself, instead of taking his place at the head of the table, had gone over to the creepie stool that sat waiting and empty, and picked it up. He had meant to place it back by the fire for everyday use, but as he carried it over to the hearth his shoulders began to shake and without warning one of the legs snapped off in his hand. He pulled the thing apart and fed it into the fire while the food on the table behind him steamed itself cold. The stool was old and dry and it gave a good fast heat. When it had been reduced to embers, he had turned around to see the members of his household standing with heads turned towards him, frightened gazes and half-open mouths. He had stuck out his jaw and looked each one in the eye in turn, until they dropped their gaze or looked away – Bessie, Helen, Will, Jane, Grizel – Gibb had been standing with his back to him, shoulders slumped, motionless. Then he had stalked back to the head of the table, muttered a grace, and forced down every mouthful of the cold, congealing, tasteless food while the room darkened as the last of the creepie stool settled in the hearth.

So that was how it had been, and how it still was, and how it had to be. Aside from himself and Gibb, it was a house of women, but in a year or two it would be time for Young Will to come back, and he would maybe bring a wife with him, and there would be bairns in the house again. Aye, that was the way it was meant to be, once more he would walk down the steps to the mill holding a wee lass's hand in his, swinging her high and making her fly with each step, laughing.

Folk had been good to them. At the Kirk on a Sunday, for quite a while afterwards they would pay a wee tribute with quiet words. 'I'm sorry for your loss.' Or, 'She was a fine lass.' Or, 'May the Good Lord gie you comfort.' Hushed words and a clasp of the hand that he had responded to with a nod and a few muttered words of his own.

But time went on and people forgot, they had their own business to attend to and their own worries to harry them along the way, and it would not be long now before the thing that had happened was forgotten. They might speak of it from time to time, when a similar story made the rounds, a young life lost in a terrible accident, but that would be it, and again it was how it should be, mainly folk would be thinking about the ones that were left and not the ones that were gone, and Jane and Bessie would be married in time and then after Kirk the Fyvie folk would be coming up to shake his hand gladly, when the banns were read, 'Ach William, you'll be pleased for your daughter, na?' And later, 'So this is your wee granddaughter, is it? Oh she's a bonnie one, look at the red hair on her, just like –.' Like what? Like your own used to be, maybe, before it turned the colour of grief. Grief, and ashes.

There were still plenty folk who shook him by the hand and drank his health when he went into the alehouse. He was glad of that one thing: through it all, he had kept his standing. It had not happened the way he would have wished. Of course not, how could he have wished that? But the thing was, a man had to keep order in his family. Order, and godly discipline. You couldna tolerate a man like that sowing the seeds of rebellion in a household. Low folk like that, without a penny to their names, dragging a good man's name and family into the dirt. He would have been a laughing stock if he had suffered the match.

But still, these last few months, there had been times when he had thought there was a change in the way some folk were with him. At Kirk there were some that turned away now and pretended not to see him, though he knew damn well that they saw him fine – that was how it seemed to him, though maybe it was only his imagination. And once or twice, on a market day, he had seen, or thought he had seen, eyes sliding sideways towards him and then away when he looked over, and the small huddles of three or four would break up all of a sudden if he went over to pass the time of day.

And once, there had been a strange thing, last month at the market young Jamie Buchan had come right up to him, humming a tune that he had not recognised. Humming away and looking Smith in the eye with a cocky look that he did not care for. So he had said, sharpish, 'What's that tune you keep humming, man?' And Buchan had answered, still cocky as anything, 'Dinna ye ken it, Tifty? Now there's a funny thing. You of aa folk. Ocht, I've nae doubt you'll hear it another time.' And he had walked off with his hands in his pockets, still humming.

But there were times when he felt weary, and he wondered how long it would be before he was laid in the ground himself in the green kirkyard, next to the grave that was there already with its simple flat stone with its skull and crossed bones and its terse inscription. He would be laid to rest, and Helen too, soon enough, and the rest of his family in time as God pleased, and they would sleep in the good rich earth, and even the stones that marked their places would be eaten by the lichens, and all their names would be forgotten, and that would be an end to it.

Epilogue

'Who gave you that song?' In the quiet of the coffee house, he leaned forward and pushed his face, with his eyes staring wide, close to that of the singer, who jerked backwards in surprise.

'Eh, well, I canna remember the first time for sure that I heard a body sing about Tifty's Annie. But it's aa over Aberdeenshire and Banff this last year or two, we like to sing it because you ken we're nae so fond of the millers, the mean bastards so they are, it gies us a wee bit spite to put in it. And those millers at Tifty, Smith they are called, father and son, they say they've a hell of a temper on them both. They say,' and here he leaned forward again conspiratorially and lowered his voice, 'neither one of them will stay in the room when that song starts. And around Fyvie, the folk like to mak sure it is sung gey often.'

'Tell me your name.'

'Duncan Nichol, frae Ellon in Aberdeenshire. And your own, sir?'

He straightened up in his chair, reached forward, and clasped the singer's hand in both of his own.

'You ken it well, Mr Nichol, you sing it many times whenever you sing that song. Andrew Lamb. But they aye called me Lammie in Fyvie.'

And he gave the man's hand a strong squeeze before dropping it. The singer stared, quizzical, uncertain, as Andrew Lammie reached inside his breast pocket and pulled out a dog-eared letter that was falling apart along the folds.

'Can you read, Mr Nichol?'

'Aye, a bit.'

He put the letter into the singer's hands, and carried on as Nichol unfolded it and began mouthing the words to himself, 'That was aa I kenned before, Mr Nichol. I've no need to read it, I have it aa by heart. She was shouting and screaming at aa her family, and then she ran awa out into the night and tripped. And she fell down the stair and broke her back. That was it, that was what he told me, but I couldny believe it.'

'It taks a wee while, sometimes, when you get news like that.'

'You tak me wrong, Mr Nichol. No, I knew she was gone, because I felt her go. But I couldny believe that was aa there was to it, tripping and falling, accidental like. I *made* myself believe it. But aa the time, I *kenned*. I kenned it was them that hurt and killed her, and there was nothin' I could do about it, no a damned thing. And the only thing I had of her was in those words there in your hand, "You must bide in Edinburgh, and think nane of coming back to Fyvie. But ken this, and it may gie you some wee bit of comfort: when I spoke to her last, she was as steady in wanting to be your wife as any man could hope." '

Duncan Nichol nodded and kept nodding as he finished reading and handed the letter back. Andrew folded it carefully and tucked it into his pocket.

'That was aa I kenned, Mr Nichol, these past three years, until you came here and gied me that song. And I thank you for it.'

The two men sat facing each other across the table, and they talked, while customers drifted in and out of the coffee-house, and dark came to the high windows, and the lamps were lit. Andrew questioned him in a low quiet voice, and Nichol told what he could of the news of Fyvie and the folk that lived there. And then the conversation turned once more to the song, where Nichol had heard it and who had sung it, and what the folk said about it, and Andrew asked, 'You say that song is being sung now aa through the shires of Aberdeen and Banff?'

Nichol answered, 'Aye, sir, it's well-loved like I say,' and he chuckled and then grew serious as he told Andrew of how it was in Fyvie, the miller and his son hounded out of every gathering, the blank faces of the Fyvie folk with their cold knowing eyes, 'Ocht it's an auld song, Tifty, havena ye heard it afore? My grandmother used to sing it.'

'I hope you'll keep singing that song wi the Buchan folk, Mr Nichol. It's a hell of a fine revenge they've given me.'

For a wee while neither of them said anything at all, they sat turning over their own private thoughts in their minds. After a wee while more, Andrew Lammie looked up and held Nichol's gaze.

'I have a favour to ask you, Mr Nichol. Will you sing that song for me again?'

'Aye, sir, I surely will. I would be honoured to do it.'

They were alone now in the coffee-house. The landlord had locked the door to newcomers and was in a back room, counting his takings for the day. Only two or three lamps had been left alight, and the embers of the fire burned low. Nichol sang, with his eyes closed, and his voice, though quiet, still had a strength to it, and long before he came to the end, his singing cut deep into the closed, tight place beneath Andrew Lammie's breastbone, and at last released the tears that were locked within him.

The spring of that year was fresh and green, and when he had the time he took himself out into the free air. Sometimes he would make the climb up Arthur's Seat, and when he reached the top he would be out of breath and a wee bit light-headed, and he would stand with his eyes fixed to the north. At first, all alone on that high place, he thought of the Deer's Hill, of the time they had climbed it together and sat looking out at the blue of the flax flowers, when she had told him how they would fall after just the one day, and their beauty would be lost. Then he would be quiet, and he would weep with his hands over his face and the tears streaming between his spread fingers.

But after a while, when the summer came, he took to thinking more of the way she had cuffed his shoulder when he said of the flowers, 'They're no as bonny as me', seeing her face, laughing at him, pretending to be indignant, both of them knowing he should have said as bonny as her, that was what he had meant, and what he would always mean. And then he would start to laugh, at that and at all the other times they had, remembering the two of them together, how the laughter had gushed out of them like a spring, welling up and filling them up and spilling over as if they could never run dry of it, the times when he had run wild with his Annie in the den of Fyvie, through spring and summer and autumn, the two of them laughing together at the world, what could it do to them when they had each other.

All through that summer he walked open shouldered and high headed through the streets of Edinburgh, with his buttonless jacket flapping open, until in the autumn his mother insisted on sewing new buttons on the thing. He protested, saying he breathed easier with it that way, and she looked at him a funny way and said, 'Aye, but now you'll breathe just as easy wi them on.'

Mill o' Tifty's Annie

At Mill o' Tifty lived a man,
In the neighbourhood of Fyvie
He had a lovely daughter dear
Her name was bonnie Annie.

Lord Fyvie had a trumpeter
By the name of Andrew Lammie
Wha had the art to gain the heart
Of Tifty's bonnie Annie

Lord Fyvie he rode by the mill
Where lived Tifty's Annie
His trumpeter rode him afore
Even this same Andrew Lammie

Her mother called her to the door
Saying Come here to me, my Annie
Did e'er you see a prettier man
Than the trumpeter of Fyvie?

She naethin said, but sighing sore,
Alas for Bonnie Annie
She durstna own that her heart was won
By the trumpeter of Fyvie

At nicht when all gaed to their bed,
All sleepit soon but Annie
Love sore oppresst her tender breast,
Thinking o Andrew Lammie

The first time me and my love met
Was in the woods of Fyvie;
He called me mistress, I said, No
I was Tifty's bonnie Annie

Wi apples sweet he did me treat,
And kisses soft and mony
His lovely form and speech so warm
Soon gained the heart o' Annie

It's up and down in Tifty's den,
Where the burn runs clear and bonnie
It's oft I've gane to meet my love
My bonnie Andrew Lammie

Her father's come to hear o this
And a letter writ to Fyvie
To say his daughter was bewitched
By the servant Andrew Lammie

Then up the stair his trumpeter
He called soon and shortly
Pray tell me loon what's this you've done
To Tifty's bonnie Annie

Woe be to Mill of Tifty's pride,
For it has ruined many
They'll not have it said that she should wed
The trumpeter of Fyvie

In wicked art I took no part
Nor therein am I canny
Tis love alane the heart has gained
Of Tifty's bonnie Annie

Where will I find a boy so kind
That will carry a letter canny
Who will run doon to Tifty's toun
Gie it to my love Annie?

Ye may come to the brig of Skeugh
And there I'll come and meet ye
It's there we will renew our love
Before I go and leave ye

My love I go to Edinburgh town
And for a while must leave ye
She sighed sore and said no more
But I wish that I were wi ye

He hied him to the head of the house
To the house-top of Fyvie
He blew his trumpet loud and shrill
It was heard at Mill of Tifty

Her father locked the door at night
Laid by the keys fu canny
And when he heard the trumpet sound
Said Your cow is lowing Annie

My father dear I pray forbear
And reproach not your Annie
I'd rather hear that cow to low
Than all the kye in Fyvie

Lord Fyvie he came by the mill
What ails ye bonnie Annie?
It's all for love that I'm cast doon
A' for bonnie Andrew Lammie

Oh Tifty, Tifty, gie consent
And let your daughter marry
It would need to be to a higher degree
Than the trumpeter of Fyvie

If she was born o' as rich a kin
As she is rich in beauty
I would ha' ta'en the lass mysel
And made her Fyvie's lady

Oh Fyvie's lands lie far and wide
And they are wondrous bonnie
But I wouldna leave my ain true-love
No for higher lands than Fyvie

Her father struck her wondrous sore
And likewise did her mother
Her sisters also did her scorn
But woe be to her brother!

Her brother struck her wondrous sore
With cruel strokes and mony
He broke her back at the hall door
A' for liking Andrew Lammie

Oh mother, father, sisters a'
Why sae cruel tae your Annie?
By love's soft stroke my heart was broke,
Now my brother's broke my body

O mother, mother, mak my bed,
And lay my face to Fyvie
It's there I'll lie, and there I'll die
A' for lovin' Andrew Lammie

Afterword

Peter Buchan, the great ballad collector, wrote of the ballad Mill of Tifty's Annie, 'This is one of the greatest favourites of the people in Aberdeenshire that I know.' (Gleanings of Scotch, English and Irish Scarce Old Ballads, 1825)

Agnes Smith is buried in the kirkyard at Fyvie under a gravestone with the inscription:

Heir lyes Agnes Smith who departit the 19 of Janvari 1673

In Edinburgh, a trumpeter by the name of Andrew Lamb served under the Earl of Balcarres and then in the Royal Life Guards. He was appointed as one of the King's Trumpeters in 1687. He died in 1707, at the age of 58.

William Smith and his wife Helen Black appeared before the Turriff Presbytery Court in 1650 on a charge of suspected witchcraft, which they denied. Along with their son William, they were still tenants of the Mill of Tifty in 1696. William senior died sometime between 1700 and 1705. It is likely that the song was already popular during his lifetime, if the tradition is true that Andrew Lammie heard it himself as far away as Edinburgh:

'some years subsequent to the melancholy fate of his Agnes, her sad story chanced to be sung in a company in Edinburgh where he was present; he remained silent and motionless till he was discovered by a groan suddenly bursting from him, and at the same time several of the buttons flew from his waistcoat.' (Laing, 1823)

Acknowledgements

This book would have been a much poorer work if it had not been for access to the extraordinary public resources of the British Library and the National Archives of Scotland.

It would not have existed at all if I had not learned to read, write and love literature under the auspices of the Scottish education system; particular thanks are due to Mrs Davies of Bishopbriggs High School for her part in my literary education.

I am grateful to Sheila Stewart and Stanley Robertson, for sharing with me their knowledge of the oral history behind the ballad.

I am indebted to the many people – friends, family and new acquaintances alike – who supported, helped and encouraged me while I wrote and researched this book. Alan Bissett's enthusiasm for the book did much to encourage me at a crucial stage.

The wonderful cover art is by my friend Andrew Shaw.

Special thanks must go to the Arvon Massive and Sheelagh Neuling for their criticism – positive, tactful and always helpful – which did much to improve the text.

Most of all, I would like to thank my partner (now husband), Nick Rogers, for his support, understanding and encouragement throughout every stage of this project.